The Adventures

of

Dogg Girl

and

Sidekick

The Adventures

of

Dogg Girl

and

Sidekick

Jennifer deBie

DREAMING BIG PUBLICATIONS

Dogg Girl and Sidekick
Copyright © 2018 Jennifer deBie

Content Editor: Jamie Zepeda

Copy Editor: Maddy Drake

Cover Art: Hope "Silver" Bob

Cover Design: Krystina Grey

Editor-in-Chief: Kristi King-Morgan

Formatting: Kristi King-Morgan

Assistant Editor: London Koffler

ISBN- 978-1-947381-24-7

www.dreamingbigpublications.com

For my family: Mom, Dad, Mary.
Thank you

Chapter 1

Karissa Dogg almost missed the boy's outstretched hand when he stood to leave her station in the tutor center. She still had a hangover slamming the corners of her skull and no one tried to shake hands after a session, the gesture was too formal for any self-respecting college student. "Thank you again, Miss Dogg." He sounded like someone from one of her novels for Romantic lit. Or maybe Victorian. The Victorians were big on formalities…

"Kary, please Johnathan." She stood and shook the hand he offered. His grip wasn't as weak as the rest of him looked. His eyes were the darkest natural blue she'd ever seen. "I'm just happy to help." She kept her customer smile in place without wincing, even though there was a student at the German tutor's desk acting like that language should be shouted instead of spoken.

She needed water. She needed Advil. She needed to sleep and eat and shower and then call her brother and congratulate him on his win the night before.

"Well then you have to call me Johnnie."

She didn't want to call him anything. She wanted to have her hand back and sit. She wanted to con Jason Dods, her co-worker, into bringing her lunch. She wanted to not be further behind on her Spanish research than she was ever going to admit to Dr. C.

"Johnnie then."

He dropped her hand. The tutor fell back into her chair and had put her head on her desk before he was out the door.

✦

"You okay, *frauline*?" Jason was standing over her, the shouty German student done and gone, it seemed.

Kary wagged her hand to show approximation. "*Mas o menos.*"

He leaned across to look at the session log she still had up on her computer. "Seventeen and in advanced Spanish?" He whistled. Kary jabbed her elbow into his gut, making her co-worker stagger back a step.

"Eyes off Dods."

He rubbed the spot where she'd sunk her elbow. "Easy there, Adamant. What's got you touchy?"

Kary rolled her eyes at the mention of their city's Register designated super and closed out of her logbook. "Seth's fight ran late. They had to interrupt coverage cause the *Dynamic A's,*" she scoffed her way through their local super and his sidekick's team nickname, "were knocking down buildings or something."

Jason retreated to his own desk, his tone became patronizing once he was out of range of her strikes. "They were bringing down White Thorn, you know, the Enlisted gang from—"

"Fanboy."

6

"You should pay more attention. Supers are important to —"

"Supers are important to *you*. Not me." Kary dug through her backpack on the off chance there was a water bottle tucked somewhere in the folds.

"They keep the peace."

"They keep the road crews in work and the rest of us in traffic." Kary upended the bottle she found and sucked down the dregs.

"You'd let the Enlisted overrun us all?"

And that was the crux: the Enlisted and their cadre of super villains and all the mayhem that went with them. The Register, the network of sanctioned supers all across the world, were necessary to keep the Enlisted in check. "Do we *have* to debate this? I've got a hangover and a hungry."

"Thought you were just sleepy."

"Why would I be *just* sleepy? Seth won last night and we closed out Jimmie's." She pitched the empty bottle into a trashcan near the door without leaving her seat and swiveled in her chair to face Jason. Her smile was wicked enough to make the German tutor gulp and wish heartily that his twenty-first birthday would come soon so he could go to Jimmie's bar, watch Kary's brother fight on the screens there, and celebrate his victories until the wee hours with the dark-headed, dark-eyed girl sitting across the room.

+

"Heyheyhey, Kary—*Kary*." She swung toward the voice and watched Dr. Constance hop-jog across the quad towards her just before her only Monday afternoon lecture. Tallish, youngish, and far too exuberant about obscure Latin American poets, her research professor was frequently mistaken for a student.

"*Hola* Dr. C." Kary planted her backpack on a bench and pretended to search through it while the professor pretended he wasn't winded.

"Do you have—"

"Those translations? Yes, somewhere, I *think*..." She flipped through the folder where she kept her Victorian literature homework. "Damn, I must've left it at my desk in the tutor center." She slapped the binder closed before he could look too closely. "Can I email you a copy tonight? It's saved to my hard drive back home."

"Yeah, that's fine." He looked disappointed. The student didn't waste energy on feeling guilty. "So how're you finding *el diario*?"

El diario de Sor Juana Ines de la Cruz? Dry. And the antiquated Spanish hurt her head.

"Fascinating, she was a poet ahead of her time."

"Aren't all poets?"

She laughed because he expected her to. "*Verdad.*" A pause grew between them while Kary shuffled her lit folder back into her bag, twisting so he couldn't see the label and catch her lie. "I had one of your students in the center today—Johnnie Foxx." She meant it as a distraction.

It worked, Dr. C brightened. "Oh? I'm glad he finally went for help. He's been needing it."

"Really?" Kary hefted her bag back onto her shoulder.

"Yeah. He's a good kid, just doesn't apply himself. Sleeps in class, comes in late. That sort of thing."

Were professors allowed to talk about their students to other students? Kary checked her watch. "Well I hope I helped him. Sorry to run, but I've got Dr. Peters in—"

"No worries, just email me that file when you get the chance."

Kary waved without looking back; she was going to be late.

Chapter 2

"You're late Bruiser."

"Shuddup Rocks." She hollered over her shoulder, striding across to the locker rooms in her gym that evening after class. Kary didn't have set hours in the gym, and he knew that. James "Rocks" Coldstone just liked giving her a hard time. He'd known the girl and her brother Seth for years; had actually been the one to introduce Seth to his trainer and manager, Rodney. Jimmie owned the gym where she trained and the bar where she drank. The old brawler and his establishments were as much a part of the college student as the muscles that lay against her bones.

Once she'd finished changing, he found her working over a heavybag trying to single-handedly scrap out a head of steam after a bad Monday. Right punch-left punch right punch-left punch right punch-left punch step back kick. Low middle high switch low middle high switch.

"What's eatin' you?" He stood behind the bag and held it while she began throwing punches again.

"Behind on research. Had to cram. Sloppy. Sloppy. *Sloppy.*" She punctuated each word with another hit, the last one carried enough force to make Jimmie take a step and brace on his back leg.

"Garth, come hold this." Kary stepped back while Jimmie swapped with one of his trainers. The younger man held the bag while his boss watched the girl's form with a critical eye. "Bruiser, you ain't sloppy." She kept up her rhythm and didn't speak. "You just need to remember that you're not punching *through* the bag. You punch *through* people 'cause they heal on their own. Bags get hurt and stay hurt."

The old brawler was trying to cheer her up. Kary dropped her fists, ashamed of her temper. Garth let go of the bag and shook the creaks from his arms. "Sorry Jimmie, Garth." The trainer was smiling at her with the crinkles at the edges of his eyes even while the gym owner tried to keep up a stern façade. Her eyes moved to the younger of the two men, "Spar with me?"

Garth was her brother's age. She and Seth met him in the gym, one of their first friends from outside their neighborhood. Seth joked that Garth was his first white friend, back when they were just teenagers Jimmie had seen something in, and Kary was just a girl skipping rope in the corner. Back before she'd begged lessons out of Jimmie too.

"No prob Bruiser, lemme get my gloves."

✝

Kary only kickboxed for fun and a workout. Her brother was making a career at it as Seth "The Mad" Dogg but he'd always been reckless. The girl knew, even if he didn't realize, that in his late twenties, his days of running with the big names in the ring might be coming to an end. The ring took a toll on the body and her brother was already starting to feel it. If he played his cards right there could be fights in Madison Square Garden or on the Vegas strip again, but the days of him headlining those venues were probably past. The big arenas in Marshal City, Andersonville, and Newtone up north though, those were garunteed invites to tournaments and packed houses for a fighter like Seth. Her brother started professional training in his late teens and by then street-brawling had already done a number on his joints. They always knew his career would be short, but he'd never admit *that* to his kid sister. In the next few years he'd have to retire from the ring officially.

Maybe he could open a gym the way Jimmie had and teach the next generation of fighters; Kary *hoped* he would. He would need something to keep him occupied besides his endorsement deals. Those wouldn't outlast his ring career by long.

Garth pegged her shoulder and brought Kary back down into their match with an audible smack. "Head in Bruiser, you're driftin'." His drawl was familiar, as familiar as the rhythm of the spar: the shuffle-skip of feet across the canvas, the smack-thwack of punches and blocks, the advance and retreat of bodies.

Kary spun away from his next punch and swung her leg up in a full roundhouse that stretched all the way to his helmet. At almost six feet, Kary was tall for a girl but Garth was at least a head taller than that and still her foot reached his cheek. The blow made the trainer step sideways in what would be called a stagger on a lesser man. Karissa grinned around her mouth-guard and closed in with a southpaw straight jab she kept back most matches because using it felt like showing off.

Garth hit the ropes, hanging there like damp laundry. Jimmie called for a halt, they were the last ones left at the old gym. Kary dropped her stance and grinned at her exhausted friend, stepping in to sling his arm across her shoulder. The man spat his mouth-guard to the side and blew in her face. "Should be 'shamed of myself, gettin' beat by a girl."

Kary tossed her sticky hair like she wasn't sore up and down. "Nah, you didn't get beat by a *girl*. You got beat by a Bruiser." As they climbed out of the ring, Jimmie asked when she was going to let him sign her up and show her off in a tournament.

"When a super saves us all, how 'bout that Rocks?" She took the bottle he held and dumped it over her head without asking if she could. Her hair hung in wet strings from thetail she'd tied it in, leaving a trail of drips down her back and onto the rubber-matted floor.

Jimmie grumbled about disrespectful kids all the way back to his office. Kary hit the showers.

✦

The block the gym stood on was quiet when she stepped out into the street, not unusual since the restaurants and bars were a few blocks north, near the university. Jimmie's was on the kind of residential and small business block that went quiet after dark. It would be a good night for a jog if she hadn't already worked out and it wasn't so late. If she stuck to the lighted paths through park that ran along the river she shouldn't have to worry about creeps but—

13

Something slammed into a building around the corner from the gym. *"Behind you Adamant."* Supers? They didn't crash over to this end of the city often. The warehouses in this part of the old city had all been turned into trendy lofts, so the gangs had moved further towards the western edge of Commonland and their supers, Adamant and his sidekick Aspect, followed.

Kary kept walking. She wasn't going to hang anywhere near here if the *Dynamic A's* were around and waiting to drop debris on her car. The news would tell her what was going on in the morning and watching TV at home was infinitely safer than investigating in person. Her car made a friendly beep when she hit unlock, the hatch lifted for her duffle the first time she pressed the button. The key fob didn't always work and she couldn't afford to go to a dealership and get it replaced.

Boom-*crash*.

Someone groaned on the sidewalk, loose pieces of brick rained from the wall he hit before tumbling to the ground, surrounding the red-suited mass of person in rubble. "You okay?" She called across the street without moving from where she stood at her driver's side door. Kary Dogg wasn't getting any closer to a super than she had to. Even from this distance, she recognized him as Commonland's resident big gun, Adamant, the one who had been assigned to protect these streets by the Register of Superheros for decades.

"Citizen, you should get somewhere safe." The voice was behind her, close enough to make the girl flinch and spin with her fists out. Her hands fell, she recognized this costume too. She'd only seen it on TV a few hundred times, the sidekick.

14

"Sure thing Aspect." He was thinner than she'd thought from watching footage on television and not any taller than her. "Just don't tear down my city." She closed the car door in his face, enjoying the shock hanging around his mouth where the black mask didn't cover. His eyes were covered in milky-white lenses, something she'd never noticed in the news coverage. He was also younger than she'd thought, maybe still a teenager. Probably not used to flippancy from real people. Kary drove away from the downtown battle without looking back.

Some business near Jimmie's was being used to launder money for guns and drugs or something like that and guarded by a few of the roid brutes the Enlisted gangs used as guard dogs. *Brute* was slang for people who took enhancers until they were good for nothing except brawn, leaving them rotted in the head while someone else did the thinking. They were insults to brawlers like Garth and her brother and Jimmie and anyone else she knew who trained to fight and think for themselves. The supers had been trying to clean up the operation with minimal property damage, the estimates the news anchors kept throwing around told Kary they hadn't been very successful.

Kary turned off the morning news without waiting for more details. There wasn't some secret nuclear plant about to blow because the *Dynamic A's* were busy knocking holes in the world and that was all she cared about.

Before she left, Kary made sure every window was closed and every light off in her apartment.

✦

"Adamant and Aspect were downtown last night." Jason greeted her with the statement when she joined him in the tutor center later that morning. "Looks like they were saving us from yet another—"

"They're not as big as I thought they'd be." She cut him off as she logged into her computer.

"Your TV okay? They looked like they always do." He visibly pouted as he settled into his own desk.

"No, I saw them. They were fighting down the block from my gym." Kary kept her voice disinterested.

"Oh, *cool.*" There was a fanboy glint in his eye. "Did you talk to them?"

"Aspect told me to scram, so I did."

"*Why?*"

"What else should I've done? Take a selfie?"

"*Ja.*" He sounded like that was the obvious answer.

Kary rolled her eyes at her coworker and fished her buzzing phone out of her bag. It was the gym's number, had the building been damaged in the fight? The idea of finding another place to train after all these years left a funny sucking place in the bottom of her stomach.

"Hello?"

"Bruiser."

"Jimmie, how's the gym? I hadn't heard it was damaged—" *How long were the repairs going to—*

Jimmie cut her off before she finished the thought: "It wasn't, I'm just calling you in on your bet last night."

"Huh?" Kary fiddled with a pencil from her desk. She didn't remember making a bet.

"You said you'd tourney when supers saved us."

16

Piss. "Yes." She dragged the word out like she was trying to remember details. She wasn't. She was trying to think her way out.

"Well kiddo, clear your calendar. You fight weekend after next."

Mierda. "But I wasn't there, and they didn't have anything to do with your place so *technically*—"

"Technically nothing, you owe me the entry fee next time you're in the gym. Try to come in at least every other day between now and your fight."

He hung up before she could protest again. Kary sighed as she tucked away her phone and checked her email out of habit.

Damn.

Chapter 3

The slim kid that shook her hand came to the tutor center again just as Kary was finishing up her lunch. What was his name? "Johnath—no, sorry, just Johnnie. What can I do for you?" She tried to brush crumbs off her desk without sweeping them into his lap as he took the seat across from her.

He was moving differently today. Slower. It was subtle, but Kary had grown up in the kind of neighborhood where it was safer to memorize people by more than their faces. To learn their walks, their stances, and to recognize when those things changed. Yesterday, and anytime before that when she'd seen this kid cross campus he moved meek and easy, painlessly except for the shyness that hunched his shoulders. Today though, today he moved the way her brother moved after a bad fight—like he hurt in his bones.

"I just wanted to thank you for your help yesterday. I did really well on my test in Dr. Constance's." The angle of his jaw was familiar from somewhere besides their tutoring session.

"Oh, well, excellent." Why would a kid like this be sore like a fighter? From what she knew, the university didn't have a problem with violence or bullying, not like the schools she'd spent time in as a kid, but if he was anyone worth knowing in the local circuit, she'd know him already. Even in the under eighteens brackets.

"Yeah, you were a huge help." Did she care? From the corner of her eye, Kary saw Jason watching them in the reflection on his computer screen. She could smell his smirk. No, she didn't care.

"That's my job." Could he leave now? She needed to work on the *diario* some more.

"Yeah, well, um." The conversation lagged. Johnathan scratched the back of his neck, blushing. "Guess I'd better— just wanted to say thanks." He scuffled towards the door, still moving like he was hurting. "Bye."

"Bye Johnathan, you're welcome." She raised her voice a hair to cover Jason's giggles and to keep her own from breaking out.

"He *likes* you." Her fellow tutor crowed when the door swung closed behind the kid. "Can't even vote and he's—"

"Oh *hush*." Kary tossed her hair; the braided ponytail thumped her shoulder when she angled her face away from her friend to hide burning cheeks. "Bet you had a crush on a pretty teacher once."

"Yeah— But I never had the balls to—"

"*Ahem*." She coughed to cut him off, "*still* don't have the balls to—"

"*Whatever*." She could hear the playful glare in his voice. "I'd never have told her at work. *Especially* if she was an upperclassman and I was some kid genius in college."

Kary shrugged and didn't answer as she pulled out her scans of the original diary and the rough translation she'd run the night before. She needed to make the text flow in English the same way it did in Spanish. It wasn't often that juniors got to work on research like this; she really needed to start acting like she cared about it.

Kary stripped out of her jeans as the door to her apartment closed behind her. Not wearing clothes was one of the perks of living without roommates, another was never sharing food. Or feeling guilty when she left dirty dishes in the sink for weeks on end.

Leaving her pants and backpack near the door, Kary flopped on the couch, letting the day wander back across her mind while she ran her hand under the cushions looking for the remote. Tonight she needed to run translations on another section of that diary and read some Browning for British lit. And she needed to put something in her fridge besides yogurt, avocados and wine. Especially since she was almost positive the avocados were bad by now.

And call Seth. She still hadn't congratulated him for his fight the other night. The remote forgotten, she reached for her phone in a back pocket she wasn't wearing.

Damn.

She didn't want to move.

The buzz sent her skidding across the floor to drag it from her jeans. "Seth?" Think of the devil and he would call.

"Kary, how's my baby Bruiser sister?"

"Not nearly as good as her *gonna be a champion* big brother, I'll bet." She grinned and paced between her bedroom and the living room. Just hearing his voice made her the happy kind of restless that she usually got from walking into the gym after being away too long.

He laughed, "Shh, don't say it out loud and maybe it'll happen."

Kary swung her leg at the knee and turned on the ball of her opposite foot in a neat pirouette. "Okay, I won't." She stage whispered into the phone like there was someone around to watch or hear.

"Speaking of fights, heard there was some excitement down at Jimmie's."

"The bar? Only a pack screaming *all Sunday night.* 'Cept during the news—"

"Not Sunday, last night. The gym?"

Last night. "Oh yeah, the supers were tearing up downtown just around the corner from the gym when I was coming ou—"

He cut her off mid word. "And because there were supers '*saving us all*' you're now in a tournament?"

"How'd you hear so fast?" She'd been hoping for a little more time to weasel out before he heard.

"Garth shot me a text." *Triador.* "I'm proud of you Sis, I'm coming down for your match."

Shit. "You don't have to do that, *really.*" Why did he and Garth have to gossip like old women? So what if they'd known each other a decade? Garth didn't need to report *everything* to her brother.

She leaped and landed spread-eagled on her back on the bed with the phone still tight on her ear. "But I *want* to Sis, you have no idea how excited I am. Me'n Bethanne'll be there to—" Bethanne, she didn't even get to see him *alone?* "—to go with you for the tests and

21

buy you supper and shout the whole time you're in the ring and—"

"Sounds great Seth, I can't wait." She could wait, a long time. She was going to get knocked out in the first round and the Mad Dogg himself, and his round-girl girlfriend, would be there to watch her humiliation.

"Yeah." She could hear his smile through the phone. "Me too Sis, it's gonna be fun." No, it wasn't.

"How's Rodney?" Her brother's coach and manager. A man who had looked out for them before their mother died and basically adopted Kary after that was all over.

"He's good. Found a new kid for me to train on that he thinks'll have a career of his own someday." Rodney was good at that, finding kids and giving them futures. Even if it meant bullying them through their GED or staying up all night helping fill a college application the night before the deadline.

"Good, that's good." She needed to call Rodney herself, catch up with him. "Listen, I've got homework to get on and—"

"Say no more, I'll let you go." She didn't really need to get on her homework right that second.

"Thanks bro, love you…. Don't wail on the kid too much." Whoever he was, if the Rodster saw potential then it wasn't Seth's place to break him.

"I'll try." She could here the chuckle in her brother's voice, mostly playful, a little dangerous. Like a wolf's laughter. He liked it when other fighters, even the ones brought in to train with him, were just a little afraid of what the Mad Dogg might do. "Love you too Bruiser, talk in a few days."

In a few days, when he called to make plans about the tournament. Kary held the phone against her chest; her cheeks hot with the anticipation of embarrassment. She threw a good punch and looked all kinds of impressive sparring with one of her brother's old buddies, but in a *real* ring, with *real* fighters? Girls who had fought before, had probably been in tournaments since their teens or before even? Who weren't going to pull punches because they were friends? She shouldn't have agreed to this.

There was a draft from her window that cooled her cheeks. Kary rolled to the edge of her bed, rummaging through the accumulated junk beside it for the photocopies of the diary's next section. Work, she needed to work now.

She'd worry about the tournament later.

Chapter 4

She saw Aspect again in person Friday evening. Kary was jogging a trail that connected all of Commonland's riverside parks when she saw his profile standing at on the edge of the dam that maintained the water level for downtown. "Thanks for not tearing up my city." She cupped her hands and called across the water to him before she could think hard about it and wimp out.

His teeth were really white beneath the shadows on his mask and above the black bodysuit he wore. Bodysuits, what was with supers and the tights? Not all of them, of course, Conjur Man and Wytch Boy both wore robes to match their magic and Mercenari wore what looked like a patchwork of military uniforms from all over the world, but the vast majority of the Register supers seemed to stick with some form of the old-school spandex, though the colors weren't as bright as she remembered from when she was a kid. His wasn't as bad as some, at least it was structured with sewn-in plates of armor, albeit tight armor. Adamant went for the classic look with full spandex but he didn't seem to demand that from his sidekick.

"Nope, no city distruction by me."

"That's a lie." He and Adamant had taken part in destroying plenty of cities, just not the one they were assigned to guard.

"Yeah." he didn't even look sheepish.

"Where's the big man? Or are you riding solo these days?" These days being the four since she'd last bumped into him. Someday Kary would learn the art of small talk with strangers, not any time soon though and probably not with masked supers.

"He's around."

"Oh, good." Awkward. "I feel safer already." She needed to get out *now*. "Well, have a good night." She took off sprinting, laughing to herself as she ran. She hadn't even *tried* for a graceful exit.

Dios, Kary was glad she didn't actually know him.

She was winding back to the park where she'd left her car when he came at her. A big guy, stinking of sweat and all the things she'd imagined a mugger would smell of back when she lived on streets where muggings were common if you weren't protected by a brother with a reputation. She reacted without thinking: shooting her elbow into his gut; the flesh was soft and loose from years of booze but her blow was sharp enough to wind him and break his hold.

Kary spun to face him right-left jab, roundhouse to the head, a streetlight behind them gleamed off the grease on his forehead, spotlighting his temple where her foot landed. Just like a heavy bag except he was a healable person she could punch through instead of just the surface. Her would-be attacker dropped like a rock.

25

She hadn't expected it to be that easy. There had to be more to fending off an assailant than two punches and a kick. She felt cheated.

Slow applause from behind her made the girl jump and pivot with her arms raised in stance. It was Aspect again, materializing from the shadows smile first like a reverse Cheshire cat. "Well I see my services aren't needed tonight after all."

Kary swept her the sweat-stringy ends of her ponytail back over her shoulder where they belonged. "Suppose not." She tried to look like someone who just took down a mugger on instinct alone, but she didn't feel it. Not when a round of *applause* made her jump.

"That was a good punch combo, you fight?" He flipped the man onto his stomach and began zip tying his wrists together with bands taken from one of a dozen pouches she could see on his belt.

"Just for exercise." Lie; she'd be fighting in a city-wide tournament in a week. "But my brother's a pro."

"Oh nice, anyone I might know?"

Kary paused, if he knew who her brother was then he would know who she was, and did she *really* want some teenager in a mask knowing who she was? "He's small time up in the Canadian circuit, so probably not." The story came easy; the girl had been a practiced Bumburyist since long before a professor assigned the Wilde play and she learned that there was a fun name for her particular flavor of fib.

"Ah, well—"

"What're you gonna do with him?" She cut off whatever platitude Aspect had to say about her kickboxing brother on the fictitious Canadian circuit by distracting him with the mugger he was heaving to unsteady feet. There was an active Canadian circuit,

26

wasn't there? Hadn't Jack London fought in it way back when? Hemingway boxed in Spain and London boxed in…

"There's a patrol car that'll be through the park in the next half hour or so, I'll leave this creep with them."

"Oh." It was *logical*. Kary appreciated good logic. "Well um, thanks for—helping me?" He hadn't done anything until after help was no longer needed.

"Yeah… my pleasure." And he knew it. This was why she'd run away earlier: because of conversations like this. "Uh, you have a good night Miss." His voice dropped half an octave on *Miss*, like he was trying to sound older than he was.

"Thanks, you too… *Aspect*." Kary dropped her voice to tease him and then took off, rounding into the park and bounding across the parking lot to her car. When she got behind the wheel she sat there for a second without turning the key, absorbing the scents of old takeout boxes and her gym bag, centering herself.

It was Friday night; Kary needed a shower and wanted a drink.

✦

There was a winery three miles past the city limits that one of her friends worked at, so that was where Kary went. Usually she did Fridays at Jimmie's, watching whatever fight was on, but tonight she needed the clean stucco walls and the CD of Chopin they played to pretend the vineyard bar was classier than it was.

The woman behind the bar, Diette, smiled at Kary when she came through the door sometime around eleven, waving her over to sit at the quiet counter. "*Finally*, someone interesting." Her voice was just a little loud for the small bar, but there weren't enough people in tonight to care. Kary had been around the older girl most of her life, they came from the same block on the western edge of the city. Diette was three years older and had made her own way out of the neighborhood working up from wiping tables in seedy *taquerias* to managing this winary on the good side of town. When Kary and Seth joined the outside world, Diette had gotten back in touch, becoming fast friends with the younger girl and turning a blind eye in whatever bar she was working to the fake ID Kary started using when she was seventeen. Now, five years away from the first time Kary'd slapped her bought piece of plastic on a bar, they were fast friends.

"Hey Die." Kary crossed the room and sank onto the scratched stool across the bar from her friend. "Slim crowd for a Friday." She took the glass Diette poured without asking for an order and swirled it without throwing wine past the rim, inhaling. "Mmm, that's nice." She strained the ruby liquid between her teeth and let the mouthful fall down her throat slowly. "What is it?" Diette had taught her the trick to drinking wine like she knew what she was doing last year, when her friend finally moved up to a joint that required more know-how than throwing together a Jack & Coke.

"It's a wine out of Texas. They've grown some nice grapes for having no water." Kary made a noncommittal noise in her throat and took another sip. "What's got you out here on a Friday? Isn't there a fight?"

Kary set the glass on the bar and twirled it by the stem. "I just... didn't feel it tonight."

"Spill," Diette took a sip from the old Patrón bottle she'd used as a water bottle as long as Kary had known her, and leaned in. "Since when do you ever *not* watch ass kicking?" A patron shot Diette a glance at her language. Both girls flipped their middle fingers at his back when he turned away.

Kary told her about the mugger, grateful that her friend was a good audience. Diette gasped in the right places and breathed *dios mios* when appropriate but didn't ask any questions until her younger friend finished the story. "So in the end, you don't need no stinkin' supers." Die put her best *Blazing Saddles* nasal into the words. "Am I right?"

Kary killed her glass of wine in a gulp. "Damn right." This time they didn't wait until the old man's back was turned before they raised their birds.

"Well in that case, we need to celebrate."

"Celebrate?"

"Your blow against the repression of women, or subjugation of the unlikely... oh *whatever*." She was rummaging under the bar, when she came up she shrugged at Kary's raised eyebrow. "I dunno, lets drink." That sounded like the right idea to Kary, so when Diette poured her a double shot of grappa she threw it back like a champ and slammed her glass down for another.

Kary woke up on her couch with a freight train between her ears and no cash in her wallet. There was, however, a cab stub tucked between the folds where bills were supposed to go, so there wasn't any great mystery about where her money went. She didn't want to look at her credit card charges online; there was no telling how much she'd run up her tab on drinks at the winery, and then later at the dance club Die had dragged her to after the winary closed.

By some small act of mercy there was half empty Gatorade in the fridge that Kary downed, only to spend the next few minutes bent over her sink trying her damndest to send her stomach down the garbage disposal with its contents. When the worst was over, Kary curled up on the floor of her kitchen and tried very hard to sleep until being alive quit hurting quite so bad.

She awoke the second time to her phone buzzing. She didn't know how it was still in her back pocket, or why she was still wearing pants, but it was and she was and the noise was murder. "Yes," she whispered into the speaker, trying to make as little sound as possible.

"Bruiser, you need to train this afternoon."

"Garth?" Why was he so loud?

"Who else?"

"I can't."

"Why not?"

"I'm sick." She was still whispering, but she could tell from his tone he had guessed why.

"You're hung over y'damn featherweight, now get out here in the next hour or Jimmie'll have your skin." His lack of sympathy was unsettling. Kary told him that as creatively as she could manage only to get a dial-tone response. He'd hung up on her.

Her keys were on the counter and her car was in its spot outside her apartment. Why was her car there? She'd driven it to the winery and then Diette had driven them downtown and Kary had a stub to show she'd taken a cab back, so how was her car here? Had she let someone drive it? Kary never handed over her keys.

She'd ask Diette later, for now, she needed to save her hide from Jimmie's wrath.

✦

"You smell like a bar." Garth told her while he held the heavy bag for her.

"Well I feel like a bitch. *You* can bugger off." It hurt to be annoyed, and soon it was going to hurt worse.

"Did you even brush your teeth, or just change clothes?" She had to think about that one too long for the answer not to be obvious. "*Wow*, Seth always said you were a slob but *seriously*?"

"I said bugger *off*," she punched the bag harder than she was supposed to and swept his feet from under him in the same motion.

Garth hit the ground at an angle that wouldn't hurt him much. "Someone's feisty. Need to nip down to Wise Guys and take a little hair off that dog?"

The idea of the warm beer served at Wise Guys made Kary feel green. "No, *por favor* no."

He grinned up at her from the floor. "Or my mama always told me that tobasco sauce in an artichoke smoothie would just—"

Kary barely made it to the bathroom in time.

Chapter 5

Monday morning was quiet, the way Monday mornings always were. Which was good, Kary needed the time to catch up on the work she neglected all Saturday and most of Sunday. "Wonder if the boy genius'll come see his lady friend again today?" Jason teased when he came in a few minutes after she did but Kary ignored him. Nothing, not even her co-worker's silly comments, was going to keep her from *finally* getting through her list of Browning's dramatic monologues in time for Peters' class.

✦

"Um?" A familiar, quiet voice broke her reading reverie some hours later.

Kary glanced up at the profile without breaking concentration. "Oh, hey Aspect."

The hand that had been going to tap her desk came down harder than she expected. "Miss Dogg, I'm not.."

Kary snapped back to where she was and what she was supposed to be doing. "Mr. Foxx, I'm so sorry I was just—wait." She'd glanced at him and greeted the profile her subconscious recognized. She didn't mess up on things like that, not ever. "You *are*, aren't you?"

He shifted under her squint. "No, I'm just here for Spanish help again, *porfavor*?" His accent was still awful.

She blew out a puff of air that made her lips buzz against each other, "Yeah, sure." She didn't believe him. "Whatcha got?" His homework was better this time, not nearly as many mistakes as before, but there was still progress to be made. Kary bent her head over the creased sheet and didn't say another word about her suspicions.

Locked in the safety of her apartment that night after the afternoon's work and an evening run to the grocery store, Kary re-examined her theory. The shy, nerd kid who struggled with Spanish was actually sidekick to the Amazing Adamant, defender of peace and destroyer of buildings in Commonland for years. The idea was ludicrous and almost plausible. The supers who were ousted by the press always had these meek alter egos that crouched somewhere behind the *nom de gurres* they wore with the spandex.

But was she *sure*? Accusing someone of being a super, even falsely, could have a huge impact on their real person lives. And if she was certain then the revelation of his secret identity could lead to all sorts of dangerous things… if the tabloids she never read were to be believed.

Yeah, she was sure. She'd known that jawline was familiar and she never forgot these things. She'd already noticed the diference in his gait after the day after he and Adamant spent a night playing rough enough to tear down several buildings. *And* he got defensive when she mentioned Aspect. Even if he walked hunched up like he was scared and wore clothes that hid his musculature, enough coincidences were piled onto evidence that Kary was still *almost* positive. She hadn't lived in a neighborhood where vigilance and the ability to recognize silhouettes at a glance was a necessary skill for a few years, but some things never went away.

If she was right, what was she going to do about it?

If she was right, then she could put an end to the Aspect, one half of the *Dynamic A's*. There would be instant fame waiting for her on the internet if she went public. There'd be TV interviews and with some luck she could probably weasel into her own terrible cable show, ousting the alter egos of supers for adoring fans. There were enough people out there resenting the Register, that she could have a niche in the trashy TV market if she wanted it. For a couple seasons at least.

But did she resent the Register *that much*? They hadn't patrolled her hood when she was a kid, hadn't kept her brother out of trouble, hell, hadn't kept Kary out of trouble after their mom died and Seth went on the road. But was it their job to be personal heroes? Was the Register... a many-headed, multinational cooperative of supers and sidekicks trying to keep an entire globe safe.... really responsible for her shitty childhood? Was Aspect, a kid younger than herself, someone who should bear the brunt of her formless anger at entities powerful enough to change the world, who hadn't bothered to change hers?

No, there were power structures and inequities that needed to be addressed when it came to the supers who fell under Register jurisdiction but outing one kid on the internet wasn't going to change any of that.

Besides, she wasn't thrilled with the idea of being a bad television personality. There was too much trash on cable already. And, as much as she hated dealing with perpetual construction and road blocks in the major cities, supers were *necessary*. With the advent of the Enlisted and its roster of super villains, supers provided valuable services that immediately resolved problems. Governments were too often tied up in red tape to do more than clean up damage or destroy even more than the supers with inaccurate missile strikes and the like.

She'd been cooking without realizing while she mused. Her hands busy with chopping bell peppers and onions, sautéing the lot with chicken and salt. It was almost done now; Kary stared down into the sizzling pan like she wasn't sure how it'd gotten there.

"It doesn't matter." She told her supper, giving the pan a shake to make the chicken and vegetables flip. Three pepper pieces fell onto the stove top; Kary picked them up gingerly with her fingertips and tossed them back in with the rest to disinfect through frying. Who or what Jonathan Foxx was in his spare time was no business of hers. Supers only brought trouble to the real people they got close to, and she had enough trouble in her life between Seth, school, and the gym. She didn't want any more.

Satisfied with herself, Kary poured the contents of her pan onto a plate, pulled two tortillas from their bag, and took the mess back to her room to eat on the bed while she watched the news on her computer.

Seth and Bethanne drove into Commonland early Friday afternoon to be with Kary for the pre-tournament blood tests. The couple chattered and flirted at each other so much they hardly noticed that the girl standing between them hadn't said a word since they got to the pit where the tournament would be held. The young fighter was too busy watching her potential competition to listen—at least that was what she would have told her brother and Bethanne if they ever noticed and asked.

In reality she was trying very hard not to look too green, too nervous. This was it. Once they had her blood on file she couldn't duck out. The line shuffled forward and a nurse came up to Kary with an impersonal smile on her face and a hand already out for the paperwork. "Karissa 'Bruiser' Dogg," she told the woman, handing over the form Jimmie had given her the night before, vouching for her place in the tournament.

"Excellent, any exposure to radiation or extraterrestrials in your childhood?" The nurse was looking the form over as she spoke.

"No."

"History of meta-genes in your family?"

"None."

"Has any of your family been tested recently?"

"My brother, he was clean." Seth's broad palms were on her shoulders, Kary tried to loosen the tension in her neck. She knew he could feel the nerve-clench in her muscles.

"Good, this way." She was sent to another nurse, her brother trailing along with her. Bethanne stepped away, pleading squeamishness around needles. Seth laughed and muttered something about getting used to it eventutally. Kary said nothing and tried to keep her mouth in a hard line.

Blood testing in competitive martial arts, hell, in *sports*, had become a necessity in the past few decades. It was the only way to make sure everyone was starting on an even playing field, physiologically speaking.

Kary turned her face away when the nurse put the needle to the vein. Suddenly Seth was chattering at her a mile a minute about how proud he was and how good she was going to do and how they needed to make sure there was steak in her fridge to put on her bruises tomorrow night. Kary chattered back with as much enthusiasm as she could until the nurse stepped away, two vials of blood in hand and the needle safely out of the girl's flesh.

"That's the worst part." Seth confided when they brushed through the curtain while the nurse labeled the vials and prepped for her next patient.

"Really? How?"

"The nurse is the one guy you can't hit back." Seth was chuckling while he waved Bethanne over. "You can hit anyone else who'll try an' hurt you but never the nurse. She's gonna stick you and there isn't any helpin' it backways or forwards."

Kary nodded, "Well when you put it that way…"

"Yes?"

"Supper's on you tonight."

"What? No—"

"I'm traumatized. You can't expect a traumatized person to pay for their own supper."

"Twerp."

"Skinflint."

"What's for dinner guys?" Bethanne had finally reached them. Seth threw his hands up and led his girls out to the parking lot without arguing further.

Chapter 6

Everyone came out to watch the tournament. Jimmie, Garth, Rodney, her brother, Bethanne, even Diette was there for Kary's first fight but had to run off to sign for a shipment at the winery after that. The second and third fights passed in a blur—a flurry of fists Seth would say and she would roll her eyes at the cliché. By the fourth and final fight, Kary was dragging from her long day. Even with the breaks between her matches, she felt the wear in her bones. Rodney had planned her snacks throughout the day, no meals during a marathon tournament but lots of high-protein, high fat little snacks... and a pair of caffine pills that Seth snuck her when the trainer wasn't looking. The pills weren't against regulations, but they made some fighters jittery and Rodster wasn't about to take that chance before the match that decided it all.

Kary twitched; maybe the pills were putting her on edge. There was a spasm in the edge of her eye, and a trickle down her face like a thought leaking from her skull. This was it, the caffine was going to be her downfall; she kept her fists up and flinched when the next blow came—

Get your head in the ring.

And then the fight focused in: Jimmie was shouting from her corner, Rodneya calm presence behind him with a glob of vasaline ready on his glove to seal in the blood that was coming down from a broken spot by her temple next time the bell called for a break. Garth and Seth were almost crawling under the ropes as they cheered. She had a solid minute left in this round and the other girl was *big*. Still technically a featherweight like Kary but even taller. She was probably one of the girls who was light in the class above and starved for a few days to squeeze down. Her legs were as long as Kary's and her reach was further but her punches weren't as hard and her feet weren't as accurate.

The next swing came and Kary knocked it aside without blinking. The younger Dogg put her heel up under the ribs of the taller girl and danced back out of her reach. She couldn't afford to get caught in a clinch with an opponent who could use her superior weight for an advantage. The bell, where was the bell? There was a funny clicking in Kary's jaw at the hinge and there were bruises all up and down her side, she needed to corner. She needed to sit. The trickle down the side of her head was distracting. She needed to be somewhere quiet where she could nurse her hurts and hide for awhile.

The other girl was jabbing but there wasn't much venom in her arm. Her opponent was just as tired and, if Kary had guessed right, was running hungry right now, whereas Kary had been carbing up for days.

Ding-bing-ding.

The bell.

Kary drug back to her corner where Jimmie put the stool under her almost as she fell. Seth took her mouth guard without making a face at the blood and spit that came with it. Garth squirted water in her mouth while Rodney ran a line of words Kary couldn't really hear in her ear and a smear of grease along her hairline. All the men in her life in one spot and not one was the least concerned with the shiner she could feel rising.

Ding-bing-ding.

The fighter swished and spat into the bucket offered to her and took her mouth guard back without protest. *Go get 'er Bruiser.* She wasn't even sure which one said it, it didn't matter. The only thing that mattered at this point was a solid twenty-four hours of sleep and a nice hot bath.

Dance dance dance, jab jab bob and weave, *step—*

Kary saw stars, a perfect right square to her mouth, her lip split like the skin of a swollen fruit and she was pretty sure her teeth moved back a solid inch in her skull. She danced back a step for space and blinked at the spinning lights and then she saw it: the other girl was dropping her shoulder. She was going to swing everything in for a second right hook but this time Kary recognized the strike and was already angled. Her leg was lifting, that perfect high roundhouse she'd worked on since Rodney taught her how to make her legs swing up over her head when she wanted them to. She hit the other girl with the sweet spot on the top of her foot, the point where all that power and all that practice came together.

KO.

The other fighter sank to her knees and then to the mat, down and unmoving while the ref beat out the count. It was over. The fight, the tournament, the day, finished.

The men were in the ring, her men. Lifting her onto their shoulders and laughing while she drooped over their heads trying to hold on with her clumsy gloves. Bethanne was over somewhere to the side screaming and Jimmie was shouting that his Bruiser would be fighting regular in the little cage at the bar starting next month and Kary didn't have the energy to tell him to shove off.

＋

They told her later that Bethanne was the one who cleaned her up. Took the fighter to the communal showers in the big gym where the tournament was hosted and rinsed her with a sprayer until her skin wasn't sticky. Combed her hair out of its sodden braid and washed it with industrial strength shampoo from the wall dispensers. Toweled her off and wrangled her limp limbs into the robe Kary woke up in.

She looked at the clock, 3AM. There was a song about 3AM, but she couldn't remember the words. It wasn't the twenty-four hours of sleep that she'd wanted, but the low hum of her injuries was going to keep her awake, so she rolled to her feet instead.

Seth was awake on the couch when his little sister stumbled out to ask about the aftermath. "Bro? wha' happen'd?" He laid aside his phone and lit a lamp, Kary blinked at the glow.

"You won." He was so *proud*; she could hear it even if she was still light-blind from the lamp. "It's almost unheard for a fighter to win their first tournament but you did and I'm just so—"

41

"Don' you cry on me." She fell into a bundle on the couch beside him.

He stood even as she sat. "Fine, I won't. But you need meat." She considered a joke about not having had a date in months but the words weren't in the right order in time for the line to land. "Here." He slapped a steak lightly on the side of her face that wasn't cut and Kary held it there.

The meat was cool on her skin and the cool felt nice. "You an' Bethanne leaving in the morning?" She was awake enough now that the bruises on her ribs made it hurt to breathe. The crack across her jaw made enunciating painful.

"Beth rented a car and drove out after we got you home. I just wanted to stick around and make sure you woke up before I headed back to Marshal."

"You're going *now*?" Kary tried not to let her wince become visible but she knew it was. Talking hurt.

"Yeah, Rodney expects me back in my gym by noon tomorrow. He only gave me Friday and Saturday off 'cause he wanted to watch your first fight." Smiling hurt too, but Kary smiled anyway. She should've expected as much from Rodster. He was there for her brother's career and wasn't about to let either Dogg forget it.

"When'll I see you?" *Next*, she forgot to peg next onto the end of her sentence but he understood her without it. Something tugged the skin on her forehead when she wrinkled it and Kary raised her fingers to feel the little tension plasters Rodney must've put there to hold the cut closed. Jimmie always sealed cuts with glue and Seth would have used a normal bandaid.

"My next fight is next week and if I win that then we move to the championship rounds. I'll have my sponsors put you up in their hotel."

42

Kary's grin got wider and she had to lick away blood when her split lip cracked open again. Sponsors always gave the best parties before and after the fights. "Okay, but no box seats."

"No?"

Kary swatted at him with her face steak and blood-spattered Seth's cheek. "No silly, I wanna be in your corner. I'll hold the spit bucket or somethin'."

His grin should've broken his face in two it was so big. "Sounds perfect, Sis."

✦

Kary waved her brother off from the landing outside her apartment less than an hour later. The moon was setting somewhere on the far side of the complex; the stars were bright and low in the sky. Kary breathed out slow and looked down the dark stretch of stairs; she wasn't sure how she'd manage them Monday morning. Right now the idea of even walking back to her couch hurt.

She washed her face in the kitchen sink as the sky outside began the slow transition from dark night to gray morning. There, hovering over a stack of dirty plates with water and steak juices running off her skin and her lip dribbling blood, her mind finally crystallized. Morning was breaking. It was time to work.

✦

Diette stopped by for supper that evening and was greeted by Kary's swollen face and a glass of wine. "The eggplant parm is almost done; in the meantime try the Chianti."

"Chianti, what're we celebrating?" Diette swirled and sniffed the wine much more elegantly than her friend.

"Mmm," Kary made a thinking noise in her throat while she peered into the oven, "call it my win."

"Okay," Diette swished a sip of wine between her teeth before swallowing, "now what's the real reason we're celebrating?"

Kary shrugged, splaying her oven mitts. "I dunno Die, I'm just… happy." She bent and pulled the tray from the oven, setting it on the wooden pads waiting for it. Her laminate countertop was too cheap to lay hot pans on without trivets; a dusty fruitbowl hid the melted spot where Kary learned that the hard way. "Hand me the spatula?"

Diette reached into a drawer and handed over the utensil like she knew her friend's kitchen as well as she knew her own. She probably knew it better. "Well, if you're not going to be interesting— have I got a story for *you*."

Kary grinned and began plating up their supper, settling in to hear something good.

+

"You look *awful*." Jason didn't mince words when Kary walked into the tutor center Monday morning. The month had turned, new shifts had been assigned and *still* her boss insisted she and Jason take the first slot of the week.

"You look terrible yourself." He didn't really. He looked disgustingly put together for eight on a Monday but Kary was never going to admit that.

"No, seriously, did you get into a fight or something?" He was coming over to her desk like she needed to be held upright.

Kary waved him away and swung her bag down to rest beside her chair. "Four actually, I had a kickboxing tournament this weekend."

"*You* fight?"

It felt like this shouldn't be new information to him but Kary shrugged. "Not as much as Seth."

"Well Seth's a pro, and a guy—I mean you're a—"

"A girl?" she cut him off and raised a challenging eyebrow. "A girl who won the featherweight title this weekend with four wins, three of them KOs?" Only one knock-out and it had been lucky but he didn't know that. Or *need* to know that.

Jason swallowed audibly. She could tell from his face that he didn't want to answer her challenge. Pity, there was an itch in her palms that only a good row would fix.

"Mind your own business Dods." She sat at her computer as brusquely as she could manage on stiff bones. "I'm fine and the others look way worse." Another lie, she had no idea how the others looked. Theoretically they looked worse because they lost but the reality was a crapshoot at best. Kary didn't look back at her coworker to see him pout.

Instead she pulled up her email and the morning news. The *Dynamic A's* had been at it again this weekend. The Black Sorcerer, a terrible name since his skin was purple, had threatened to raise the seas until they swallowed some little town on the east coast because centuries ago the town citizens burned his lover as a witch. Adamant and Aspect and a whole slew of others from the Register had been called in to put him down or bring him to justice or whatever it was they were supposed to do.

Idly Kary played a clip of footage, watching Aspect fall fifty feet to crash into the rocky beach they were fighting on. When he stood up it was from the bottom of a sizeable crater. What was his power exactly? Most supers' powers were public knowledge but Aspect's seemed to change fight to fight. Watching him dust off his uniform and climb out to start the attack again Kary assumed it was something to do with durability and closed out of the window, glancing toward the door in time to watch Jonathan Foxx shuffle through the tutoring center door. *Think of the devil...*

She smiled as he sat down and her lip split open again. "Oh, 'scuse me." Kary tugged a Kleenex from the box on her desk and pressed it to the seam she'd thought was finally sealed enough for her to quit worrying it. "I had a kickboxing tournament this weekend and I'm looking a little battered." He was squinting at her the same way Jason had, like she might fall over at any second.

"Are you *sure* you're alright?" His hands were inside his bag but they weren't rummaging.

"*Sí*, what've we got today?"

He pulled out his homework and a tube of ointment. "Try this on your lip." He held it out to her. Kary eyed his hand, it looked like a normal over the counter antibiotic but if he was who she thought he was then his Neosporin might not be what he said it was. "It's *just* ointment, I promise."

There was a low note of authority in his voice that made her smile inside. *She knew it.* That was Aspect's voice, somewhere buried under the squeak he used when he pretended to be a real person. She *knew* she

46

hadn't missed her guess. "Thanks." Kary took away the tissue and smeared a tiny dab of ointment on her lip. By the time she handed the tube back she could feel the skin knitting together. "*Just* ointment, huh?" She kept her pitch normal, rather than lowering it. If she lowered her voice too much Jason would get curious and try to listen in. If they sounded normal he wouldn't give them a second thought.

"*Good* ointment." She swiped her still-greasy finger against the break on her forehead and felt it too start to smooth over.

"Mhmm," Kary made a noise like she didn't believe him and spun his homework on the desk so it was facing her. "Okay, now with your preterit conjugations—"

✦

There was someone leaning against her car when she walked out of her gym that evening. The medal Jimmie had presented to herthumped a hollow stutter against her chest when she stopped and recognized the now-familiar profile.

"Aspect? Why're you— Shouldn't you be off saving a city or something?" He shouldn't be here. Her plan to quietly keep his secret didn't involve him actually hunting her down and them *talking* about it.

"We need to talk."

No panicking. Doggsnever panicked. "A super needs to talk to a civilian, why?" She hit the unlock button on her key fob and brushed past him to the open trunk and tossed in her bag.

"You know."

She went still. "Maybe." Not panicking.

47

"No, you *know*."

Kary felt tension in the backs of her hands and an itch in her palms. She flexed her fingers without realizing, like she was prepping for a fight. "So?" She didn't appreciate his vague phrasing.

"Is there somewhere we can talk… privately?" Kary squinted at him in the bad lighting and her fisted hands fell limp. He sounded like the kid who shuffled through her tutor center. He was so *young* and probably just as baffled by the situation as she was.

Split second decisions rarely ended well in her experience but Kary made one anyway. "My apartment, 6301 in the Grove. See you there." She slammed the trunk and stepped past him again to her driver's side door.

"See you there."

Chapter 7

A kid in an oversized hoodie and loose jeans with a backpack slung over his shoulder knocked on Kary's door less than five minutes after she got home. A look through the peephole showed her a glimpse of a raised hood and a black half-mask. "You look like a creep." She told the sidekick when she opened it to let him in.

He swept past her in a swirl of cool autumn air. "Would you rather I came in through a window?"

She was on the top floor and had no balcony except the landing at the top of the stairs leading to her door, "Could you?" He laughed like it was a silly question but stood awkwardly in the center of her living room while she re-locked the door out of habit. "Sit and lose the mask. I know who you are Johnathan."

"Johnnie." He sat and pulled the mask from his face with a funny sucking sound.

It felt weird to call him the name he'd introduced himself with a lifetime ago. "Still, Johnnie?" There was a red crease pressed around his eyes where the mask had been and his hair was unruly, it was humanizing to see a super like this.

"It's what my friends call me."

"Supers have friends?" This was getting weird. She needed to stop asking questions. Uninvolved people didn't ask questions.

"Sure, the norms we meet in day-life. Other supers we've collaborated with." What were they, bands on albums? "All supers on the Register know each other, *lots* of friends. It's a small community." For some reason she didn't believe that *lots* was as large a number as he wanted her to think it was.

"Small community, lots of friends… Huh." Why was she having this conversation? "*Please* tell me you came into my home to talk about something *besides* super social networking."

Johnnie shifted uneasily. "Yeah, um, how'd you figure it out?"

"Figure what?" She knew exactly what he was asking but she wasn't going to give him the satisfaction of filling in his gaps.

"How'd you find out who I am?"

Kary felt sly and tried not to let it show. "Your jaw, I don't forget facial structure."

"Plenty of people have seen me on TV and in day-life, what made you special?"

What made her special? How deep into her backstory did he really want to get? How many times it saved her skin growing up being able to peer down the darkened block or across an alley and recognize who was coming at a glance and know whether she just needed to duck her head or cross the street or get ready for trouble.

Aguas-aguas-aguas.

Watch out-watch out-watch out.

Cops who dragged people away, gangs with their stray bullets and empty cruelties, supers who could tear the roof off a house and didn't care where the debris landed or how long it took the city to fix the road afterwards.

After their mom died and before Rodney came into the picture, she and her brother had to watch everything. Seth had grown big, tall and broad with thick calluses across his knuckles and a brawler's walk even before the trainers started paying attention to him. Kary though, she hadn't. For years, seeing everything had been her best defense.

Even now, with a tournament medal on her chest and the thickened skin of a fighter laced across her own fists, old habits died hard.

But was she going to tell him that?

No.

Kary sucked in and spewed what felt like dialogue from every bad romcom ever. "How many people actually *see* you? You walk like you want people to look right through you, and you talk like you don't wanna be heard. I just happened to actually *see*, that's all." Exactly like a line from the protagonist in a bad *teenage* romcom. Not even a real, big girl romcom with gratuitous sex scenes and lots of drinking.

"*Really?*"

Was he buying this? Were *all* sidekicks saps? "*No,*" Kary couldn't let him believe some shit line she didn't even understand. "I had a hunch, I watched: you limped the day after *Aspect* took a beating. I put two and two together. Don't flatter yourself."

"That's exactly what you said the first time."

"Maybe, but the second time it sounded a lot less cheesy."

"That's true."

He was flexing his hands the way her brother did when he wasn't sure what to say. "Hey, if you're worried about me telling people, I won't." His eyes widened when she said it. "I don't want to deal with the press that comes with being a super outer any more than a super wants to be outed, so just—you do your thing and I'll keep my mouth shut like a good little civilian."

She paced toward the kitchen, swooping to drag bottles of water from the torn-open case on the floor as she walked. "Want one?" She glanced over her shoulder, "What?"

"You flinched. When you bent over you flinched."

Kary tossed him a bottle and cracked open her own. "Told you earlier, I got a little dinged up in my tournament. They're just some bruised ribs."

"Let me see?"

"A teenage boy trying to talk a woman out of her shirt. Original."

He blushed and tried to cover it by breaking the seal and taking a gulp from the bottle she'd thrown at him. "I deal with lots of bruised ribs in my line of work. I just want to make sure you're okay."

She brushed off his concern, "It's fine Johnnie. *I'm* fine." Her stomach growled. She hadn't re-loaded on calories since before her workout. "Well, I'm hungry but that's a whole other problem." She opened the freezer and dug. "You eaten? I've got three pizzas I can bake."

"What, we each get one and split the third?"

"*Claro.*" Cheap frozen pizzas weren't big enough to share any other way.

He laughed; she liked making the sidekick laugh. He sounded like the kid he was when he laughed. "Then go ahead but no telling when I'll need to run." It sounded suspiciously like he was giving her permission to do

52

something in her own home. Kary was hungry enough not to lecture him.

She spun the dial on her oven and rustled through a cabinet for foil to bake them on. "Adamant keeping you on a leash?"

"I have to always be reachable but it's a quiet city. I *might* get a night off, since it's Monday." Kary slowed in her cabinet rustling but didn't stop. If he had the night off, then what did his being here mean? Exactly how long was this little visit going to take?

Offering to feed him probably wasn't her best move if she really wanted to stay uninterested.

+

"Not all of us like having alter egos." He told her while they blew on their slices. "Some supers barely try to hide, they want the recognition."

Kary had seen that on the news, supers who tried to claim credit for their actions when they looked like real people. It never ended pretty. There always seemed to be hateful crowds outside their mild suburban homes, at least when the cameras were there. "Do you want the limelight?" She bit and chewed gingerly.

He shrugged. "Some, but it's nice to not have the pressure of being Aspect all the time. I must not want to hide very bad though, not if some *norm* could figure me out in a couple of weeks."

She flicked a string of cheese at him. "That norm just fed you, *chico*, show some respect."

"Mmm." He made a playful humming sound like he was considering it but a tiny beep cut him off. He put a finger to his ear, "This is Aspect, go." A pause. "I'll be right there."

53

"Trouble?"

"The good kind." He was halfway to her door, pizza forgotten on the coffee table.

"You're going like *that*?"

He paused, hand stretched toward her deadbolt when Johnnie seemed to realize he was still in his hoodie and jeans. His mask was on her coffee table between their plates. "Mind if I change here?" He looked embarrassed at being caught forgetting himself.

Kary didn't bother to cover her amusement at his discomfort. "Bedroom's on the right, help yourself."

He took his backpack to her room and came back out bare minutes later. Kary looked up from scrubbing their dishes in the sink. "So how'd you get here anyway?" Her voice made him turn but his eyes were already off toward whatever he was called about.

"Trade secret. Mind if I leave my clothes?"

"You're a minor and I could be arrested if someone took that the wrong way."

"There anyone here to take it but you?"

Another sentence that could be misconstrued. Kary raised an eyebrow and he blushed. "You're on a roll."

"Can I leave my stuff or not?" He was getting antsy and she was just getting warmed up.

Boom.

The windows rattled and Aspect, not Johnnie, lost his flush, turning pale. "*Please?*" Something was happening out there, something he had to go help stop.

"Yeah, sure. Just—be careful?"

He grinned over his shoulder and crossed her living room to the outside wall rather than going to the door. The young super opened the glass and climbed out the window and up onto the roof of the apartment building. He stuck to the siding like a fly or a frog and when he flipped up over the lip of the roof and out of sight it was like a move a gymnast would do for the judges. There was a hum she never would've heard if she hadn't been listening for it and a whole section of sky gave a shimmer like a heat wave, moving away from the apartment complex *fast*.

Kary breathed out; some sort of ultra quiet jet with camouflage technology? She walked across the living room to slide her window closed while she wrestled fresh temptation. She could be *major* internet famous for reporting that a mere sidekick had tech like that. The television crews and eventual TV show hostess gig wouldn't be far behind if...

Deciding that her homework for the night could wait until morning, Kary flicked on the 10 o'clock news to figure out what exactly was going down in her *quiet* city.

Conjur Man and Wytch Boy seem to be having difficulties holding the line. We have conformation that Adamant and Aspect are en route, but will they be here in time to help fend off this alien scourge? Cat, back to you at the desk.

Thank you, Jack, in other news homelessness in both Marshal and Commonland cities seems to be droppi—

Kary flipped the TV off, uninterested in local fluff when there were bigger issues at hand. Conjur Man and Wytch Boy? They usually stayed further east and south, around Lake Alexandria, so why would they be in Commonland before the supers who lived here? Kary squinted at the computer in her lap; she had live footage of the scene pulled up online. Wherever the camera guy was he wasn't at a good angle. All she could see was lots of dust and the familiar bolts of gold and silver light from the super sorcerer's spells and the black flares from his apprentice. There was a flash of dull red and the windows of her apartment shook again, that must be the alien weapons.

Zap-zap.

There he was, zipping across the sky in a mottled black-and-gray jet, shooting lasers from the nose into the swirling haze. Aspect fell from a porthole in the belly and the plane kept switching angles to shoot into the fray. Adamant was coming across the skyline in great leaps, his super strength letting him jump building to building like a giant frog. The animalistic outline of another super/sidekick duo could be seen on the edge of the mêlée. Bearkat? The Register wasn't messing around if they'd called *him* in.

There was no reason for her to watch; the aliens, whoever they were, didn't stand a chance against three full supers and their sidekicks. Something swooped in Kary's stomach and she closed her laptop. She couldn't be worried about them, they were practically indestructible. And with the sorcerers around there they could be healed from anything instantly.

She went to bed early that night and tried to sleep through her windows rattling.

+

"Hey, can I swing by and get my stuff?" He was grinning at her like a kid when he found her reading Tennyson in a secluded corner of the library. Kary was struck again by how young Jonathan, Aspect, Johnnie, *what'shisname*, was: just seventeen. A genius and a super and a senior in college, but only a teenager.

"Can you really not get into my apartment without me opening the door?" Kary doubted that was the case.

56

"It's not polite."

"Uh-huh." There was a detective super on the west coast who was notorious for snooping through all sorts of places without permission when he was on the hunt. "Since when do sup—*youlot* have ethics about breaking and entering?"

"Since I know the *nor*— *person* who owns the place." He was mocking her.

"Point." Kary made a scratch with her pencil under the last line she read and looked up at him properly. "You okay?" It had been two days since the aliens decided to invade Commonland and he looked like he hadn't slept since.

"Been a rough couple days." He scrubbed his hair and sunk onto the arm of the overly-boxy, modernist chair she was curled up in. "But we got 'em."

"Who were they?"

"Militants from Binyon—" one of the planets Earth had friendly relations with, "—guess even aliens have radicals." The Binyonese were supposed to be a unified and peace-loving society, that they had any form of militant faction was disconcerting.

"Why here?"

He shrugged, "That's someone else's job."

"Oh." He wasn't concerned. He looked tired, but the alien invasion obviously wasn't high on his list of worries. How often did the Register deal with threats like this, and what percentage of them did civilians actually hear about? "Yeah, sure, I'll be home by seven."

"Huh?"

"Your stuff? I'll be home by seven, swing by anytime. I'll be up late with homework."

"Thanks."

Had he really forgotten the whole reason he came over to talk to her? "Some genius." She muttered, laying the book aside while she dug through her bag for a sticky note to make a memo in it.

"What was that?" He leaned over her, his face playful.

"I *said*, some genius—if you're gonna forget the whole reason you found me *all* the way back here." She was in a back corner of the basement stacks, the end where the hard copies of newspapers and old city records were kept. No one came this far back except couples who wanted to have sex and couldn't book a study room.

"Oh *yeah*?" He looked like he was gearing up for something. Kary didn't wait to find out what.

Thwump.

Both of her feet shot into the chair arm, making him shake off balance. He had already been leaning, now he was falling. The fighter rolled out of the seat in the same motion she'd used to piston her legs and stood over him as he flailed on the furniture. "Yeah."

He was up almost as soon as he was down. They locked arms against each other's shoulders and strained, sneakers grappling on the ancient, indeterminately colored carpet that covered the library basement. Kary swung a leg up to put her knee in his hip. Johnnie twisted with her motion and she was falling, except he held her up, suspended a foot over the floor dangling from the ends of his arms like she didn't weigh anything.

"Give." He grinned down at her like he'd already won.

"*Nunca.*" She hooked an ankle around his knee, pulling his weight down against hers. He staggered and his hands loosened enough for Kary to yank away, dragging back to her feet. "You're not half bad." They were circling each other theatrically.

"I hope so; I got sent to Recluse when I was a kid."

"Recluse?" She hadn't heard of that one. She feinted left and slid in toward his right.

"Yeah, he's one of the trainers. No official Register work, just lots of meditating under waterfalls—" Johnnie dodged her swipe, "—and fighting bears."

Yeah *right*. "Now I *know* you're fibbin'." She came in again to lock arms with the young super, he barely braced while she threw her weight into a twisting throw. "*Cheat*." There were *reasons* supers and meta-humans and whoever else weren't allowed to compete in professional sports.

"*Yup*." He twisted back the opposite way and Kary's weight fell almost to the floor a second time. "Still wanna go?"

She was winded, why was she winded? Even sore from her fight last weekend she shouldn't be *winded*. "Nope." She reared back and headbutted him square in the jaw, making Johnnie drop her in surprise. Kary rubbed her forehead and stood up. The super was massaging his chin. "I need to keep reading, or are you going to attack me again?"

"Oh, *I* attacked *you*?" He straightened today's oversized hoodie like he was offended but there was a smile crawling along his mouth.

Kary shrugged and pretended to straighten her own shirt to mock him. "A girl's got a right to protect herself when she feels threatened—" She felt something wicked pulling her lips back. "—'specially when there's no big strong super around to keep her safe."

Johnnie gripped his chest melodramatically, "My heart, that *hurt*."

"Good."

+

Kary went to bed just after midnight. Johnnie never came by to claim the bundle clothes that he'd wedged into a corner of her couch but she wasn't worried. The news hadn't mentionedsupers besides the continuing cleanup from the attack on Monday, so he probably wasn't hurt.

Not that she would've cared if he was hurt 'cause he was a super and likely had some healing ability. And it wasn't like they were actually *friends*. Acquaintances if anything. He was probably just busy or sleeping. He sure looked like he needed the sleep that afternoon. Kary hoped he was getting some rest; college kids got precious little shut-eye without running around in costumes most nights. Kary rolled over, balling her body in on itself; that had to be it. He was somewhere sleeping.

+

It was almost two when a breeze from her bedroom window pulled her from deep sleep. Kary opened her eyes without stirring, calm, breathe, *wait*. Someone was moving across her floor. Wait. She could almost smell them. *Wait*. One step closer.

Now.

Kary surged out of bed in a flying tackle toward the movement's source, her fists going fast and her bruised ribs protesting the awkward twist she'd had to perform.

60

Hard hands caught her and held her at arms' length. Familiar hands.

"Easy there, Bruiser."

Kary jerked away. "*Johnnie?* It's the middle of the night, what're you *doing* here?" she slept in a t-shirt and panties. Why, *why* did she only sleep in a t-shirt and panties? It was dark, he probably couldn't see.

"You said I could come get my stuff."

"Through my *bedroom?* Your stuff's in the living room, you could've just gone there." Kary ripped a blanket from her bed and draped it around herself like a cloak.

She could hear him scuffing his feet in the dark, like a kid caught red handed. "Well actually—"

"Actually *what?* And how do you know my nickname?" He scuffled again. "Did you spy on my *gym?* Unbelievable." Not really, she already knew he spied on her gym. It was how he found her Monday night but Kary wasn't in the mood for rationality. "This is an *invasion* of privacy after I *swore* to keep your secret and a *violation* of civil rights and a—"

"*Adamant wants to see you.*" He cut her off mid rant in a fast burst of words. Like he was afraid if he didn't say them fast he wouldn't say them at all.

"What?" Johnnie reached over and turned on her lamp like it was an old habit. In the golden light Kary saw that he was in uniform even though there hadn't been any report of the Dynamic A's being out tonight. "What *happened* to you?" Her conclusion that he had been sleeping evaporated as she stared at his face.

His black eye was big enough to spill down his cheek under the mask and there was a scrape on his jaw that was starting to scab. "Training, it's nothing. Will you come? Adamant really—"

"Did *he* do this to you?" She'd never seen him with an injury on his face. She'd seen him walk like he was sore and heard him talk about battles, but never seen him with evidence on his face that someone else might notice and recognize.

"Doesn't matter, Kary, please?"

Kary nibbled her lip, did she really want to go meet some pissed off super who wasn't afraid to rough up his own sidekick? In the middle of the night? When she had classes and work in the morning? No, no she really didn't.

"Gimme a minute to get dressed."

Chapter 8

Kary spent the ride dozing and blindfolded in the back seat while the jet hummed around her like a big cat and Johnnie exuded tangible disapproval for her lack of awe. "You know you're the first norm to see the House in, like, *ever*, right?" He asked when he shook her awake.

Instinctively Kary's hands went to remove the blindfold but he caught them before she could. "See, huh?" She yawned while she let him guide her out of the jet. "You know it's some ungodly hour in, like, the morning, *right*?" She retorted out of habit as fear began a slow pulse in the back of her skull. Real people didn't see super lairs 'cause they weren't supposed to—it was a division that shouldn't be breached.

"So *this* is the norm that's got you charmed, *eh* Aspect?" His voice was big, booming even without the bullhorn he used sometimes to tell civilians to get out of the way when the big disasters struck. It echoed all around her and Kary tried not to visibly cringe against the warm presence that was Johnnie on her right.

"She's a friend Adamant, she promised to keep our secret."

"She *promised*? Well that changes *everything*." His sarcasm was bitter on her tongue when she tried to swallow and speak.

"I *trust* her."

"*Why*?" Kary said the word and felt them staring at her even though her eyes were still bound.

"Um, Kary? Defending you here?"

"But why trust me? I helped you with Spanish a couple times and figured out who you were. Why do you trust me?" Go down swinging. *Always* go down swinging.

"Kary, not helping."

"Why am I here Johnnie? You said Adamant wanted to talk and now he doesn't sound like he even wants to see me. Take me back. I have class in a few hours."

"*Kary.*"

"*What*?"

"Take the blindfold off." Adamant's voice shivered through her bones and left the girl hollow inside. Johnnie untied the bandana before Kary could raise her hands to do as she was bid.

The cloth fell away and the entirety of the House was laid out for her. It was a cave, wide and deep with the jet parked behind her; just one in a long line of sleek, animalistic vehicles lining a smooth runway that sped away into the gloom. There were grottos along the walls where Kary caught glimpses of furniture and large glowing screens. "*Eyes here.*" Adamant still didn't sound happy but at least she could see him now. "Karissa Maria Dogg. Twenty-two years old. Junior at Commonland State University. Born and raised within the city limits, west side. What is your interest in us?"

"Nothing."

He snorted like he didn't believe her. Kary raised her voice a hair and hoped she could manage sincerity on half a night's sleep. "No, *seriously.*" Her voice cracked, she swallowed and tried again. "You have no idea how little I care about getting to know *any* super, much less the baby one going to my *college*. My life is a hella lot simpler without you." Without *either* of them

"Hella?"

She'd gotten a *super*, a big name, inherited title super like Adamant, to say *hella*. What was this night coming to? "Yes, *hella.*"

"Why should we believe you?"

Kary shrugged. "Don't you have truth serums or something? Drug me up, ask your questions and send me home. I've got class tomorrow and I'd like to get *some* sleep."

Adamant and Johnnie shared a look that made her fidget. "Wait here." Chorusing supers were creepy. Kary sat cross legged on the tarmac between the jet and some sort of reptilian motorcycle while they paced away, heads bent together. Their voices were low echoes made musical by the reverberations from every side of the House. In a matter of minutes Kary had curled down against the friction-warm tire of the jet and slipped back into sleep.

"What's with you and sleeping when you should be impressed?" Johnnie was shaking her awake from what felt like a winter's hibernation. He was still wearing his mask and costume but the skin of his face was smooth and unblemished again, like he'd never been injured.

"Why should I be impressed with a place where I'm not wanted?" Kary grumbled back, taking the hand he offered and letting him pull her to her feet. "Can we go yet?"

"Yeah, Foretoken vouched for you."

"Four what?"

"Foretoken, she's a truthspeaker, can't tell a lie even if she doesn't know what she's talking about. We asked if we could trust you and she said yes, *empathetically*."

Emphatically, probably. Kary didn't bother correcting him. "Some chick I've never met vouched for me, *gee* thanks."

"It's an honor. Foretoken doesn't give yes or no answers often. There's usually too much in between for that."

"Great, I'm estatic. Can we go now?" Kary spoke in sarcastic monotone.

Johnnie popped the roof on the jet and laced his fingers together in a step to boost her up. "Your chariot m'lady."

"*Largase*," she muttered as he lifted her without strain. Stupid skinny sidekick with his stupid super strength. She took the bandana when he handed it up after her and had it tied on by the time he was in place at the joystick in the front seat. "Wake me when I'm home." They didn't bother telling Adamant goodbye.

Kary woke to her alarm at eight the next morning with no memory of what happened after she put the blindfold on the second time. She was also still in the jeans she'd put on to go meet the hostile Adamant. "*Punk kid thinks he can carry me into my apartment asleep, no*

respect these days, stupid supers with their late nights and not needing sleep—bah." She kept a steady stream of angry mutters flowing the whole morning.

Chapter 9

Her brother won his fight that weekend and Kary was hammered by the end of the celebration. Jimmie bought a round for her andGarth in the bar that night and then another and another. They both ended up smashed enough that he bought them cab rides too. Jimmie was always generous when one of his alumni was doing him proud and Seth had *always* done him proud. The Mad Dogg and a hotshit new kid were going to duke it out the next Sunday for the title and Kary was going to be pressed against the canvas shouting for him the whole time.

The whole world was gold Friday night while Kary packed her weekend bag. She was leaving first thing Saturday and she already had a good feeling under her skin—a *winning* feeling. Seth was going to bring home the championship belt for the fourth year in a row and she was going to watch from the ground and be right *there* for him. Nothing was going to ruin this weekend for her. *Nothing.*

"Watcha doing?"

The fighter jumped and turned with her fists out, then dropped them and turned back to her packing. Aspect was curled and draped across the top of her half open bedroom door like a cat balanced on a fence. "That can't be comfortable." Couldn't be good for the hinges either. She spoke with her back to him while digging through a drawer for socks and underwear. There was barely enough room between the top of her door and the ceiling to fit the skinny teen, much less fit him comfortably.

He flipped over, still balanced on a surface two inches wide and stretched his back down the corner at an angle that made three vertebra sound out satisfying clicks. "It's not bad." Kary tossed a ball of socks over her shoulder and heard his suit creak when he reached to catch them. "I hope these are clean."

"You think I keep dirty socks in my drawers?" She asked without looking away from her bag.

The ball bounced off the back of her head. "I don't know your life. How you like your cereal, how you take your steaks."

Drowned and bloody. Kary walked to her closet, rummaging through the hangers. "Hey," she pulled two tops from their fellows on the rack. "You think this one, or this one would be better?" One was red and tight with a zipper up the front, the other was black and metal studdedand barely covered the essentials. She didn't try to hide how much she enjoyed making her uninvited guest blush.

"Is there a right answer?" He wasn't looking her in the eye.

"Not really. I'll take both." She slipped them off the hangers and tossed them into her duffle.

"Take them where? Not a street corner I hope, 'cause Adamant and I've shut down all the major pimps in Commonland and he's gonna be *majorly* PO'd if we've missed one."

"Nope, they're going with me to Marshal. Seth's fight's Sunday and Saturday night the sponsors are hosting a party for him."

"Sponsors?"

"Yeah, he's got endorsement deals with two different sports drinks *and* Nike's working with him to design a line of athletic wear." She was so proud of her brother for the last one: *finally* Seth was thinking about his future, beyond the next fight.

"So much for your small-time kickboxer in Canada, huh?" Kary wasn't even embarrassed about that particular whopper. Her logic at the time was flawless; it was the events that followed that were flawed. Events that somehow led to a sidekick deciding he could come and go as he pleased in her apartment; someday she'd sit down and map out how exactly the flaws culminated this way.

"He's done good and Sunday night he'll do better. I *know* it. And get down from there."

"I could always ask Foretoken if you wanted a hint." He slung down from the door and landed beside and a hair behind her.

Kary jabbed her elbow at his kidney and he took the hit even though he had to know that she *knew* that he could've dodged it. "I'll wash your mouth out with soap if you spit junk like that again, *chico*."

"What's with the kid stuff? You know I turn eighteen soon, right?" He was massaging his side even though she hadn't hit him *that* hard. Even puffed with indignation he was barely as tall as the girl.

70

"So? You're still ages younger than me."

"Four years give or take—" he shrugged, "*massive* difference. You know in Register time we're the same age and you probably'd have had my kid by now? Continuing the super legacy and all." He turned away from her was looking at his hands like he was examining his fingernails through the gloves he always wore with his uniform.

Kary considered her list of possible reactions for a half second. "Oh yeah?" She leaned against her young friend's back, draping her arm so that it rested across his flat stomach on the points of his hips. She let her fingers tease along the top of his utility belt. "And if I liked the sound of carrying on a... legacy with you, what would Adamant say about *that?*" She tucked her face around his throat until her lips were under his jaw.

"He would say... that—what're you doing?" She had pulled away a fraction and was blowing in his ear. Johnnie was getting fidgety, nervous. Men, *boys,* were so predictable.

"Relax kid, I'm not gonna go around playing with jailbait." Kary unwound herself from him and tossed her hair, she was trying hard not to laugh and probably failing.

"Why'd you—"

"Because I'm too old for you, Johnnie. You still look like a baby to me, even if you're a baby who can leap small mountains in a single bounce or whatever it is you do." She was being too harsh on him. She was used to telling men to piss off, but not used to turning them down while still trying to stay friends. She needed to lighten the mood. "So you just go find yourself a nice sidekick girl your own age to play footsies with or however it is you supers flirt and leave this norm out of it."

Did he understand? She couldn't see his eyes when he wore his mask, only a pair of blank white orbs. He was smiling but there was something tight around the edges of his mouth. "You thought I'd want an old lady like you?"

His laugh was strained, hers was too when she joined in. "What can I say? I'm vain and I thought it was a standard fantasy."

"Nope, besides, Adamant's got another sidekick coming on pretty soon and she's *hot*."

"Oh yeah?" Kary dug through the bottom of her closet and could only find the left half of every pair of shoes she wanted to take with her.

"Yeah, Adamant Girl."

"His daughter?" Was Adamant old enough to have a daughter old enough to go public as a sidekick? He hadn't looked much older than Kary.

Johnnie chuckled a little, but it still sounded tight. "Fat chance of him having a kid anytime soon." Really? There had to be loads of willing baby-mamas out there, the fem versions of Jason and all that. "Nope, she's his niece. All supers are related."

"*Seriously?*"

"Small community, remember? My mom was a super and my dad was scientist."

"Anyone I'd know?" It was the first time he'd talked about his origin story.

"You might know my norm name but I'm not spilling *all* my beans."

"No, you've gotta save some for Adamant Girl, remember?" When he laughed this time he didn't sound strained. Neither did she.

✦

Johnnie left to patrol the city in the jet just before midnight and Kary went to bed not long after. It wasn't a good night's sleep, by the time her alarm rang the next morning she'd been awake and lying there for an hour waiting on it.

Her bag was packed and her hotel reservation was confirmed. She had a suite in the Marshal downtown Hilton on the same floor as the representatives from her brother's big three sponsors and a microchipped invitation to both the pre and post match parties they would be hosting at one of the downtown clubs. They were going to be invitation only shindigs with bouncers to keep gatecrashers out and all sorts of "live entertainment" Seth told her when she called Saturday morning as she was locking the apartment.

"Strippers, Bethanne's letting you have *strippers* at your sponsor party?" Kary had asked when she heard the tone her brother used. "More importantly, why're you inviting your *baby sister* to a party with strippers?"

"They're not *strippers*… they're dancers." He'd been defensive. She'd been amused.

"With clothes on?"

"*Eh*," she could picture him wagging his hand at angles to indicate approximation, "*mas o menos.*"

"See you in a few hours Bro." Two, she would see him in two hours.

"See you then Bruiser, call if you run into trouble." She hung up without responding to that. He'd been ragging on her driving since she put a dent in that Oldsmobile they nicked for a joyride back when she was too short to reach the pedals properly, a lifetime ago. Before they immigrated to the other side of the city and she started at the high school and he began winning prizefights and the world changed. Before Rodney made sure their world changed.

Pulling her sunglasses down onto her nose, Kary unlocked her car, tossed in her bag, and swung down into her seat.

As she pulled out to the highway to head north she didn't notice the heat shimmer following her in the sky.

Chapter 10

"***Bruiser!***" Kary hugged her brother in the lobby of the hotel after handing her bag off to a bellboy with instructions to take it to her room. "How was the drive?"

"Not bad." She rolled a crick out of her neck. "Mind poppin' my back?"

✦

"Bruiser, I want you to meet—" the base thrummed and she missed the name. "He's the..." Her brother trailed off and waved a hand for the handsome man in an expensive shirt to fill in.

Handsome and expensive was obliging. "Director of creativity for—"

"—for my athletic line with Airwear." Seth cut back in again.

Airwear? Kary was certain he had a deal with *Nike*. At least he *used* to have a deal with Nike. Airwear was still good stuff, quality products, but he wouldn't get half the exposure from a company like that as he would've had with a big, international brand. "Pleasure to meet

75

you." She had to shout to be heard above the music pumping across them in physical waves.

"*Enchanted.*" When she gave him her hand to shake, he kissed her fingers instead. Kary hoped the club lights were low and pulsing enough to hide her blush. "Can I buy you a drink?"

She shot her brother a *go-away* glance that he picked up on in an instant, shuffling back into the crowd without handsome noticing. Kary smiled at him, a run of goosebumps sneaking along her spine under the red top that had made Johnnie uncomfortable. They were good goosebumps. "That'd be great."

He was clever, for a club pickup artist, this creativity director of Seth's. Clever enough that she didn't ditch him after the first round. Kary laughed at the right lines and sipped the cocktail he bought for her without asking what she'd like. She ate the pineapple garnish off the toothpick in a way that made his fingers bounce against the back of her hand when he reached for it to lead her to the dance floor.

He smelled good when his body pressed against hers in the center of the crush of dancers. Like he picked out his cologne for the express purpose of pressing against girls in clubs and making them want to comment on it. His abdomen was firm, not ridged with muscle, but solid enough that Kary didn't walk away fast. She never respected a flirt with a weaker stomach than her's. His breath on her ear was cool when he muttered a suggestion she hadn't heard in a long time.

From the car she shot Seth a text saying she'd see him at breakfast.

✦

Karissa turned over and looked at the glowing alarm clock on the nightstand 7:02. "*Mierda.*" She was rolling towards the edge of the bed as fast as the tangled sheets would let her.

"What's the rush, love?" An arm snaked around her waist, solid but not gym muscled.

"I've got breakfast with Seth in twenty." Breakfast with Seth in an hour but if she admitted that he'd try to hold her for another round and Kary hated being called love.

"You *sure* you couldn't be late?" He was running his lips down her spine.

She unwrapped the arm and slid away. "Positive." She wasn't sure what his name was. Jack? Jake? Jeremy. "Thanks for last night…" Kary trailed off and could tell from his face that he was annoyed she didn't remember his name.

"Johnny," he supplied.

"Johnny," she repeated, what were the odds? "Johnny the creativity director." She was already bouncing to wiggle her jeans on.

"See you at the fight?"

"Um," in the morning light he was older than she'd thought at the club. Maybe in his early thirties? Not unacceptably old but older than she wanted to encourage. "Maybe, but I won't be in the box." She buttoned her fly and grabbed her top from the floor.

"Oh."

"*Yeah.*" She dragged the word out, the red thing zipped up her front like a vest. Kary pulled the tab as she turned toward the door. "*Bye.*"

✦

"Good night?" Seth quirked an eyebrow at her over the rim of his coffee mug at the bistro where they met for breakfast.

Kary was feeling nicely pliable after the evening's exercise and not nearly as hungover as she'd expected. Leaving the club early had advantages besides light cardio. "Not bad, great party."

"You were there for what, ten minutes?"

"*At least* twenty." She signaled the waitress for her own coffee and settled her elbows on the table. "Where's Bethanne?"

Seth shrugged, nonchalant. He looked fresh, well rested for all Kary was certain he wouldn't have left the party before the club closed at two. "Still asleep when I left. She doesn't do a lot of late nights."

Kary snorted at his lie and thanked the waitress when she brought the coffee. "Johnny was nice."

"Thought you might like him."

"*Really* wanted me to skip breakfast with you."

"*Cabrón.*"

She giggled at her brother's faux venom and looked at the menu. It was *good* to see him like this. No one else, no pressure, no depth. Just them, the way they'd always been. When she glanced over the edge laminated pages at him, she could tell he felt the same. There was a warm spot in her tummy even before she sipped the artisan coffee they served at this overpriced little café with the sun running across the tables and the staff dashing around in organic dyed aprons.

"So what's good here?"

+

There were echoes from the crowd down the cement block halls of the dressing rooms when Kary slipped past the guards to see her brother before the fight. The fans were screaming for the warm-up fight like it was a main event. Even in the hollows behind the scenes, she could feel the pulse, the adrenaline sweet and heavy in the back of her throat.

Tonight. *Tonight.* Tonight. *Tonight.*

Tonight was gonna be good.

"Ready?" Seth turned toward her question from the doorway, but his eyes were a million miles elsewhere. He was already in the gold and black silk robe, his gloves strapped on and his feet wrapped in tape. He was perfectly still, every muscle taut, ready in the middle of the floor.

Rodney was walking a slow circle around his fighter, picking up first one glove and then the other to re-check the tape sealing them to his hands. Bending down to check the wraps on his fighter's feet, running a hand over the smooth bands, he was trying to hide his nerves from his fighter and his fighter's sister. His kids.

The coach answered when Seth didn't. "He's ready. Born ready."

"Damn straight." Her brother's voice was low and smooth. She grinned: his serious voice. His gonna win it *all* voice. "How're you Sis? You look like a round girl." Round girl equaled whore and they both knew it. Seth was dating a round girl and they both knew what that meant too.

She was in the metal studded, black top, the structured leather bra Johnnie had been unable to look at. It made her feel dangerous, the way it showed off how cut her abs were and pushed her tits up around her ears. "Like a distraction Bro," she corrected him, "I look like a distraction."

"You think a champion level fighter's gonna get distracted by a girl in the other corner?"

She shrugged, probably not. "He might. Or it might do nothing. Either way I look *good*." He saw through her bravado and she knew it. She shot a play punch at his shoulder and he swatted her away.

Jab-jab. His right glove flew towards her face twice, just barely tapping her nose each time. Kary didn't flinch even though she saw the second one coming. The fighter felt the air move with the force behind her brother's arm, if he'd extended all the way—if he'd actually *hit* her—even on accident, she would've walked away with a broken nose and fractured cheek bones.

But he wouldn't hit her. He'd *never* hit her full out. He knew his body and he knew her trust and those were the two things that he'd sworn all his life he would never corrupt. Seth grinned at his sister with a mouthful of teeth that had been battered in a dozen times when they were kids, before Jimmie found him, turned him into a real fighter instead of some street brawler. The dentists had done a good job over the years but his left canine would always be crooked. He liked it that way—it added flare to the *Mad Dogg* name.

A bell sounded somewhere in the distant pit. A blurred voice came over the speaker in the dressing room announcing that it was time for the fighters to move to where they'd make their entrances. Rodney came up behind Seth, straightening his robe and flipping the hood up over his fighter's head.

Seth winked at her from the hood's shade. "Well Bruiser, we gonna go win ourselves a few rounds?"

80

Kary rolled her head and heard her vertebrae click. She gave her brother the same, slow smile. "Yeah, *let's.*"

Chapter 11

The pit roared. The canvas thrummed like they were dancing on a drumhead. Kary had been screaming for years and minutes, watching, analyzing, drinking in every punch, every elbow drive and heel strike and it was all too *much*. Her brother was too good. He knew everything, anticipated everything, countered and blocked and battered like the fight was scripted. This was it. She could feel in her bones that this was the best fight of his life and she was right *there*.

She squirted water in his mouth between bouts and held the bucket when he spat. She toweled his face. Checked his gloves. Handed Rodney the ice pack and vasaline. Slapped his shoulder and told him to mind that southpaw and watched from her place at eye-level with the fighters' calves with bated breath. The other fighter was young, maybe even her age but his youth showed. There was a lot to be said for that kind of vigor but here her brother's experience carried more weight.

The stands agreed. Half of them were barking the way only true Mad Dogg fans supported their fighter. Kary barked too. She growled and slavered and howled victory when Seth connected a punch to the kid's jaw that should laid the kid flat, but only for a second.

The referee made them step back and did a spot check on the kid's eyes for concussion. The stands went quiet: if he was deemed unfit to continue, the fight would go to Seth and there wouldn't be a judge in the world who could take it away from him. Kary was leaning so far forward she was almost under the ropes, onto the canvas when the kid shook the ref off and wheeled his gloves for the match to keep going.

In the lull before the crowd exploded Rodney muttered something about updating the super screening tests under his breath. "*What?*" She shouted at him over the roar that surged up to wrap and tie them like a present.

"Nothin' Bruiser." He called back. That wasn't like him, not telling her something. Rodney didn't have much backbone except when it came to Seth's training. All the skill and none of the spine, it was something the entire fighting community laughed about on a regular basis—when they thought the Doggs were out of earshot. Everyone knew how protective they could be over the trainer who was more than a trainer to them.

She kept her eyes on the fight but was preoccupied. Who'd fooled the tests? *How?* The tests couldn't be fooled—that was the whole point. They were randomized and constantly evolving. It was big business to keep athletes at all levels of competition from doping or cheating by dent of being latent supers. Huge companies made lots of money on those tests. Why hadn't anyone noticed? At this level there was so much scrutiny on the fighters that—

Crack.

His arm was limp, why was his arm limp? *Pick it up Seth, what're you doing?* He was screaming, his mouth guard spilled from his teeth on the ground and the kid was backing up with his hands raised over his head and his eyes wide.

The shoulder. The shoulder. *The Shoulder.*

It was hanging different. Wrong. It was hanging *wrong.* Broken. It was hanging broken and limp and her brother was kneeling on the canvas holding it with one clumsy glove while the stadium howled confusion and the bell rang that the fight was over.

Dislocated, fractured in three places, broken clean in one, muscles disconnected from the bone in two: he'd never fight competitively again. Kary absorbed the information mutely while doctors and nurses murmured around his bedside and sponsors swamped the hall outside waiting to find out if they needed to start severing contracts. Johnny stared her down from where he leaned beside a fake fern; she walked into her brother's room without glancing sideways.

Rodney was there, so was Bethanne. Her brother's found family in one antiseptic little hospital room circled, hovering, while he sat like a rock waiting for something. Waiting for someone to tell him what to do. He looked like a child; lost, stoic, patient even if he wasn't sure what for.

There were words she could say. The empty, comfort-words people used when they couldn't really understand someone else's pain. Tonight, they would just be wasted air.

She kissed her brother's forehead and told him she needed to get back to Commonland for class in the morning. She told him he had her number and to call any time, she'd leave the ringer on. He didn't respond, and she left. There was nothing she could do.

+

She slept on top of her covers with the light on that night, still in the black top and jeans. She didn't remember falling asleep, only waking up the next day in an unhappy fog and dragging herself through her morning routine. It wasn't until she got to the tutor center and Jason said he was sorry about her brother that the whole thing came crashing back and Kary wept for the first time since their mom died a decade before.

+

Johnnie came in for Spanish help about the time the fighter finally got ahold of herself. "How was your weekend?" There was a bitter note in his voice that made her twitch.

"Not now Johnnie." She breathed, taking the homework from his fingers unceremoniously. Jason was watching their reflection on his computer screen again; she didn't have the energy to deal with either boy right now.

The sidekick went quiet, mutinously quiet. Kary glanced over the paper, his answers were flawless. He'd been using the tutor center as an excuse for morning visits instead actual academic help for a couple of weeks. "Don't forget the accents on your preterits." She told him crisply, handing it back.

He glared at her, but when he turned toward the room at large his face was blank. If Jason was looking for evidence that she and Johnnie knew each other outside of the tutor center he'd never find it on the incognito sidekick's face. Kary wasn't so sure her poker face could match his. "Mind if I cut out, Jason?"

She didn't look away from her computer to watch him answer. "Go ahead, I'll cover for you."

"Thank's Dods, I owe'ya one." She lit out of the tutor center and skipped class to go home. It'd been too shitty of a Sunday to deal with more people than she had to.

Johnnie knocked on her door while she was making lunch. When Kary let him in he was still in street clothes but his hoodie was gone, replaced by a black athletic shirt, the kind that clung to his pects and outlined the ridges on his tummy. She rolled her eyes but only after she'd turned away. "What do you want Johnnie?"

"Just seeing how you are."

"I'm fine."

"*Really?*" He dragged it out like he didn't believe her.

"What do you *want?*" She was angry and it had nothing to do with him and she knew it. She considered telling him that and apologizing but didn't.

He looked sulky. "You fucked a guy this weekend."

Kary went still, Johnnie *never* cursed. "*That's* what you're on about?" Of all the idiotic, pigheaded, *childish* things, he was worried about who she chose to have her one night—"How'd you know that?"

He didn't budge. "Did you even *know* him?"

86

"It's none of your business."

"Did you?"

"*Johnnie*—"

"*Did you?*"

"*No.*" Why was she blushing? "I didn't know him, okay?" She didn't care what he thought about her sexcapades. "That's the *point* of a one-night stand." She didn't care. She didn't *care*.

He looked like she'd kicked him. "You *do* that?"

"Have sex? *Still* none of your business."

"But—"

"Johnnie you petulant *child*, I make my own decisions." He still hadn't told her how he knew about her one-night stand. "Do you have anything you *actually* wanna talk about or are you just here to ask about things that aren't your business?" She should pull back on her temper. She didn't want to pull back. She wanted to rip and tear. She wanted *blood*.

"I just—"

"My brother's career is *over*, Johnnie. He's *broken* and his sponsors're leaving him and there's no backup plan so if all you're doing today is lecturing me about the choices *I* make Mr. follow-a-super-never-question-orders, then you can get the *fuck* out of my house." She wasn't crying, she was shouting. She was angry. Hurt. Ready to fight. Ready to run. Ready to curl up and sleep until Tuesday morning came and she could focus back in and ignore the rest of the world.

She couldn't look at him. She wouldn't.

When he finally answered, his voice was small. Shamed. "I'm sorry about your brother, I didn't know. We were called off Sunday night so I didn't get to watch the fight." Didn't get to watch the *fight*. So what

87

was he watching that he knew about her going back to the creativity director's hotel room?

Not looking at him.

He sighed deep and kept going. "And I'm sorry I followed you to the party. It was stupid."

Yes, yes it was.

"Forgive me?"

She pulled in a deep breath through her nose and released it slowly through her mouth. No. But anger cost energy and she didn't have any of that.

"Grab us some waters, the pasta's ready."

They watched movies all day. Children's movies where the conflict was always resolved, and friendship trumped evil in ninety minutes. Action flicks where the explosions were always perfectly timed, and the hero always got the girl in a hundred and twenty minutes. Military films where the soldiers were always just and true and the foolish foreign country was always saved from itself and the snipers only hit the bad guys in a hundred and forty minutes.

"Why aren't there any supers in movies?" Kary asked in the break while they looked for their next one.

"There were, in the beginning before the Register was formed. The Firsts—" the original members of the Register back at the turn of the century, "—went to court over it. Called it an invasion of our privacy and a danger to us and by extension the world we protect."

"Feels thin."

"For today, yeah. But back then it worked and Barrister," an early super known for quoting law at criminals as he incapacitated them, "wrote some sort of ironclad bill, law, earmark, whatever prohibiting us from even being *referenced* in film."

"Huh, boring."

"What, did you want some secret war between Hollywood and the Firsts?"

Yes. "Maybe?"

"Typical norm." he muttered, and she kicked at him from where she was leaned against the opposite end of the couch. "*Hey.*"

It had landed with more force than she intended but Kary didn't apologize. "Typical sidekick, can't take a hit."

"Touché."

He picked the next film, some hopeless sci-fi action flick involving oversized robots and aliens. "So aliens can be shown on film but not supers?"

Johnnie shrugged. "As long as they're not *super* aliens." She kicked at him again because she wasn't sure if he was teasing her or not.

"And *what* do we have *here?*" The line was a cliché of magnificent proportions and it *still* sent a crawl up Kary's spine. Johnnie was moving faster than she could see; pinning the intruder by the neck against the wall so hard he shook the frames of the kickboxing posters Kary hung as decorations. "Testy, testy Aspect-boy, since when do you hang out with *norms?*" There wasn't any fear in the smooth, female purr coming from over Johnnie's head.

Kary edged around the corner in time to see her friend slowly lower the intruder back to the ground. It was a woman, maybe Kary's age, maybe younger, she couldn't be sure in the iffy lighting. "Kary—" he didn't turn to look at her. "meet Mynx, Foretoken's sister, Bearkat's sidekick, and my future partner."

Chapter 12

Mynx hissed when Johnnie mentioned her sister then slid into a purring string of words. "Don't go spilling *all* my secrets Aspecty dearling, haven't I taught you slower's better?" She trailed one hand across his chest as she slunk around him toward Kary. There was feline grace in the way she moved, and feline menace. Kary took an unintentional step backward. "Come now sweets, not *scared* are you?"

She was close, too close. "Just wondering how you got in, *chiquita*." Kary was sure she didn't sound nearly as brave as she wanted to. When she met Aspect, he had been a known quantity, always on the TV and running around Commonland destroying buildings and saving lives. Bearkat and his sidekick Mynx were shadowy at best, drifting from city to city as needed. They shunned the cameras and only seemed to show up when things were at their direst.

Mynx swung her leg up and placed it on the seat of one of Kary's bar stools, her whole body flowing after it until she was perched there with her knees wide and her hands on the cushion between her feet. "Oooh, norm wants to know how kitty got in." She was talking to Johnnie over Kary's head. "Should we tell her Aspect boy, or just let her... *wonder?*" She cocked her head sideways when she said the word. Kary had to clench her fists and remind herself that she'd look silly trying to punch a super. "*Look*, she's *mad.*"

"Mynx, why're you here? This is a civilian home."

"Because I *care* about *civilians.*" She was off the stool like water and circling him. Kary could picture this cinnamon skinned woman with a cat's tail that wasn't there, flicking it under Johnnie's nose to watch him squirm. But he wasn't squirming, he was stone.

Stone from the boy who'd blushed while she packed club clothes? Almost like he was used to... "*Mynx.*" Used to her. His tone was the kind of heavy paitencethat only came from long exposure to someone. Partners, he'd said they were future partners.

"Adamant and Bearkat want you. We've got..." she was behind him with both hands on his shoulders, fingers stretching down, her eyes green and narrow on the other woman, "*business,*" she turned her head and clicked her teeth in his ear, "to discuss."

Johnnie sighed and the stone cracked from the edges inward. "Kary, I gotta—"

"Go." Kary stared Mynx down across her friend's shoulder. "Get out of here super kid. I need to get to the gym and console Jimmie anyway."

"Will there be alcohol—" Now he was being patronizing again "—involved in this consolation?"

Yes. "No, just a few bouts between me'n Garth to give the ol' boy a show. I *might* promise to fight at the bar."

"Call if you need a ride." She didn't have his number. His eyes were earnest even if his mouth was hard. *"Please?"*

Who was he? *Rodney?* Worrying over her like he had a right to. "Will do, now *go.*" He and Mynx left via her bedroom window but Kary didn't watch to see exactly how they did it. Instead she cleaned the living room from her day of sloth, waiting until she was sure they were long gone.

It took her over an hour to muster the courage to gather her gym bag, drive downtown, and view the carnage.

"How's he?" Kary asked the girl at the front desk when she came through the door.

The girl shook her head, her eyes sad. "Inconsolable." If the desk girl was using thesaurus words, things must be serious. Everyone knew Jimmie hired his desk girls for the same reasons arenas hired their round girls.

The fighter walked into Rocks's office without knocking and sat a bottle of Johnny Walker on his desk without speaking. "Bruiser, I don't want that." He looked about as lost as Seth had in the hospital after his fight.

"Sure you do." She shrugged her bag off her shoulder. She might not've been able to help Seth but Jimmie she could fix. "You wanna take three fingers of that and come out here and watch me knock over whoever's around. And then you'll take another few fingers and I'll grab another body and we'll keep on 'til there's no one here, or you finish the bottle." Whichever came first.

Rocks looked up at her with gray eyes that'd watched too many good fighters get hurt. "Promise?" He sounded younger than he should when he asked like that.

"Cross my heart Rocksy, lemme get gloves on and we'll have a big time."

Kary KO'd the only lady trainer Jimmie employed twenty seconds into the first round with a fierce southpaw uppercut. There was no use holding her left in reserve tonight. Not when all Jimmie wanted to see was a line of wasted fighters. Tonight was about numbers: about hits and points and damage done to someone he hadn't put time into the way he'd put it into Kary.

Someone he didn't care about.

She beat through every person who would climb into her ring. She went rounds with all of the trainers, including Garth, and as many of the regular gym goers as would step up. None of them lasted longer than the second bell. She was faster and angrier than anyone on the canvas.

After she made eight wins in a row, three of them one strike knockouts, Garth started calling around to the other gyms, asking them to send over anyone who wanted to face the Mad Dogg's little sister.

They came in droves.

Seasoned lady kickboxers who wanted to see if the kid from the tournament matched the hype. Guys who wanted to see what the younger one looked like compared to the champion, a champ who should've by rights won his fourth belt the night before. Trainers who thought the blooded thoroughbreds over at Jimmie's place were getting soft from being in the pasture and not in the ring came to try and humble the famous Rocks on his own canvas.

Tonight Rocks would not be humbled and his Bruiser would not go down.

She took all the punishment and dealt it back double, her expression the same dead stare that made arenas across the country bark and howl for her brother once upon a time.

Kary knocked them flat or went her five, two-minute rounds with each and came out the lead in points. It didn't matter. She was on her groove. She was past feeling pain. She wanted *blood*. Jimmie's gym stayed open far later than the typical 10 o'clock close that night.

The only reason the bouts finally came to a halt was that she couldn't walk anymore. She stood on the canvas instead of dancing and that was Garth's cue to step in. He caught her when she started falling, kicked everyone out and set his friend's sister on the bench beside their sloshed gym owner. He left them leaning on each other while he locked the fire exits.

"Kary, can you drive?"

She was punchdrunk. She shouldn't drive. She could hardly stand. She should tell him that. "Gimme ten and I'll'b good."

Talking and thinking had become difficult. The processes were slower than they should be.

He didn't look convinced but didn't protest either. While Garth helped Jimmie to the office to sleep it off on the couch, Kary nodded on the bench between awake and elsewhere. The open water bottle in her

94

hands tipped steadily toward the floor. "You *sure* you're good?"

His touch on her shoulder was enough to make the fighter rocket to her feet, brushing him away from her bruises. "*Sí señor.*" She saluted with the bottle and sloshed water across them both. "Where's my duffle?" Garth shook drops from his hand and hooked the bag over her shoulder. She didn't wince when the weight fell across her battered flesh. "Thank'y."

She didn't let him carry her to the car but she did let him walk with her. "Bruiser, your eye's swelling shut."

That's why her depth perception was going screwy. "That'll be fun in the morning." She told him in turn, hitting the unlock on her key fob, and then hitting it a second time when nothing happened. This time it grumbled out a reluctant beep and Kary looked down the little Chevy's scuffed flank. The idea of sitting inside the car and then climbing out again at the apartment was exhausting.

"I *really* don't think you should drive."

"S' midnight on Monday, ain't nobody on th' road." She was slurring like she was actually drunk when a drop hadn't passed her teeth. She squinted at the trainer in the streetlight's glow.

"*Kary.*"

"G'night Garth."

"Text me when you get home, *please*?" He looked concerned and sweet. Her brother's friends had always been sweet to her. They deserved better than the infrequent communication Seth offered from the road, or the little thanks Kary gave them.

"Will do bossman." She saluted with the arm that didn't have a duffle hooked over and crawled into her car. She could feel him watching her worriedly until she was down the block, around the corner and out of sight.

✦

Kary filled her tub with ice and water and dozed there until the ice melted. When it did she pulled the drain and slept the rest of the night without moving, cushioned and covered by every towel in her bathroom. When she woke the next morning in time for her 11 o'clock class, her joints had locked up and her bruises *hurt*, but she was only half blind.

That had been stupid. Helmets and other guards aside, she could've easily concussed herself. She could've broken a bone. She could've torn a muscle. She could've lost teeth or done all sorts of terrible things to herself just because she had a temper and she wanted to let Jimmie live vicariously for a few hours.

Stupid. Stupid. *Stupid.* Stupid.

She texted Garth as she went in for her first class: apologizing for making him worry and thanking him for taking care of her and Jimmie.

Her phone was buzzing when she sat down and began pulling out her spiral but Kary ignored it in lieu of explaining to the girl she shared her table with that *no* she did *not* have an abusive boyfriend and *yes* she would be sure to get help from the authorities if she ever felt threatened.

Stupid. *Stupid.* Stupid. *Stupid.*

She should've been expecting the looks she was getting. The whispers. Her face was probably swollen beyond recognition; her eye was certainly swollen beyond being useful.

The idea of feeling threatened when she had been trained by Jimmie for years, and a teenage super made it a point to hang out on her couch, was laughable at best but she didn't mention that. She had to make the same explanation three other times that day, once to a campus police officer who Kary was fairly certain would've followed her home if she hadn't lived off campus and out of his jurisdiction.

Garth's text told her that the end total had been thirteen for thirteen, averaging under two rounds a match. The number was staggering, especially since the longest she'd taken between fights was the ten minutes it took an opponent to warm up. The stat was followed by an assurance that she was slated to fight at Jimmie's bar Friday night so clear her schedule, nurse her wounds, and no excuses. And last, a three-word question. *How's he doing?*

She didn't know.

✦

Kary had a long talk with her brother that night over the phone. He sounded like he was still waiting for something to happen but at least he was forming full sentences now. He did manage to say how proud he was of her performance Monday night, that he'd heard through the grapevine she KOed twenty of Commonland's best in a never before seen spontaneous brawl fest. Kary assured him that it had not been *that* many, that she had only KOed a few of them, that they had certainly not been Commonland's *best*, and that she looked the worst out of anyone this morning which probably meant she *really* lost.

She also told him that with last night's stunt she destroyed any chance she had of ducking out of being in the Friday night lineup at Jimmie's place. He laughed like he was hurting when she said that. "Get some rest Bruiser." He told her, "you're gonna need it if you're up Friday."

She hung up without protest and filled her second ice bath in as many evenings.

✦

"Kary?" The voice echoed through her dark apartment from the living room. She hadn't heard the door but the windows in there were quiet and it was late enough that he could use them to get in. He only used her bedroom when it was light out because it had the fastest roof access and the most difficult vantage point for passers by to notice. At least that was what he *claimed*.

"*In here,*" she called painfully. She was soaking in a sports bra and jogging shorts, anticipating that he might come over before going on patrol.

"What happened to *you?*" He was staring down at the girl, up to her neck in ice and bruised across her face from a hundred punches that couldn't put her down.

"Went to Jimmie's, reminded him there's still a fighter left in this town."

"And how many are left after last night?"

She grinned. Two of her teeth felt a little loose, she hadn't noticed that. "*Me.*"

Chapter 13

"**Haul** me up, I've been in almost an hour." She stretched up a hand and Johnnie took it in both of his. He'd pulled his gloves off and his fingers were hot against her deadened skin. Kary groaned when he tugged her from the ice in a surge, water and cubes falling away from her in cascades. When she staggered, unable to get her leg over the lip of her tub, he lifted her bodily up and over. "Thanks." She yanked a towel from the rack and rubbed feeling back into her flesh with as much vigor as her stiff arms would muster. She wondered idly how close she was to hypothermia.

"You look *dead*." He took her hand towel from its loop by the sink and began chaffing her shoulders and back with it.

"Do I?" She looked in the mirror. Her lips were blue, her skin was pale, the bruises and scrapes covering her face, and chest, were livid. "*Huh*, I do." Could he leave and let her put on dry clothes?

He was kneeling behind her now, scrubbing at one of her calves while she worked on the other. "Seriously,

I've seen corpses with better color. How many did you fight?"

She wanted to ask about corpses but couldn't think of how to say it. "I'm told I lined thirteen up and knocked thirteen down but I can't testify. After bulling through everyone at Jimmie's I quit counting." Why hadn't she worn a bikini, instead of the sports bra? The ties would've made it easy to drag off.

"You beat everyone in your gym?" He made her balance on one foot so he could massage the other. She braced her hand on his shoulder and tried to lean against his warmth without letting him notice.

"They probably went easy on me."

"And then what? Took to the *street* looking for partners?" The blood returning to her foot *hurt*.

"*Ow*." She said it more from reflex than a complaint. "Garth called around. People came over." She put the foot down and raised the other without being asked or lifting her hand from his shoulder.

"How *many* people?"

Felt like she'd answered this question already. It'd seemed like hundreds, but the gym wouldn't fit that many. At least not *comfortably*. "Lost count."

He finished with her feet and stood again, squinting across at her. "You busted your lip again." Johnnie pulled a tube of the same stuff he'd given her weeks ago from his utility belt without looking away. "Here." He smeared ointment on his finger and his finger across her mouth before she could react. Just like before, her split lip started knitting together almost instantly.

"*Ew*, foot hands." She teased instead of thanking him. Kary took the hand towel he'd draped on her shoulder and shooed him out so she could begin dragging her wet clothes off and pulling dry things on. She kept talking once there was a door between them. "So what's up with that Mynx girl?"

"She's a super, couple years older than me. I trained with her. Her mentor, Bearkat, he and Adamant are… close. They wanted to talk to me about the Register."

"The Register?" Wasn't he already on it?

"Yeah, my eighteenth's coming up and when I'm eighteen I can finally go on the Register as a full super."

Oh. "*Really*? That's awesome." She winced when the sports bra stuck on her shoulders on the way off. "*Ow.*" Did she have scissors somewhere? This wasn't one of the good ones, she was willing to mutilate it for the sake of painless removal.

"You okay?" The bathroom door creaked when he touched it.

"Don't come in, my shoulder's just jacked."

"And your ribs."

"Legs."

"Knuckles."

"And my jaw," *Face.* "what of it?" She was getting tired of listing her hurts. And tired of standing with her arms and shoulders at odd angles trying to get the damn bra off. Any time she started to tally the injuries she was reminded of how many there were, and they just hurt worse.

"Can I *please* take you back to the House for first aid?" She was fighting on Friday. She had to heal fast and he and whatever enhanced medicines he had access to were probably the only way that was would happen in time. "*Please?*"

It was cheating. There was no way his med stuff would fly under a drug test for another tournament. There was no way *anyone* who saw her today and would see her tomorrow was going to believe whatever lie she spun. She should tell him to shove off and chew an asprin and go to bed like she usually did when she took a beating this bad.

"*Please?*"

The sports bra came off with a graceless yank and the fighter scraped through the pile of dirty clothes behind her door for a real bra. "Lemme finish getting changed."

✦

Kary was blindfolded in the jet again but this time she didn't have to wear it once they came to a park inside the House. Fully awake, she worked to maintain the same indifference she'd shown Johnnie during her last visit to the supers' lair. It was difficult; the cave with its chamber full of vehicles and offshoots full of secrets was much bigger and much more interesting when she wasn't half asleep and cranky.

"Welcome back Kary." Red spandex tights, bulging muscles, and white mask: Adamant was there waiting to greet them on the runway.

He'd been less than friendly the one time they'd met. She hadn't been at her best either. "Thanks Adamant." She shook his hand when he offered it. His grip almost crushed her already beat-up fingers. "I'm glad you trust me." Of all the awkward things she could say, that was her first choice?

"We're glad we can trust you too." He wasn't any better at this than she was. Now that she was up close she could see Adamant wasn't much older than her, maybe her brother's age even. And possibly not used to talking to real people. Certainly not real people who knew the things she knew.

"Yeah, so um, Johnnie says you've got something that'll help with my ribs?" Johnnie winced when she said his name, "Sorry, Aspect, *Aspect* said you had something to help with my ribs." Her friend was in uniform, calling him by his super name was probably expected when he was in uniform.

"Yes, right this way." Right this way? Who said right this way anymore besides rich old people? He led her to a grotto along the edge of the runway that was outfitted with a metal table and medicine cabinets like in any trainer's room in any gym anywhere. "Aspect will fix you right up."

Kary hopped onto the table and tried a disarming smile but it felt funny with her jaw jacked like it was. "Thanks Adamant."

"It's good to see you again Kary." He strode out like he had something important to do all of a sudden, but the girl would've bet money it was just for show.

"You too Adamant," she called after him, and then leaned in toward Johnnie, "and I thought *you* were awkward."

"He's just not used to norms knowing so much. When he's in day-life he's pretty suave." Johnnie looked defensive under the mask he'd put back on before leaving her apartment. "Now what hurts worst?"

Kary let a jibe about Johnnie noticing suave older men pass her by. "Shoulders and ribs."

"Bruises?"

"Mostly."

He rummaged through a cabinet. "Get your shirt off and get over your modesty, this stuff is going to have to set on you for awhile."

"*My* modesty?" She muttered, pulling her t-shirt off with another wince. He turned toward her holding a jar of thick orange paste, poker face back in place. "You look like a real super when you do that, kiddo." He'd even managed to get his blush down to a bare glow.

"I *am* a real super, just not Registered." He walked around the table, his gloves were off again, and began daubing the goop on her shoulders. He held the jar where she could reach around to it without straining. "Paint it an inch thick over everywhere that hurts."

There was a lipstick on pigs joke somewhere in there if she cared to look for it. "This isn't gonna stain my bra is it? I don't have any others this color." The girl began smearing the stuff as instructed.

"Don't know. I've never gotten it on clothes." His fingers were gentle, and still warmer than her skin as he moved the straps on her shoulders to spread ointment across what felt like one long scrape. Was her skin temp still low from the ice bath?

Guys had it lucky. Being able to strip out of their shirts and deal with chest injuries without the world going crazy. It was enough to irritate her on days when she needed something to be irritated at. His hands were steady like he'd treated injuries like this a thousand times. He might have. "You get a lot of practice with this?"

"Told you after your tournament, didn't I? I've dealt with a lot of dinged ribs."

He had. "I thought supers didn't get hurt."

"A lot of us are sturdier than norms and have higher pain tolerances but we still get beat up. We train to deal with pain in the field and keep capsules that speed the healing process to take while we're in the middle of long battles."

"And all this stuff?" In the cabinet he'd left open she could see piles of gauze and dozens of jars like the one he was holding.

"For after the fact. We have to maintain our covers as norms and that means getting up and going to work or class the next day without looking like we spent the whole night foiling plots to end life as we know it."

"Then why did you limp into the tutor office that day I figured it all out?" She hadn't exactly figured it out then and there, but it was definitely a big piece to the puzzle.

He thought for a minute, "Late August or early September, right?" She counted back in her head and nodded. "Our usual shipment of med-supplies was delayed enroute from the Register manufacturer and we ran low. Adamant needed them more than I did that night, so he got the last of our stock."

He turned away from her and walked to wash his hands in the sink while she considered that. Why shouldn't supers have shipment problems like everyone else? It was so mundane, in its own way. *First world problems.*

"So now we wait?" He was pacing back towards her, his eyes on her hands. Should she wash them too? She'd tried to descreetly wipe the ointment off on her jeans and only succeeded in leaving orange streaks in the fabric.

"Now we wait. What's your question? I can tell you've got one." He had taken her hands and was examining where she'd broken the skin of her knuckles. She hadn't wrapped her hands nearly as well as she should have.

He was good at reading her; she wasn't used to being read. "Mynx, it seemed like you had… history." More than just training.

He'd let go of her hands and she left them hanging in the air while he dug in the cabinet again, emerging with a different, smaller jar. "Yeah, there's some history."

"Gonna share with the class?"

He shrugged and began smoothing something chilly and green on her knuckles. "She's nineteen? Yeah, I think that's it. It's hard to remember because age for us isn't nearly as rigid as it is for norms."

"How do you mean rigid?" Kary was going to be seriously pissed if his healing junk kept her calluses from re-forming.

"Well... for norms age is almost set in stone. When you're this old you can drive a car and when you're this old you can vote and this old go to a bar or whatever." He left off looking at her hands to look up at her eyes. "We're different. I think I was twelve when I was trained to fly the jet, younger than that when Adamant taught me to drive a car. I was six when I was sent to the Recluse for training and nine when I came to live here, ten the first night I went out in the field."

"You were still a *kid*." She remembered him being young when he first started appearing on the news, she just hadn't done the math to realize *how* young.

"A child who'd been training every day for four years by the time I debuted in public. A child who was gifted with abilities above and beyond those of a normal child."

"But still—"

"What I'm saying is that age is a different concept for us. Mynx might be a little older than me but she's been in the field the same amount of time. A lot of supers don't survive their first decade of training or time spent being mentored. Fewer still survive the second decade, after they leave their mentor. So, where you see me as a

106

kid whose age means he should be in high school, other supers see me as a man who's been active almost a decade, has proved his mettle and'll strike out on his own soon."

It made sense but Kary didn't have to like it. "It's not right asking so much of supers so young."

He shrugged. "Maybe not, but those of us who go through the training do it 'cause we want to. I've been told we have more developed empathy cortices and stronger protective instincts than most norms. It's why we cling to each other so much, and why I latched onto you when you figured out who I was. I'm built that way."

Instincts, great. So *that's* why she had her little sidekick friend. Why he'd decided it was okay to just start showing up in her apartment. The afternoon she'd finally, *officially*, given him permission to just drop by he'd been really abashed, realizing he'd never asked. "Okay, guess I get that." Still didn't like it. "But how does this tie back to you'n Mynxy?"

"Oh, *that?* The Register expects us to marry and form an official partnership at some point soon if we both survive."

Marry? "Nice deadpan there, totally can't tell you're joking."

He was putting up the jar of stuff he used on her knuckles. Already it was sinking in and new skin was forming over the broken places. "No, it's no joke. That's another thing Adamant and Bearkat wanted to talk to me about. Trying to find the best time for the wedding."

Chapter 14

"**Okay.**" She dragged the word out, waiting for the punchline. It never came. He kept watching her with the same bland expression and she kept trying to wrap her mind around the idea that her super human friend who wasn't even old enough to *vote* was going to get married to another super just barely older than him. "Congrats?" *Felicidades*? How was she supposed to respond to what sounded suspiciously like a child marriage?

"Thanks but you're a bit early. I told them it'd have to wait 'til after graduation." He handed the fighter a damp rag and motioned for her to start wiping the orange gunk from her skin.

"Oh, well that gives me time to plan my gift." She was stalling and she knew it. "Have you picked out your colors?"

"Red, like the blood of our enemies." Mynx came slinking in from somewhere Kary hadn't noticed before. Tonight she was in full costume, a black leather body suit that stretched and bent like her skin. In the apartment the night before she'd only worn a mask with civilian clothes. "Discussing our encroaching nuptials, dearling?" She purred in his ear as she circled the other sidekick.

"He was actually." Kary was talking shit to keep silence from stretching tight between them. "So red, have you started a registry yet 'cause I saw—"

"Sweets, the norm seems to think I'm actually *listening*. Do set her straight."

He was still stonefacing like a champ. "Here Kary, I'll get your shoulders." He held out a hand for the rag but she didn't give it to him.

"Can't do that Johnnie, not with your *affianced* here. Kitten might get hissy." She was staring him down, daring him to say something, *anything*. "So're we done here? Can you take me home? I've got a fight Friday to rest for and a weekend's worth of homework to burn through."

"Soon as you're cleaned up. You sure I can't do something for your face?"

"People'd notice and we're aiming for discretion, *aren't we*?"

"How novel, a norm with a sense of prudence."

He ignored his fiancé entirely. "That we are, ready?"

Kary dragged her shirt back on and hopped off the table. She was still sore but the sharp pain she'd felt every time she breathed was gone. "Ready."

He led her from the first aid grotto back toward the runway and the line of vehicles. "How do you want to get home?" He asked, gesturing to the options.

Kary noticed the way his hand lingered towards the car and the bike, the slower methods of transport. She walked to the jet, climbing into her seat without letting him help her. "Just take me home Johnnie, I'm tired."

His face was resigned when she tied the bandana over her eyes.

Her bra straps were stained from the orange stuff, so was her skin. It took a solid half hour of scalding water before her flesh quit looking like a bad spray tan; she doubted the bra would ever be the right color again. It was a small price to pay for being whole and healed in a couple hours but that wasn't enough to keep her from being peeved in general.

He was just so *young*. Teenagers shouldn't get married unless there were unexpected babies imminent. And now here were these *supers* tasked with saving the world and humanity and peace and all that bullshit getting hitched because some decades old society of supers expected it?

What was this, the dark ages?

Kary stepped out of her bathroom in a cloud of steam. She wouldn't think about it. There wasn't any point in fussing over something that wasn't her business.

That didn't stop her from being exceedingly scathing in her response paper on *The Scarlet Pimpernel* that night even though she'd enjoyed the assigned reading and the class in general.

Friday night came quicker than the preoccupied the college student would've imagined given what happened in the first half of the week. Jimmie's bar was wall to wall with the people from all branches of

110

Commonland's fighting community and Kary was fairly sure she was going to be sick before her match even happened. Nerves were hitting her hard and Jimmie's assurances that tequila could calm them if she'd just let him pour her a shot were not comforting.

Diette slapped Kary on the back. "I'll take that Cuervo Jimmie, if you're pourin'."

"You made it." Kary swung an arm around her friend. "Thanks for coming."

"Wouldn't've missed it. Jimmie, make hers a *tequilito* and if she won't take it I will." Diette's old accent, the one she usually kept back because customers liked a more polished bartender at the winary, was leaking out. Kary wondered exactly how hard her friend was planning on playing after the fight.

Kary knocked back the half shot and leaned on the bar beside her friend. "See anyone you know?"

"Well… where's that strapping fellow who cheered you on at the tournament?"

Which one? Most of her male friends were fairly strapping, with one notable exception Diette didn't know about. "My brother?"

"Not him, *that* one." Diette tipped her chin toward Garth where he was weaving through the crowd toward them at the bar. "*Quiero.*"

Garth? *Guapo?* Weird. "Hey Bruiser, you drunk enough to fight yet?"

"Who says I gotta be drunk?" She shouted back over the crowd noise. "Kicked *your* ass dead sober."

"Eh, you were punchy by the time I got to ya."

"*Maybe.*" She drew the word out slow. He leaned against the bar stool on her open side. "Garth, you remember Diette, yeah?"

"Yeah, glad you could make it out again." He reached across Kary to shake her friend's hand. Diette's fingers looked like matchsticks wrapped in Garth's massive paw.

"Wouldn't miss it for the world but I hate not knowing anyone here."

"Well you know me."

"Well I guess I do."

"Watcha drinking?"

Kary melted away while her friends started getting acquainted against the greasy oak that was the bar. One of Jimmie's waitresses, a girl who was a regular in the weightlifting section of his gym, caught Kary as she was in the process of melting. "Time to get ready, you're up in twenty."

"Thanks" Kary siphoned through the crowd to the storeroom that doubled as a dressing room for the fighters. "Hey." She recognized the girl who was already in there but didn't know her name.

"Ready for our rematch?"

Rematch? Was this one of the girls she faced Monday night? She couldn't remember. "Yeah, it'll be fun." Great, a grudgematch. Jimmie'd best be paying her *well* for this beating.

The girl wasn't any taller than Kary but she was heavier by a solid thirty pounds of muscle. They never would've been paired up in a league match, not with the weight difference, but Kary was still quicker. Duck dodge *punch* the girl must have a jaw made of *rock*. Kary danced out of range of her legs and kept moving while the crowd screamed and drinks sloshed through the ropes onto the canvas.

Thwack.

The other girl's heel hit Kary square in the stomach, how'd she manage to down this girl when she was punch drunk if she couldn't do it sober and healed with super-meds? Kary ducked out of the corner her opponent was trying to hem her into and prayed for the bell to come fast.

Ding-ding-ding.

"*Corner.*" Kary hobblewalked to her corner and fell heavy on the stool Garth slung between the ropes for her. Diette passed over a water bottle but she waved it away. "What's happenin' out there Bruiser? You're hurtin'."

"She's *heavy* Garth, what was Jimmie thinking?"

"That she was number ten on your docket Monday and you didn't have a problem then, what gives?"

"She's grudgematchin' and I'm here for a payday. Who'd'ya thinks more motivated?"

"You'd best be, Jimmie won't pay for a bad fight." Kary knew that was true, Rocks was notorious for not paying fighters he felt came to the canvas without caring. The bell rang again. "Now get out there and earn your paycheck."

Kary shoved her mouthguard back in and smacked her gloves together. He was right. It was time to settle in and earn her keep.

✦

Bob and weave jab-jab catch that leg knee up *hook.* Kary caught the girl by her calf and released it at the same time she landed another solid blow to her jaw.

The girl staggered towards the ropes, eyes murderous when they focused back in. Kary wheeled her gloves and advanced without giving her recovery high-low high-low knee to the hip and swing that leg up all the way—

KO.

Someday Kary's legs would stop swinging up over her head in that perfect roundhouse but this Friday night in this seedy bar on this worn canvas was not that time. Garth and Diette were in the ring before Jimmie finished the countdown, raising Kary's arms over her head while the whole bar bayed for more blood.

"*I'll* give her a shot." The voice was quiet but the world stopped to see who spoke. "If she'll have me." The woman swinging through the crowd was tall, buxom, not known at any of the local gyms if Kary was reading the faces in the crowd right. She climbed through the ropes and shook out her long black hair, her eyes were slim and green on Kary's.

"And what do we call you little lady?" Jimmie asked. Kary swore she could've heard a bug breathe the bar was so quiet.

There was a sink in Kary's stomach. She'd never seen her without the mask but that didn't mean she couldn't put a name to those cheekbones. Kary pulled her hands free of her friends and wished she wasn't wearing the bulky sparring gloves so she could cross her arms over her chest while the other woman answered: "Kitten, you can just call me *Kitten*."

Chapter 15

Why was Mynx in her bar? Didn't she have better things to do on a Friday? Like save civilians from cataclysmic events? *"Next up, Kitten and Bruiser. Bout starts in twenty."* Great, and *now* she couldn't duck it without major loss of face or death by enraged Jimmie. Neither option was welcome, so Kary brushed off her friends and retreated to the storeroom to wait for Mynx and will this into nothing but a bad dream.

"A norm who can throw a few punches, how *quaint.*"

The voice made her skin crawl but Kary tried for a sardonic smile. "A super who beats up real people for kicks, how... sad." Her stomach *hurt*. "Shouldn't you be off saving the world and screwing a teenager?" When was the last time she'd felt nerves like this? Kary bent her head towards her wrist, loosening her glove's laces with her teeth. For a brawl like this she wanted her fingerless fighting gloves, for harder, faster strikes.

Mynx stretched, flexing her entire body like a well strung bow. "It's early yet. Why shouldn't I get in a warm up?"

The college student wedged the loosened glove between her side and her other arm, yanking her hand free and starting on the opposite laces. "Just remember you have to fight like a norm tonight." Her eyes never left the sidekick.

"Oh? You worried about me?" She blew her opponent a kiss. "I'm touched."

Maybe in the head. "Bearkat know you're here? Or Johnnie for that matter?" Or Adamant. Or the Register. Or the bouncer since Kary was almost positive Johnnie had mentioned the girl was too young to be hanging around in Jimmie's place. The second glove fell away and Kary rummaged for her other pair.

"And what if they didn't?"

And she called *Johnnie* childish. "Then what if they can't find you and they need you? No phones in the ring, remember?"

"Supers don't need norm tech like cell phones."

"Even so, wouldn't you feel bad if your fiancé died 'cause you were trying to beat up on little old me?"

Mynx swung around and circled Kary like a shark. "And why should you care one way or the other about *my* fiancé? How well do you *know* Aspect boy?"

There was a drawl in her tone that implied carnal knowledge. "Pretty well." Why was she letting herself get baited into a pissing match with a kid over a kid?

"How's his power work?" Mynx had her there; Kary had never asked nor really cared what Johnnie's power was. It kept him safe and meant he had access to the House with all its enhanced medical supplies when she needed them.

Kary set her mouth in a hard line. "How often does he skip theoretical math?" Mynx stared her down with pupils that were sliced into diamonds like a cat's.

116

"Favorite movie?" She still didn't speak. "How's his Spanish grade looking?" The super was quiet, seething. "You might know him as a super but to me he's…" What was he? A friend? She'd never had a friend that was also a secret, could he be a friend if he was a secret? Should she tell Diette and Garth and—

A hard fist on the other side of the door saved her from finishing that thought. "*You're up girls, Bruiser first.*"

Kary checked over her gloves one last time and straightarmed the door without looking at Mynx again. Behind her the super couldn't resist a parting shot. "May the best fighter win, *norm.*"

She was fast and strong but she didn't know how to kickbox and if anything was going to save Kary's hide, that was it. Jimmie kept calling 'Kitten' out on attempting throws or elbow strikes that were prohibited, meaning more points to the younger Dogg. Even so, his Bruiser was hard pressed to keep the sidekick from boxing her into a corner and wailing on her 'til the bell.

Kary swung her leg up in a kick that connected just under Mynx's ribs, the first successful kick she'd used all match. The other girl was too *fast*. Every opening was a trap, every trap was just another blow from one of those slim arms that left Kary staggering.

She could hear the incredulous crowd all around them. By now they'd heard about her brawl Monday or at least seen her earlier fight. They couldn't believe she was being beaten by some unknown. Some unknown that was her equal in height but didn't carry as much mass as the Mad Dogg's little sister. They shouted for her to get her head in the game, to quit fucking around, to hit the bitch, *anything*. When that failed they started shouting for Mynx instead.

When the final bell rang Kary left the ring without waiting to hear the verdict. The scoring system at Jimmie's was informal to say the least, but no amount of favoritism was going to tip the points in her favor. The fighter took her bag from the storeroom and left the bar before her friends could find and try to console her. She knew there was no shame in a real person losing to a super, but she wasn't sure she could stand her friends buying her round after round in sympathy. She also wasn't sure how locked her tongue would stay once she had a few drinks inside her. Kary couldn't take that chance.

Johnnie was leaning against her car looking taller and broader than he did normally. He looked... "Older, why do you look older?" Having to look up to see his face was disconcerting.

"Borrowed a few years so I could go in after Mynx. Saw your match."

Borrowed years? Kary would have to ask him for clarification on that at some point. "Yeah, she's a gem, that girlfriend of yours."

"She's not my girlfriend she's my—"

"*Don't care* Johnnie. Tonight was supposed to be fun with my friends. Now I've gotta leave early, *and* I'm gonna spend weeks keeping them from looking for her for a grudgematch." She unlocked the car and tossed her bag in. "Tell her that, please? Tell her that she might not care but a *norm* is going to be paying for her pointless pissing contest for the next month give or take."

"Kary—"

She shouldn't take her anger out on him. It wasn't fair and she knew it and even as she said it she was repentant. "Just, tell her. Maybe if it comes from you she'll actually listen." Since they were partners or lovers or whatever. Kary slid into her car and drove off with an ache already creeping back into her shoulder and a sneaking suspicion that she was going to live to regret tonight's fight.

✦

Her brother called the next morning. "Heard you got schooled by a *nobody*." She put thirteen up and thirteen down, it took him a whole day to hear. A stranger knocking her around the ring for three bouts, he heard about *that* by morning.

"Yeah, she whooped me good."

"How're you feelin'?"

"More sore pride than anything. Jimmie's gonna have my hide if I ever get up the courage to show my face at the gym again."

"Jimmie's pretty soft on fighters who take hard knocks, he took me back."

"*No.*" She couldn't believe it.

"Yup, I start as soon as my shoulder's healed enough to demonstrate a proper hook."

"*No.*"

"Mhm, it'll be like old times. You'n me in the gym, just two Doggs in a pit."

"*No.*"

"Can you stop saying that?"

"I will as soon as you start telling the truth, Jimmie's not hirin' trainers Garth told me weeks ago."

119

"That was before I came up as a candidate. Can't you just be happy for me?"

"*No.*" But she was laughing now, it really would be like old times. Seth and Kary, two Doggs in a pit and the whole world wishing they could be in there too. "How'd Bethanne take it?" Princess round girl wouldn't be happy if her boyfriend was moving back to Commonland. And Rodney? What did his coach think of the Mad Dogg retiring to trainer life?

"Oh, we broke up."

When? She'd seen them last weekend—was it just last weekend? "I'm sorry to hear that." Yeah, Bethanne'd been at the hospital. "She was nice."

"She was never gonna be a keeper anyway."

"I see." She didn't like her brother talking about a woman like that, even one like Bethanne. "So when're you moving up this way? You know I've gotta couch you can crash on for a while if you need it." Theoretically Johnnie should quit being a frequent in her home now that he was officially *engaged* and his fiancé was staying in Commonland.

"Thanks Sis, I might for a couple days while they finish getting my house ready."

"House?" Since when did he have the cash reserves to buy the sort of house that other people got ready for him? Even when he was fighting every week and earning obscene amounts, he'd been more of a spend-it-all than a save-it-back.

"Yeah, I bought a nice place over on Concho Park. My decorators oughta have it almost ready by the time I'm packed here."

"That's great." Concho Park wasn't a cheap neighborhood. "What number? Can I run over and bully your decorators sometime?" See how deep in debt he'd put himself.

"Sure, house 69 on the north end."

"69?"

"Yup." He was snickering and she could hear it.

"Very mature Bro, I'm proud of you."

"That's good, I live to make you proud Bruiser." Sure he did.

✦

Diette came over unannounced not long after Kary hung up on her brother. "*There you are*. We looked for you for *ages* after..."

Kary cut her friend's trail off before it got awkward for both of them. She could feel the heat dragging up her throat and onto her face. "Sorry 'bout that. I had to get out of there." She should've at least texted them after leaving, instead of storming out and ignoring her phone.

"That fight was bullshit."

"Agreed."

"*So*, to make up for it I brought enchiladas from Tony's." One of the places she had worked after leaving their neighborhood, a *taqueria* that claimed to be *almost* authentic.

"Nice, very nice."

"And mimosa makings from Dom's—" The cheapest liquor store on this side of town, "—because if it's got orange and pineapple juice in it it's not an alcoholic beverage, it's a classy brunch drink."

"So for classy brunch we're having smothered enchiladas and cheap champagne?"

"Yes."

Kary pulled out plates and her long-stemmed wine glasses, since they were being *classy*. "Sounds perfect."

"Good, 'cause I've *gotta* tell you about Garth."

"Please don't tell me how good he is in bed."

"Oh have you heard stories? Dish 'cause he wants to go on an actual date and I don't think I'm gonna get a piece of that *gringo* without putting at least a *little* time in—"

"Stop, Garth's like family and that's just—"

"Well if your brother was on the market I'd—"

"*Diette.*" He was, but she'd never wish her brother on a woman she actually cared about.

Her friend grinned at her over a forkful of cheese-dripping enchilada. "*What?* I'm just being honest."

"And who ever said that was the best policy?"

"Big Bird I think, maybe Elmo."

"I never liked that show."

"Agreed, now back to Garth…" Kary could tell she wasn't going to divert Diette from her latest prey and so settled in to enjoy daydrinking with her best friend because they were young and it was a Saturday.

Chapter 16

"**How** was your weekend?" Jason asked when she came in Monday morning. There was a distinct gloat on his face that made Kary wary when she answered.

"It was fine, yours?"

"Better."

"Than what?"

"Hmm?" He was feigning disinterest and she *knew* it. Kary was sure he was dying to spill his guts. She didn't want to give him the satisfaction of asking again. That didn't mean she was disciplined enough to stop herself.

"Better than what?" The question came from between her teeth.

"Than *your* weekend or anyone's weekend *ever.*"

"Seriously?" What happened? Did Dods finally get himself laid?

"Aspect and Mynx are a *couple*. I saw it. And they were on our place and it was *awesome.*"

Johnnie and the kitten? Old news. "Oh yeah?" What did he mean on his place? On his land?

"Why aren't you happier?"

"Why should I be happier? Are they making super sex tapes that I should be seeing?" Masks and all? That'd be a hoot. And illegal for a few more weeks. Possibly illegal for forever if what Johnnie said about the Barrister and film was true, or was that covered when the laws were written? Was porn exempt? Was there a whole market of superhero pornos that she just wasn't aware of? She certainly hadn't plumbed the depths of the—

Jason cut her wondering short, before Kary made the mistake of looking for answers to these questions on a university desktop. "Where's your pride in humanity? *Super* couples mean *super* babies that'll become *super* grownups who continue to save our civilian asses for generations to come."

He was so passionate. Too passionate. "Uh-huh, and what makes you think sidekicks'll be making super babies anytime soon?" How did that translate to pride in humanity anyway? She was still more curious about the porn.

"'Cause I *saw* them."

"Well aren't you the peeping tom." Maybe she could just ask him instead…

"Is it *really* peeping if they're perched on the power line pylon making out in the aftermath of utterly *destroying* Tituba the Witch Saturday night? *Is it?*"

Kary wondered how she'd missed this epic battle; she really should get back to watching the news regularly. "Well that is something, I guess. Where was this exactly?"

"I went home to the ranch over on past the south side of town this weekend and the whole thing was *way* on out in the riverbottoms where the pylons stretch across our place and—" and just like that Kary quit caring. A showdown between two sidekicks and a second-string villain on private property out in the boonies wouldn't have made the news circuit unless it was a *really* slow day everywhere else in the world.

"—And I shot this great video with my phone—"

"Of two supers suckin' face?"

"*No*, of the fight, *see*." He tossed his phone at her and she caught it on instinct, her thumb hitting the play button when she did. There was a surprising lack of shouting going on, just the smooth movements of Aspect and Mynx and a dim, throaty voice coming from the distant pixels that represented Tituba. Kary watched the way her friend and his future partner worked around each other, the feline grace of Mynx against the athletic prowess Aspect was showing. The pair made a good team.

She handed the phone back. "They are impressive." Her voice sounded funny, far off.

"*Yeah,* and after the fight and the smoke cleared and Tituba was tied up on the ground they were both just standing up on the pylon looking at the moon or whatever and it was like a scene from a *movie*."

"There aren't super movies." Kary corrected automatically, turning back to her computer and pulling up her email.

"Well, if there *were* this'd be a scene from one and I'm the only person on *earth* who knows it happened." He was practically swelling with the importance of the secret he now had, she almost hated to burst his bubble.

"Except for them."

"Huh?"

"Except for them, the supers. You might have the video but they probably had to do some sort of report

125

for the Register which would mean that by now all the supers know and have probably started leaking it to the papers and—" She watched him shrivel in a few inches and took mean satisfaction in it. "—really you don't have anything all that interesting except for some grainy footage and a story that some reporter's gonna tell much better third hand than you did first—" Johnnie edged inside the door somewhere in the middle of her bubble bursting and Kary became self-conscious, breaking off mid-rant.

"Spanish help?" Johnnie still looked like a wilting daisy when he came into the tutor center but he spoke clearer now and didn't lurk by the door frame.

"Over here Johnnie, what can I help you with?"

"We're not done Dogg, Aspect and Mynx are an item."

"Go away fanboy, no one wants you here." She glared casually at Jason as her coworker spun back to face his station. Johnnie was waxing between staring at the table and turning subtly green. "Now, homework?"

He was slow fishing out the worksheet they both knew was probably perfect. "What were you talking about?"

Maintain cover. Maintain *cover*. She couldn't let Jason know that she knew anything more about Aspect and Mynx than what he'd told her. "Dods over there claims he saw a pair of sidekicks sucking face back on his parent's ranch this weekend. Now *personally* I don't see the big deal since sidekicks are free to suck all the face they want but fanboy says— you okay?"

She hadn't known people could be green and red at the same time. His voice became a low buzz between them. "A norm *saw* us?"

"Apparently you were tearing up his back forty, was he supposed to *miss* you?"

The green was getting darker than the red. "What am I supposed to *do*?"

"Was that rhetorical?"

"*No*." She could feel the mortification rolling off of him and it only amused her more. "I mean in the heat of the moment—"

"I don't really understand your problem here." She was pointing to a grammatically perfect response to a question in the Spanish present perfect tense. Jason looked over at them, curious at what they were whispering about. "You followed the instructions and you're getting the result that's expected, so why're you asking me?"

"'Cause I'm not sure I understand the reason for the... the *instructions* and sometimes I get a little turned around." No one could say he wasn't fast on the uptake, in some things at least.

"Because people older and wiser than us laid them out. Any other questions?"

He was quiet, obviously wanting to discuss further and without eavesdroppers. "No, thanks for your help." He took the paper from her and slid it between the books stacked inside his backpack.

Kary waved him out and logged the session on her computer.

✦

"You know at some point pretty soon you're gonna have to quit coming over unannounced." She told him when he walked out of her bedroom a couple hours after she got home that evening. "And why'd'ya use my bedroom window anyway?"

"Easiest roof access." Oh yeah, he'd mentioned that before at some point. "Why can't I be dropping by?"

"Seth's moving to Commonland soon and might be staying with me for awhile."

"Oh." He sounded surprised.

Kary craned around on the couch to look at him. "Did I forget to tell you?" Whoops.

"You did. Got anything to eat?" He was already rooting around in her fridge.

"Not much, I've been needing to get to the store." Paying rent always put a damper on the excitement of grocery shopping.

"But I'm *hungry.*"

"Well then start doing my shopping. There's cereal in the pantry and milk in the fridge."

"And not a clean dish in the place."

"Pretty sure the sauce pan's clean." She'd been avoiding doing dishes for almost a week. The sink was starting to smell but only when she stood close to it. She could febreeze the whole thing and probably get away with ignoring it for another few days as long as she was okay using a paper towel for a plate.

"You're disgusting."

"Says the sidekick who's the ward of a super who's probably a jillionaire."

"Who says I'm Adamant's ward?"

Jason the Fanboy. "Lucky guess, isn't that how it usually goes?" He didn't say anything about the money. Kary filed that away for future reference.

"Not always but it makes things easier." That made sense, trying to have a real people family and maintain a secret identity would be a pain. "Don't you have anything besides Raisin Flakes?"

It was the cheapest high-protine cereal the grocery store stocked, but she wasn't about to admit that. Not now. "Don't knock my fiber, keeps a girl regular."

"*T-M-I.*"

"Kids these days even know what TMI means?"

"You keep saying that like you're not a kid too."

"At least I can *vote.*"

"I can too, in three weeks."

"No, seriously?"

"Yep, Thanksgiving weekend." Kary did the math in her head, was it really almost Thanksgiving?

"Huh, so what does one get the sidekick who has everything, including a hot fiancé he sucks face with on power pylons after routing baddies at midnight in civilian's back pastures?"

He didn't turn around to look at her. "Better cereal."

Chapter 17

Kary jerked awake early Tuesday morning, squinting at the figure in the gray, pre-dawn light from her window. "Johnnie, that you?" She *really* didn't like him using her bedroom window as a front door. Especially if he was going to be entering while she was sleeping. "If you need to crash, go to the liv—"

"Were you *expecting* him?" Well he was the only person she'd given express permission to wander in through her windows, even if she didn't always like his window of choice.

"No." She rubbed at the sleep in her eyes. "But he's the most frequent visitor to my third-floor window." What time was it? Four? Why was Mynx even here?

"I'll *deal* with that *later*."

Kary was sure she would. "Why're you here, Mynx?"

"Can't a girl visit her …*friend*?" The word friend sounded like an insult in her mouth.

"Not at this hour." Whatever that was. For a half second Kary wished she was back living in the dorms, where she could scream and bring throngs rushing too her door to save her. It'd be embarrassing but at least

Mynx would have go away or risk being caught in full costume.

"But *Aspect* can come at four in the morning?"

Was Aspect old enough to cum at any time? "He would've gotten an earful and a stern boot out, like you are. Leave."

"No."

"Why not?"

"'Cause."

"How old are you, six?"

"Not moving."

Kary considered her options and picked the one that would end poorly for her if she'd judged wrong. "Suit yourself." She rolled over and went to back sleep.

When Kary's alarm went off for class every poster on her walls had been drawn on with black ink. Kary leaned in and squinted at the mustache scrawled across the faces of her brother and one of his championship opponents from three years before. Not just ink. Eyeliner. Sidekick bitch decided to Banksy using Kary's best eyeliner, the expensive liquid one that she only used when she really wanted to get laid.

Why? It made no sense. Kary ate the last bowl of Raisin Flakes with angry crunches, staring down the graffiti the whole time, before dragging off to class for the day.

"Shouldn't Mynx be too busy to wander into civilian's homes at four in the morning and scribble on posters?"

Kary was panting as she and Johnnie jogged the trail along the river that evening.

"You'd think."

"Keep a handle on your girlfriend, she's annoying."

"Still not my girlfriend."

"Fiancé, crime fighting partner, casual fuck buddy, whatever you call her."

He spluttered as he ran and she pushed on. "I told you that—"

"Don't care."

"*Kary.*"

"What-y? Register got you down?"

"They heard about us taking out Tituba."

"Well I hope so, there's video." She leaped an uneven place in the concrete and felt every muscle in her leg stretch like cables inside a machine.

"It's online." He sounded disgusted, and barely winded. That was annoying.

"Oh?"

"Sidekickcouples4life posted it last night. Watch the root."

She skipped over the root. "You guys're official, why's she after me?"

"Jealous, probably."

"What? Branch." Talking in full sentences was a strain after the first mile.

He ducked the branch and kept talking without panting. "She keeps trying to get me to spar outside of training and getting mad when I tell her Ineed to study."

Kary had a sneaking suspicion that Mynx was suggesting more *intimate* sparring sessions than her friend wanted her to know about, but didn't have the wind to tease him. Instead she gasped: "Petty much?"

The fighter felt like a bellows when she tried to force out air and words at the same time.

"But we'll make pretty babies." She hip-checked him into the river and opened her stride to a sprint giggling and gasping as she went. "Kary, *Kary,* wait up!" She could hear him calling behind her. The water was cold enough that for anyone else she'd be worried, but he was a super. He'd catch up in a minute.

Kary skipped up onto a bench and used it as a springboard to leap back down, continuing to run faster like they were playing tag. On flat ground again, she glanced back to see if he was gaining on her yet.

"*Uf.*" The runner sucked in a bellyful of air in surprise as she reeled away from the hulking figure she'd run into while being distracted by her own cleverness. "Sorry, didn't see... you." The rapidly descending night made a simple turn menacing from where she had been knocked to the ground.

His voice was a pleasant tenor. "No problem Miss, let me help you."

He stretched a hand down, but the college student avoided it on some instinct she couldn't name and bounced to her feet, ignoring the scrapes on the heels of her hands and other little aches that she'd normally check over after a fall on her run. She tried for a disarming smile when he looked hurt but wasn't sure she managed it. "Thanks, but I'm fine. My friend'll be here in a minute." Where was Johnnie? Supers should shake off a little water faster than real people. Her nerves were singing. This guy was even bigger than her brother and heavier than Garth.

He advanced a step and she retreated one. "Now I think we both know that's not true Miss, let me help you to your car." Her car was a good two miles back down the river, and Johnnie some quarter mile down the trail if she was gauging distance right.

Her fists came up. "I'm fine, thank you." One fast pivot on the ball of her foot and she could be flying back down the path toward Johnnie, her personal sidekick. She just hated to turn her back on this guy when he was so close. One surge at her while she was running away and he could lay her flat on her stomach, defenseless.

Aguas-aguas-*aguas*.

She still couldn't name the warning bells in the back of her head but she wasn't about to ignore them.

"No, no, I insist." He stepped forward and reached for her again.

Kary bobbed around the hand the size of a bear's paw like it was a thrown punch and bounced back three steps. Enough distance, pivot and *spri*—

"*Huk.*" She coughed painfully when the punch landed on her spine, spinning towards it and countering with a left jab on instinct. *Ow.* Punching people without gloves *hurt.* She backed away and slung her leg up in an arc meant to catch him under the ribs and leave him winded. *Where was Johnnie?* This guy'd probably run if there was a witness to his attack.

The stranger caught her leg, his palm on her bare shin and wooziness passed through Kary like a wave. Why was she—where was she—what was she—the edges were falling in together and the ground was rising up to swallow her. Johnnie? Seth? *Johnnie?*

Nothing.

Chapter 18

Kary came back to the world screaming. *WhereamIwhereamIwhereamI?* Her wrists and ankles were chained. *WhereamIwhereamI?* Her head hurt like she'd gone five rounds with her brother on a bad day. *WhereamIwhereamIwhereamI?* Her voice bounced like she was in a cave. *WhereamIwhereamIwhereamI?*

"Oh *look*, it wakes."

Mynx, that was Mynx. Why was Mynx here? Where was here?

"Kary?" Where was Seth? She wanted Seth. "*Kary.*"

"Where'mI?"

Johnnie leaned against her bed, his face dragged deep with worry lines. "Thank goodness, you're back."

"Seth?"

A pause, "Your brother's still in Marshal."

Why wasn't he with her? Seth was always with her. "Where?" Speaking felt like reaching for objects under clear water, distorted and further away than they looked from the surface.

"You're in the House. I brought you here after that guy drugged you."

Guy? "Why?" She rattled the chains on her wrists and hoped he'd understand.

"To… whatever he gave you was—" He broke off while removing one of the cuffs on her wrist. When it came away she could see blood and torn skin. "You were thrashing so hard we were afraid you'd hurt yourself."

"Hurtself?" More than this?

"Yeah, it was…bad. You had us worried."

"How?"

He was down at her feet now working on their bindings. His hands were shaking. He looked ashamed. "Remember a few weeks ago when I said we'd gotten rid of all the pimps?" That sounded familiar, it'd been right before she went to visit Seth—*Seth*? Where was he? She wanted her brother.

Johnnie continued like she'd nodded, maybe she had. "Well there's a new player in town. Abducts girls and a couple weeks later they turn up working a street corner."

"Samecity?"

He nodded. "With no memory of who they are or who they work for."

"How?"

"Handlers, middle men like the one that attacked you. Just as disposable and as blank as the girls they work. We could turn them in by the dozen but the hospitals can't fix their memories or break the mind control and until we find the mastermind there'll just be more made."

"Oh."

"You'll be okay. I came up just after he slapped this on your leg." He held out a Petri dish with what looked

136

like a square Band-Aid in the center. "You went down and I handled him."

"Whereshe?"

"Adamant's going a few rounds with him in the interrogation room but we're not hopeful. He's been drugged or brainwashed same as the others."

"See?" She wanted to look at this person in the light.

"I'm not sure you should be moving."

Her fist was hard on bedside table, rattling its spindly legs on the stone floor of the House. She glared at Johnnie and he looked away.

"This way *norm,* if you can walk."

Why would Mynx help? Mynx didn't do *helpful.* Kary looked down at her legs, free from the cuffs but they didn't feel like hers. They felt separate, distant. She wiggled her nerves and at the other end of the bed her bare toes wiggled too. "Coming." The disconnected feet swung off the bed and planted against the House floor, it was warmer than she expected for a cave. When she lifted from the bed, her legs held.

Kary staggered after the graceful sidekick with her mouth set in a grim line. Aspect followed, wishing she'd go back to bed.

⚓

"Canhesee?" They were staring into one of the antechambers through a window set in the cave wall.

"No."

Kary braced her hand on the glass and watched Adamant pace around the man who'd tried to abduct her. Mynx flicked a switch somewhere on the wall and their voices came through in a monatone stereo: *"Who are you working for?"*

"I dunno man. Last I remember I was walkin' the dockyards out in Marshal." The dockyards were the nightlife

district, where the bars and clubs were. Seth's party had been in the dockyards.

"Tell the truth."

"I ain't lyin'."

"Different." The water was getting shallower; she could catch her words easier. "His voice was different." Johnnie came up behind her with a chair and she sank into it without thanking him.

"How do you mean?" The three turned away from the glass to face another figure, another super. *Bearkat*, Kary recognized him from the rare glimpses and dim outlines that showed up in news reels. He was even bigger in person. Adamant looked like a normal guy in tights but Bearkat looked *different*. His walk was even more animalistic than Mynx's, and there was something inherently menacing about a seven-foot man wearing nothing but furs around his waist and a tribal mask covering his face. "What do you mean about his voice?" Kary couldn't remember hearing Bearkat speak before this moment. He shunned the cameras and it was always Adamant with the bullhorn. There was lilt in the super's words, something not quite Caribbean, but similar.

"Not his voice exactly." The speakers were rendering both Adamant and their captive toneless. "His words, he was more… articulate."

Bearkat appraised her and Kary tried to meet his eyes without looking away. Mynx was expressionless beside her mentor. "He could be acting."

Kary nodded, he was right.

"You do not think this is the case."

No, she didn't. Johnnie fidgeted behind her, and then she heard his steps retreat. She glanced in the window to watch where his reflection was going, but the glass was too clear. She could only see the interior room; Adamant and the stranger staring each other down across a metal table. Adamant was reaching for their captive, moving like he was going to take his hand.

Bearkat followed her eyes and knocked on the glass. On the other side, the big super pulled away instantly, leaving the abandoned captive staring around confused as Adamant left the interrogation room to join them. Bearkat gestured for Kary to repeat herself. "He was different when he attacked."

Adamant looked down at her. His mask was Johnnie's but opposite, white with his eyes shaded in black lenses. The effect was unblinking; Kary realized suddenly that she'd never met his eyes for this long. "How so?"

Kary paused, choosing her words carefully. "He had perfect grammar and he sounded smoother, I think." The speakers made it hard to tell.

"Like he was using a different accent?"

"Like he was a different person." Mynx snorted behind her and a blush hit Kary's cold cheeks. "Believe me, he didn't sound like *that*." She staggered back a little and hands, familiar hands guided her back down into the chair. She hadn't noticed Johnnie's return.

"We believe you. Aspect did some… reconfiguring on him after you passed out and that seemed to jog his memory a bit but didn't give us anything useful. We just need to cover our bases. Aspect, go finish analyzing that sedative patch. Bearkat, you and Mynx should patrol the city."

Kary was as surprised. "You do?"

"Foretoken said we could trust you." Mynx muttered something but Kary couldn't hear her properly. The feline super and sidekick duo left before she could call the girl out on it. Aspect's hand was on her shoulder for a second, the glove making his slim fingers feel heavy as it sat there, and then he too was gone. Adamant's mask wrinkled when he furrowed his brow at the sitting girl. "Kary, you should go back to the sick bay and rest. You aren't well."

"Can I go home?" She wanted to see her brother or at least talk to him.

The super sighed. "We need to keep you for observation a while longer, at least until Aspect finishes his analysis." He reached down to help her up and and began leading her back toward the room where she'd woken. The fighter touched her sore wrists and had a sudden powerful revulsion to the infirmary.

"Is there somewhere else? Another room?" She cupped one wrist protectively.

Adamant's voice was understanding when he told her *yes*. Kary followed him to a room filled with computer equipment and monitors and dozens of techy panels that she didn't care to try and understand. The leather couch along the back wall was the only thing that interested her. "You can rest here. I'll be running scans of the city and verifying what our guest claimed, just speak up if you need me."

"Thanks Adamant." She stretched out full length on the couch to let every muscle flex, before curling into herself like a wrinkled crescent moon.

"Adam." He spread a quilt worn soft with long use over her like he was accustomed to tucking people in. "Call me Adam."

"Adam Adamson, reclusive telecommunications mogul and hottest billionaire under thirty-five, *I knew it*." She mumbled against the couch arm, turning her face away from the light.

If Adamant was surprised that a twenty-two-year-old college student guessed his norm name from a given name and a hunch about his wealth, he showed no sign. He sat in front of his computers and began searching for the person responsible for hurting her.

✞

Kary slept deep and woke without any sense of how much time had passed. When he heard her move, Adamant turned around and she was pleased to see he wasn't wearing his mask and costume anymore. "Civvies? In the House?" She stretched and scratched at a kink in her spine. The water was gone.

"No point in masks when the secret's out." She hadn't dreamed it. She *had* guessed his identity before falling asleep. "You've only been out an hour and a bit. Bearkat still hasn't come back from booking your friend at the precinct."

It felt like she'd been asleep for ages. "No chance I can go home?" There was no way Johnnie could've figured out whatever it was he was figuring out in an hour, even if he was some sort of child prodigy.

"Maybe. We can check on Aspect and see."

So stage names were still in, even if costumes weren't. Supers were silly. "Why's he the one doing sciency stuff? He doesn't even have a degree." *Yet.* She followed Adam into the main shaft of the House.

"He really never told you what his power is?" Second super to ask her that, the student was starting to think she was missing something important. "Let's say he's got a head for this sort of thing." When she walked this time, Kary felt stable on her feet.

"A head for what sort of thing? How does *anyone* have 'a head' for microwhateverology?"

141

Adamant laughed and sounded more human than she'd ever heard him. A motion sensor door slid open for them with a pneumatic hiss. "He does and if you want more you'll need to ask him yourself."

"Ask what? My brilliance?" Johnnie was standing in the middle of a laboratory that put the university labs to shame; he was holding the Petri dish with the bandage in one hand and a test tube of something in the other. "'Cause I *am* brilliant." He continued, "unequivoally so."

"You mean unequivocally?" Kary hadn't always had a vocabulary like this. It wasn't until the GED night classes Rodney signed her up for that she'd gotten interested in fun words.

"Either way, look at *this*." He handed over the tube for Adamant to look at. "Do you see it? Sniff it, it won't hurt you—not *you* Kary. I mean it won't hurt Adamant." His friend backed her nose away from the tube and made a face at him but didn't say anything because Adamant was speaking.

"An organic compound made entirely from locally grown plants and naturally occurring minerals." What? There was no *way* he got that from sniffing some test tube. "What is it?"

"The stuff that this," Johnnie pointed to the Petri dish and the innocent looking knock out Band-Aid isolated in its center, "was soaked it. Which means the sedative—"

"Is likely manufactured in Commonland using easily accessible materials." Johnnie beamed at his mentor and Adamant continued. "That makes this a local operation and not one we need to tell the Register to worry about widespread—" This wasn't science. There was no way real people science worked like this and super science couldn't be *that* different.

"Yet. The formula's volatile when not paired with certain fibers. That's why it's soaked on that sticky pad instead of being sprayed from a mister or something like that." Kary had the sudden image of baddies running around with water guns full of knockout juice and had to fake a coughing fit.

"How are you keeping it in this tube then?"

"Short periods of time, I'm storing it in a sponge." He took the tube back and dumped its contents on an already sodden sponge in a metal basin on one of the tables. "The good thing is, it doesn't have any long term affects by itself. So Kary, you're in the clear and can go home as soon as we find your shoes." Oh yeah, she had been wandering around barefoot this whole time. The floor of the House was so smooth and warm it hadn't bothered her enough to really notice.

"The bad news?"

"I still don't know what's being used to mindwipe the girls, or the big guy for that matter. There wasn't anything unusual in his blood sample, same as the ones we collected earlier." Earlier? How long had they been working this case?

"So you can't make an antidote."

"Not 'til I have a viable sample."

"Damn." They both looked grim, their faces identical masks of responsibility even without the matching masks they wore to fight crime. Kary wondered briefly if she was necessary as a witness, decided she wasn't, and slunk out of the lab without either super calling after her.

Chapter 19

Kary paced across the floor of the gym grotto toward the reflex bag in the corner.

This cavern, it was really much too large to be called a grotto, was an offshoot of the main level of the House and contained a full-size basketball court. The court floor was covered in other training equipment and the baskets didn't look like they'd ever been used.

If there'd been a ball around Kary might've checked how bad her shot had gotten, but since there wasn't she went to the corner with the bag on a bendy stick and looked for gloves. There weren't any. She dug through a handy first aid kit and used the bandages she found for wraps instead.

Jab-jab swoop jab-jab side jab-jab back.

She fell into the rhythm of punch and dodge, relaxing herself and flexing her muscles. The fighter still felt like she'd been sleeping for days.

Jab-jab left jab-jab bob jab-jab weave.

So, she'd been almost abducted by some dasterdly prostitution ring. The only reason she wasn't there now was that she happened to jog with a super these days.

Jab-jab bounce jab-jab right jab-jab deflect.

And now she was recovering from some new sedative that was absorbed through the skin and produced locally, according to the super noses back there in the lab anyway.

Jab-jab advance jab-jab retreat jab-jab slap.

"Should've known you'd find this place." Johnnie, she hadn't heard him come in. Except he wasn't Johnnie: he was in full gear, and even smiling, the blank, white eyes made his face stern. Like he had other things, important things, on his mind. He looked older when he was in full gear.

"It's nice, you've got good equipment." She put a hand out and stilled the reflex bag when it bounced back towards her.

"We do, not that it protected your hands very well."

There was blood running down her elbows; she hadn't even noticed it. Kary unwound her wraps to figure out where it was coming from. "It's just my wrists where you had to tie me down. People're gonna think I'm into all sorts of fun play."

From the twitch beside his nose, Kary knew her super friend was raising a mocking eyebrow at her behind his mask. When he told her to come with him back to the infirmary she didn't argue.

"So I've been told I need to know what your powers are." She remarked from where she sat on the metal table waiting, once again, while he dug through a cabinet.

"You have?"

Not exactly, but close enough. "Yes, so're you gonna spill or do I need to take to the internet?"

"Please don't, they've got some terrible theories and none of them are very true."

"*Very* true?"

"Most of them sort of understand: I'm called Aspect because I can borrow an aspect of any person I meet."

"*Okay.*" That sounded pretty basic to her, so why was he talking like it was a state secret? "Big deal?"

"It is when I don't ever lose them."

Don't ever lose—*Oh.* "You mean…"

"There's a reason the Register wants my genes hitting the pool soon."

"Every villain, every super, every—"

"Every normal person I brush past on the street, I can get something from all of them. I've got something from you."

"Me?" It made sense, as long as they'd been hanging out, but what would he have wanted—

"First time I met you. I shook your hand and borrowed your Spanish." She'd *known* that was weird. No self-respecting student shook hands these days.

"So you've got what? Adamant's strength and Mynx's—"

"—her flexibility, Bearkat's durability, Hyperdrive's mastery of vehicles, Mercenari's krav maga, your coworker's German, Tituba's flight as of last week. I've got hundreds of tricks and skills and attributes from supers, villains, scientists, specialists, and norms from all over the world."

All that knowledge and those talents and strengths and powers must mean her little friend Johnnie was one of the most powerful supers on the Register. "All that must make you incredibly…." She didn't want to call him *dangerous* to his face.

His hands were gentle when they smoothed ointment on her torn wrists. "That's what they tell me." He didn't look up from their hands. "That's why they sent me to Adamant, because if I ever go rogue he *might* be strong enough to put me down."

Put him down. That's what people did to sick dogs, not other people.

"Take me home please." She didn't want to think about it. About mentors who adopted little boys and raised them to be good and kind and save others being ready the whole time to kill those same little boys. About little boys who grew up knowing their father figure might kill them. About a mysterious guiding council of supers who only thought of such little boys as breeding studs to be exploited. About the way it would affect a psyche of a little boy who grew up knowing all this and knowing that if push came to shove he could still probably destroy them all.

Kary looked up at her friend, her poor manipulated, kind friend and the mask that was hiding his reaction to her reaction to his plight. "Please? I want to call my brother."

✦

It was dark when she swung off the back of the animalistic motorcycle Johnnie drove her home on, pulling off her helmet and blindfold in the same move. "You know you don't need the blindfold anymore, we trust you—" he paused before finishing, "with everything."

Everything? She handed him the helmet, fingering the bandana thoughtfully. "Maybe, but I don't trust myself. Anyone finds out how much I know and you could lose your identities because of me. At least this way you won't lose the House too."

"We don't deserve a norm like you."

His sounded serious, too serious for an almost eighteen-year-old. They'd both been too serious lately. Kary tossed her hair and gave him her best devil's grin. "I know, scram kid. You've got a load of brainwashed hookers to find and save."

He jammed the helmet on his head and raised a hand in farewell. Then he was gone and she was left standing barefoot on the chilly parking lot of her apartment complex thinking that he didn't deserve her, he deserved better.

✦

It felt like years since she'd been in class but in the real world she'd only missed a day. One day of drugged sleeping and thrashing around. One day off and the whole world should've changed. It hadn't, but it should've.

Her car was parked in its usual place and when she checked the hide-a-key on her back-left fender she found her key exactly where she left it before going for her jog. Her apartment key was still in the center console where she'd put it after locking her front door. Her duffle bag was still in the back seat, her shoes laid below it on the floorboard. The supers had moved it back for her. A small gesture. A powerful one.

Kary took her bag and keys up the stairs and began getting ready for her day.

✦

She called her brother that evening. "Hey Sis, how's it?" He sounded cheerful, happier than he'd sounded since before that awful fight that she was just going to blame everything on because that was the easiest thing to do.

"Not bad." Why was she lying? If she could be honest with anyone about even a part of this mess, it was her brother. "Just been a little stressed. You?"

"School, huh? That sucks." She didn't correct him. "I'm good. My rehab's going awesome and they tell me I'll be okay to move down there over Thanksgiving."

Thanksgiving, Johnnie's birthday. She needed to do something for Johnnie's birthday. "That's fantastic; your house'll be ready by then?" She'd driven by the site a time or two but never stopped. The building was too big and the workers hiving all over it too focused for her to think about stopping and trying to figure out *exactly* how exorbitant her brother was being.

"Yup, and there'll be a whole suite on the second floor for you. Say goodbye to that ratty apartment and paying rent sis, I've got you taken care of."

Kary looked at the graffitied posters she still hadn't taken down and the stack of dirty dishes in her sink. She poked her nose into the bathroom with soapscum buildup that she hadn't scrubbed for a month. She paused over the sweaty clothes piled behind her door. It'd been so long since her last load of laundry that she was almost to the washing-underwear-in-the-sink stage of clothing desperation. Undoubtedly, Seth would have some sort of maid come through a couple times a week

149

and she would never have to worry about these things again while she lived in Commonland. "Sis? Bruiser?"

He'd spent a good chunk of his life paying to move her up in the world. He'd gotten her out of that neighborhood and into the better high school. He'd helped her pay for college the first semester, until she started finding jobs on campus. He'd bought her car when she moved off campus and into the apartment. She owed Seth a lot, but she was in a good place. He didn't need to keep trying to move her up in the world, she could do that on her own now.

"No thanks Seth, it's ratty and renty, but it's mine and I like it." Besides, if she lived with Seth, Johnnie wouldn't be able to pop over and hang out, and she wouldn't be able to disappear to the House without making up excuses and cover stories.

She heard a rustle that meant he was shrugging, "Well, if you ever change your mind, it'll be there."

"Thanks Seth, that means a lot." She wasn't lying.

They made plans to do Thanksgiving lunch at his place and watch the football games on the cinema-sized, flat screen he was having installed in his new home. Kary offered to attempt a ham and the fixings. "I know I'm not up to a turkey but a ham—" Seth cut her off and Kary tried not to be hurt when he told her his cook would take care of everything. She just needed to bring chips and dip for game watching snacks.

Kary hung up on her brother and laid on her bed willing the day over and most of the events of the week to have been a dream.

Chapter 20

"**I'm** making Thanksgiving dinner at the House Thursday night." Johnnie was reading on her couch while she worked through a translation when she made her announcement the weekend before the holiday.

"You're what?"

"I'm making Thanksgiving dinner Thursday for you and Adamant and whoever else's hanging around the House."

He thought for a moment, looking across at Kary where she and six books and half the translation file were spread out in a circle on the floor. One of them was a volume of British poetry that never moved from the rug where she usually did her homework. Tonight it was flipped open to *Rime of the Ancient Mariner*, the verse about something lurking *ninefathomdeep*. "Any special reason why?" She wasn't looking up from her research while she talked.

"Seth is having his *cook* make lunch and I wanna try and bake a ham."

Johnnie decided not to mention that generally he and Adam ordered a Thanksgiving dinner from one of the

151

nicer restaurants in Commonland and microwaved it when they had time. "Sure, gimme a list of what to buy and it'll be waiting for you in the kitchen."

A paper airplane landed on the open pages of his book. He glanced it over, "Okay then.

✦

Seth looked *good* when he answered the door of his new home. "*Bruiser.* Come in." He wrapped his uninjured arm around his sister and pulled her in for a hug. For a second she relaxed against him, he was her brother and they were going to be together for the holiday. Even if this wasn't how she pictured it. "Oh good, you brought the chips, we're almost out."

We? "Who all's here?"

"Oh just Garth, Diette, a few of my boys." He was leading her through a foyer to a room that echoed with broadcast noise and human voices. "*Okay guys, time for lunch.*" Seth still had the voice, the one that made everyone go quiet and pay attention. It was good to hear it, good to be able to hear anything after the clamor that'd echoed in the hall.

The TV went off and the whole party filed into what could only be called a formal dining room, even though Kary was certain her brother had never eaten a *formal* meal in his life, and turkey was served. It looked like a true fifty-pound bird, steaming and dripping and smelling like something off a cooking show. Kary resented its perfection. She'd asked Johnnie to get her a pre-glazed haunch and it wasn't going to be near as nice as this professionally basted bird. But it would be personal, and the sides wouldn't be served from tin takeout trays.

She comforted herself with that while she poked at her stuffing and leaned across the table toward Garth. "Where's Rodney?" It was weird for her brother's trainer to not be somewhere in the crowd, he always did holidays with his Doggs. Jimmie too, for that matter. She didn't know most of the people here, they all moved and talked like fighters and hype-boys and the girls that attached themselves to that crowd, but they weren't the ones she remembered swarming Seth at Marshal. They were all so loud that she had to pitch her questions low to have a hope that her friend would be able to make them out across the table.

Garth looked guilty, "Hasn't Seth told you?" Told her what? Since when did her brother not tell her stuff? "He and Rodney got into a huge fight over his coming down here. They haven't talked in a month."

A month? Rodney had been her brother's coach since before Seth started the circuit back when he was eighteen, almost a decade of working together. What on earth could they be fighting about that got in the way of *Thanksgiving*? What did Rodney have the nerve to fight her brother about? Usually he only had the backbone to argue about training stuff. She wanted to ask, but Garth was concentrating on something Diette was saying and her brother was at the other end of the table, too far away to ask without shouting.

She addressed her response to her plate instead. "That's too bad. Rodney's been a friend for a long time."

✦

The quiet of her apartment was a relief after the noise and crowd in her brother's house. So many people, all friends from the gym or Jimmie's or whatever but just so *many*. All drinking from the keg her brother brought in and shouting at the television even though none of them cared anything about football.

And then the gradual dropping off, people just falling asleep there on the couches or slinking away to find quieter places to nap off their indulgences. Her brother grinning and asking if she was *sure* she didn't want to see the room he'd set aside for her and then inviting her to come back in a few hours when they all woke up and started partying for real.

This was the first year her brother wasn't competing in the Turkey Tourney in Marshal and he was determined to create a new tradition even if his sister was less than enthused. Kary told him she'd think about swinging by. They both knew it meant she wouldn't show but the offer stood.

Johnnie knocked on her door around seven that night, after evening had blended into true dark. "Ready?" He was in a leather jacket and had a helmet tucked under his arm.

Kary grabbed her jacket too, knowing it wouldn't be enough to stop the wind. "Yeah, all the stuff in the kitchen?" She turned off lights and locked the door behind her while Johnnie bounded down the stairs. She should've called Rodney this afternoon; they hadn't caught up in a long time. Too long, if the fight between he and Seth was really that bad. She filed that away under things to do when she got back tomorrow, he'd be busy tonight anyway.

"Everything's there, ham's been thawing all day."

Thawing? Why was it frozen in the first place? It was a moot point, if it had been out all day then it was ready now. "Excellent, new bike?" It was shiny and red and civilian looking.

"Early birthday present from Adam, you're the first to ride it besides me driving it out of the dealership."

Kary thought about the slim envelope tucked in one of the inside pockets of her jacket alongside her folded-up recipe printouts. "Well that was generous."

"I know, right? He's the best." The helmet hooked on the back of the seat had her bandana tucked inside. When she pulled it out Johnnie said: "Thought you'd fuss if it wasn't there."

"You thought right." She swung her leg around the bike to settle in behind him and tied her blindfold in place. "Now let's get going, dinner isn't gonna cook itself."

                    ✦

The kitchen in the House was small with counters carved directly from the grotto wall and polished until they shone brighter than the marble in the kitchen her brother had paid for but would never use. It was warm and had excellent acoustics when she fiddled with the stereo in the corner to break the quiet. The cabinets were illogically organized and the water from the tap came out scalding—it was perfect.

"Really? 'Cause Adamant's been complaining about it for years." Johnnie had been banished to a bar stool on the far side of the counter bordering the kitchen while Kary worked.

"No home kitchen should be logical." She told him while she cranked on a can of green beans. "Only industrial kitchens are organized and they're not for serving families." At least according to the movies.

His laugh was cut off in the middle and she turned to see him with two fingers against his ear. "Aspect... the kitchen... yessir, two minutes."

"Duty calls?"

"Pretty often, no telling when we'll be back."

"No telling when it'll be ready, *go*." He went. She turned back to the illogical kitchen and mounds of ingredients. "I'll be here."

It was just before one when they came back, Aspect, Adamant, and Bearkat, and a girl she didn't know. "Adamant Girl, I take it?" Kary took a guess on the similarities between her and Adamant's costumes.

"Uncle says I can trust you, even though you're not Registered." She couldn't have been older than fifteen. "Call me Audra."

Audra Adamson, the alliteration that came with knowing supers real people names was going to be the death of her. "Nice to meet you Audra, I'm Kary Dogg."

"The norm bitch, that's what Mynx calls you." She would've hoped Mynx might be more creative than that. Adamant shifted and coughed like he was embarrassed, his niece rounded on him. "It's *true*, that's what she—"

"Maybe we should wash up?" Uncle cut off his niece and she looked petulant, exactly like a teenager about to scream it out.

Kary intervened. "Yes, *vamos*, all of you. You smell funny. Supper'll be laid out by the time you're cleaned up." She dipped her voice as close to her brother's quiet authority as she could and made shooing motions with the big, two-tined fork she was testing the ham with.

"So where is Mynx this fine evening?" Kary asked from the kitchen while at the table Adam carved the ham and Johnnie began passing carmalized sweet potatoes.

"She's visiting her sister, she'll be back this weekend." Bearkat told her, shaking out the cloth napkin she'd wrapped the silver in and laying it in his lap with casual grace like he was accustomed to dining in nice restaurants. *Formal dinners* and all that. He'd laid his tribal mask aside for the meal, revealing his face to the girl for the first time. His eyes were light and observant and there were ceremonial scars carved into his cheeks in a swirling pattern.

"That's why I'm here early." Audra cut in, turning up her nose at the sweet potatoes.

"Ah, I see." Kary set the normal mashed potatoes beside the teen on a hunch and pulled the mask from the girl's face when she turned toward the bowl. "No masks at the dinner table." If Bearkat was going barefaced she wasn't going to let a teenager get away with hiding her eyes.

"*Hey*—oh." Adam shot the girl a look at her protest and she lapsed into sulky silence, a sulk marred somewhat by the double helping of Irish potatoes she took before passing the bowl on.

It was a quiet meal. The supers were all exhausted from whatever crime fighting they'd been called to and Kary hadn't slept since she woke up Thanksgiving morning. But the food was good, the ham was warm through and only dry on the outside inch, the dressing only a little bland and the rolls were maybe a bit burnt but there was plenty of gravy to cover all of that. For dessert there was a real pumpkin pie, crimped crust and whipped cream like the picture on the website.

"This is delicious Kary, what's your recipe?" Adam asked while they all savored the feeling of being full.

She was almost certain he was just being kind. "It's an old Smith family recipe."

"Oh? Is that your family, the Smiths?" Audra must not've seen Kary's file, or she would've known better.

"No, that's the website I got it from—Smithfamilyrecipe.com."

"Ah" She looked embarrassed. "Even the pie?"

Kary fiddled with her fork. "That one came from the internet too. They all did. We don't really have any family recipes." Did frozen pizza count? Even after their mom died and Rodney took Seth on the road, the old lady the trainer had landed Kary with made most of their meals with a can opener.

There was some awkward shifting. "Keep these." Bearkat's lilting timbre brought Kary's eyes to his. He looked the college student up and down across the table. "You do them proud."

"Thank you Bearkat." It was awkward not knowing his real person name when she knew everyone else's but Kary didn't have the nerve to ask. He smiled at her and even smiling he was intimidating. Never mind that the teenagers on either side of her were possibly more dangerous, Bearkat was the one Kary wouldn't want to meet down a dark alley. She stood up abruptly and began clearing the table. "Do you guys have to go back out on patrol?" She couldn't look at her friends, they were being too kind.

"Not unless—" Adamant broke off, put his hand too his ear, took it away, and sighed deeply. "—not unless the scanner picks up something." Bearkat stood to help her carry the dishes, his hand landing briefly on the other man's shoulder.

Kary kept her eyes on Adam as she asked. "Something?"

"There's a fire in Marshal City at one of the big gym complexes, apparently there was some sort of late-night tournament going on? They need help with evac."

Her stomach dropped. Somewhere behind her in the kitchen, a stack of plates rattled as they were set down on the countertop. "It's an all-night tournament." Seth wasn't a fighter anymore. Seth wasn't there. Seth was safe. "A big one." The cutlery she was holding fell from her nerveless hands. She needed to get ahold of her stomach. But who else was there? Had Jimmie run up to watch a few rounds? What about Rodney? If he and Seth were on the outs and he was still in Marshal he'd probably be—

"Kary, you look…." Johnnie was worried but she couldn't look up to see it.

She was on her knees, picking up the silverware with trembling fingers. "Nothing, go." Every time she grabbed a piece, it fell again.

"*Kary*—"

He was bent towards her, his hand hovering over her shoulder. The rest of the heroes had already left to gear up; it was just two of them now. "*Go.*" She sounded cruel. She didn't mean to sound cruel. He left at a run, leaving Kary crouched beside the table holding her stomach like she could push her knotting insides together from the outside.

Chapter 21

She was in the library of the House when they dragged in near daybreak. Johnnie, still reeking of smoke, was the one who found her. "Hey." She whispered across the room, her eyes wide when she heard the door open.

"Hey." He sat on the floor in front of the leather arm chair Kary had been curled up in for hours, dozing fitfully and always waking with a jolt and the smart of bile high on her tongue.

Before he turned to lean his back against the chair arm her head was propped on, she saw his face. He'd taken off his mask and left the ghost of it in clean skin around his eyes; the rest of his face was flushed with burns and streaked with soot. "How'd it go?" She sifted her fingers through his hair. Her hand came away sticky with sweat and smudged gray with ash.

"We recovered twenty bodies." He mumbled, leaning his head back into her hand. "But there will be more under the debris."

Twenty. Twenty bodies and probably more to come. Fighters and trainers and fans gone from the local circuit. Seth wasn't there. Seth was safe. Seth wan't a fighter anymore. "I'm sorry," she murmured, continuing to scratch and stroke his scalp. She could feel his exhaustion; it oozed out like a scent from his pores. She wanted to tuck him into bed like a child and leave her friend there until the worry creases around his eyes and mouth smoothed away.

He relaxed his weight under her touch, how long had he been going? Supers who went to class or work or some other sort of cover must never get proper sleep. How long had it been since any of her super friends had more than a few consecutive hours of rest? And meals, how often did they get fed properly? Carrying the weight of the world and not getting the proper rest and nutrition, no wonder supers had low life expectancies. They probably keeled over all the time from exhaustion.

He was asleep. His face hanging slack, making him look young, the way he was supposed to look. He turned eighteen at noon today; he'd told her that at some indistinct point she couldn't really remember. Finally old enough to vote for the country he'd been actively protecting for years now. Calling the situation ironic was the wrong word, but she couldn't remember what the right word would be.

Kary kept scratching her friend's head gently. "Happy birthday Johnnie boy."

Adamant drove her home in an inconspicuous sedan Friday afternoon. He'd found her and his sidekick sleeping in the library and left them in peace until they emerged to scrape together leftovers for a late lunch before Kary asked to go home. She needed to call around and count her friends.

✦

"Rodney's dead." Garth answered his phone on the sixth ring, he sounded like he had a hangover and a cold at the same time. "Service's Sunday."

Rodney? Rodney, who'd seen her brother at Jimmie's back when Seth was a teen and angry at the world and known the kid had potential on the circuit? Rodney who had all of the skill and none of the aggression to be a fighter, so he trained fighters instead? Rodney who picked her up from school when Seth was busy and pretended to be her dad when she got into brawls and needed someone for parent-teacher conferences. Who signed her up for night classes after she got kicked out and didn't let her skip? Rodney who taught her the roundhouse, *her* roundhouse—that perfect, tall arc that she'd used time and again, that smooth motion that made her feel like the most powerful person on earth.

He couldn't be gone, she still hadn't called him. "Bruiser?" There was a shuffle and mumble on the far end of the phone, she heard Garth mutter *it's Kary* to someone and the phone changed hands.

"Kary? You there?" Diette, why was Diette talking on Garth's phone?

Wait.

Oh.

That.

"Diette?"

"What *mija*?"

"Is he really—" She couldn't say it. She wouldn't say it. If she didn't say it, it wasn't real.

163

"The list is online, your brother went to identify the body and make the preparations this morning." Why hadn't Seth told her? There weren't any texts in her inbox or voicemails waiting on her, surely Seth would've wanted her with him. He needed her—

"Kary? You there?"

She wasn't. She was twelve again and mourning a mother who'd never been a presence, with her brother in the next room working a speed rope while Rodney stroked her hair and wiped her eyes on a handkerchief. He was the only person she'd ever known that carried a real hanky everywhere in his back pocket.

She was fourteen and sulky because her brother was on the road all the time. Shouting at Rodney for taking her brother from her. Resenting not being allowed to live alone. Sneaking past Rodney's maiden aunt until she found out the woman left a window open on purpose every night so Kary could get back in.

She was sixteen and landing her roundhouse perfectly every time on the bag. Rodney holding the boxing pads for her to test her accuracy on taller and taller targets. Her brother leaning under the ropes from the floor shouting encouragement until she was hitting the pads even when they were held way over her head.

"Kary?"

"I'll see you Sunday." Her hands were cold and her chest was hot. Her stomach was trying to drag up out from her throat on a fishook. She was breaking, like a doll, a machine, a tree blasted down the center by lightning. She was breaking like something that only had sharp, hard pieces inside.

✦

Seth wasn't wearing the brace and sling at the funeral. She almost asked him about it but they were greeting mourners and thanking people for coming. They were hugging strangers and telling them Rodney would be missed. They were delivering their awkward, joint eulogy where they talked about how Rodney didn't know he was adopting two kids when he agreed to coach one fighter.

They made people smile while they sniffled and were two of the pall bearers across the hard ground to the hole that had been prepared. Kary laid a bouquet of bay branches for victory and bellflowers for loss on the casket before it was lowered into the cold dirt. She called five different florists looking for someone who could put the flowers together on short notice. Calla lilies had been suggested, and wine-dark roses—typical flowers, but Rodney had given her a Victorian flower language dictionary her sophomore year and she'd be damned if she wasn't going to use it to send him off.

Garth and Diette invited Kary back to Jimmie's bar to toast Rodney's memory but she turned them down. "I just need some time to myself." She told them by way of explanation and they walked off arm in arm, no one else tried to get in her way when she left.

There were cops knocking on her door when she climbed the stairs to her apartment. "Can I help you officers?" She asked, and they jumped, hands moving to their belts automatically.

They looked uncomfortable when they realized what they'd done. Even more so when they saw that she was in funeral black. "Pardon us Miss Dogg but we have a few questions about the disappearance of Miss Bethanne Rogers."

Bethanne was gone? Kary stepped past the officers to unlock her door, making her movements slow and trying to keep her hands visible to them. "I had not realized she was missing. She and my brother broke up over a month ago. I haven't seen her since Seth's last fight." She was glad the keyring was already looped over her fingers coming up the stairs; jumpy cops didn't mix well with purse-rumaging.

"That's just it Miss, no one's seen Miss Rogers since the week after your brother hurt himself."

"*Was* hurt, officer." She sounded angry, dangerous. Did she mean to sound that way?

"Pardon?" They were shuffling their feet like they didn't want to be standing on her doorstep. She didn't want to be standing on it either but she wanted them in her apartment even less.

"My brother was hurt *in the ring* by someone else, officer. There was no accident." She didn't like that they were wearing jackets, it meant that she couldn't see their muscles tense. Even their fingers were in gloves so she couldn't watch for a white-knuckled warning.

"Oh, I'm sorry Miss. We just need—"

"Need *what* officer?" She shouldn't take this tone. "The last time I saw Bethanne was in the hospital after the fight. When I left that night she was fine." She was being aggressive. She knew better than to be aggressive with cops.

"Could you calm down Miss? We just want the facts." There was a vein throbbing in the nearest one's throat. They were as on edge as she was.

Calm. Breathe.

Kary gestured for them to continue, lowering her eyes in what she hoped at least looked like a repentant stare. "Miss, could you tell us where you were Thursday night?"

Her head jerked up guiltily before she could control it. "Why Thursday? I thought Bethanne disappeared weeks ago?" That was what they had said, wasn't it? Why did they care about Thanksgiving night?

She couldn't tell them she was home alone. Someone had to have noticed Johnnie's hot new bike, she'd just look worse if that someone was found. But she couldn't tell the truth—these were real people cops, they couldn't know supers' secrets. And she couldn't—

"We have reason to believe the disappearance of Miss Rogers and the tragic fire at the Marshal City Coliseum are connected."

Bethanne and the fire? It almost made sense, she was a circuit employee and the Coliseum was hosting a massive cage tournament when it... "Bethanne was—I don't understand." She needed more info. She needed these cops to think she was shocked and helpless. She needed to know if someone was targeting people connected to the fighting community 'cause that might mean that—

Aguas-aguas-aguas.

"I'm sorry Miss. We're not at liberty to say anything more. Your whereabouts Thursday night through Friday morning?"

Seth was safe. Seth was safe. *Seth was safe.*

She needed to be softer. "I was...I don't want to say." Look down, blush, what was her alibi? She needed one that could be corroborated, but that meant it was either up to Johnnie—a teenager, Bearkat: whose real name she didn't know, Audra who she'd just met, or "Adam."

"Miss? Could you repeat that?" They shifted again and leaned in toward her like they wanted her to be intimidated.

Kary tried to let them think it worked. There was a set of hard gears turning in her head. She raised her eyes and was suddenly very glad that the cold was making her flush. "I was with my boyfriend all night."

"And what is his name Miss? We'll need to collect his statement to corroborate your story."

"Adam Adamson, CEO of Adamson Industries."

Chapter 22

As soon as the cops left, Kary bolted through the apartment to her computer. The only phone number she could find went to the front desk of Adamson Industries. There was no number for Adam's office, not even a secretary she could make personal appointements with. She didn't have *time* for this, why hadn't she gotten Johnnie's number months ago? She needed a surefire way to speak to the quiet billionaire she'd now met several times in his secret super lair and the closest she could get was some desk clerk who was going to think she was a crank caller.

Kary gritted her teeth and dialed. "Adamson Industries, how may I direct your call?"

"Yes, could you connect me to Mr. Adamson please? Tell him Kary's calling."

"Miss, I'm afraid that Mr. Adamson does not take calls unless they go through his secretary—"

"Then could you connect me to Mr. Adamson's secretary please?"

"Miss I'm afraid that—"

This wasn't working. "His secretary, *please*? I just need—"

"Miss it is company policy that Mr. Adamson not take—"

"Just tell him Kary called. That's all. *Please*?" This wasn't going to work. She was going to be sunk. The perfect alibi and it was going to be thwarted by some desk jockey with a company policy manual. "*Please*?" she put every ounce of *help me I can't help myself* she had into it. When this was done she was going to need to shove someone around the ring a time or three to feel like herself again.

A deep breath that sounded more like a growl. "*Fine*." Wait, it worked? "Hold please." She wasn't relaying the message. She was putting Kary on indefinite hold and hoping the college student would give in and hang up.

Fat chance.

Kary didn't know how long she had before the cops worked up the courage to interview a billionaire telecom mogul about his relationship with a college student some ten years his junior, but it wouldn't be long. At most she had an hour to get this story straightened out.

If Adam agreed. What if he didn't? What if he—

There was a beep and a click, *seriously?* Just like that? They were gonna disconnect her, well then she was going to— "Kary, what's wrong?" Oh, that was the sound of him answering his phone, not some secretary hanging up on her.

"Um." Now how was she going to explain this, again? She couldn't come out and say she'd lied to the cops and needed help. If secretaries were shown with any accuracy on TV then there was no telling who was listening in on the line. "*Darling*, how are you?"

170

"Kary?" He sounded worried; it was sweet how the supers got concerned over her. She just hoped that concern stretched far enough to cover her lying ass. "Are you okay?"

"Not at *all*." She made her voice as sugary as she could. "The *nastiest* thing just happened, I got home from Rodney's funeral and there were two *cops* outside my apartment, imagine that?" Please understand, please understand.

"That's *awful*…sugar plum." Sugar plum? Was that *really* the best endearment he could come up with on the fly? "Are you hurt? What did they want?" Thank goodness he was playing along.

"It was the *strangest* thing. They wanted to know where I was Thursday night 'til Friday morning."

There was a sound like a breath cut in two. "*Oh?* And what did you tell them?"

"The truth, *silly*." Be teasing, be light. "That you and I were together *all night* over at your place. What was I *supposed* to say?"

"Oh yes, you *did* have… pumpkin pie with me Thursday night, I almost forgot." Terrible euphemism but at least he was on board. "Honey, it seems my secretary wants my attention." A pause, "Speak of the devils. I believe it's those same cops from your apartment. Is there anything I'm forgetting that you'd like me to pick up for tonight?"

Was that code for other details? Did he honestly think she'd thought this out further than turning him into an accomplice? "Nothing *cariño*, just that I can't wait to see you again."

"I feel the same—actually I can't wait at *all*. Come to my office Kary, we need to… talk." Holy *piss* his *voice*. Kary hoped the cops were embarrassed after hearing the drawl he put on that last line; she sure was. She hung up, tossed the phone behind her on the bed and paced toward her closet, mourning didn't suit her.

✦

"Darling." Kary slammed through Adam's office doors running, at least three secretaries scurrying protests in her wake. Kary ignored the stares and wrapped herself around Adam, kissing his cheek and staying snugged against his chest to stare at all the on-lookers. "Officers." She pretended embarrassment but wasn't sure it sold without the cold to make her blush. "Are you *still* here?" She was wearing a top cut lower than the chilly weather warranted, her jacket was open and she had no scarf.

"We were just leaving. Thank you for your time Mr. Adamson." They looked like guilty children. Just what had he said that made them not look her in the eye? Had her entrance *really* been that convincing? A real flush hit Kary's throat and kept traveling up. Adam's fingers curled inside the collar of her coat, smoothly stripping it down and off her back, it fell to the floor unheeded.

"Of course officers, have a good day." His hands free and jacket gone, he was now rubbing her back like the officers weren't there, for all intents totally engrossed in Kary's shoulders and moving lower.

Day. It was Sunday, why on earth was Adamant, the man strong enough to juggle semi trucks and rich enough to buy out small countries, in his office on a *Sunday?* As soon as the door closed and they could step away from each other she asked him.

172

"I spend every other Sunday in the office catching up on paperwork. You're lucky I'm here, usually I leave by three." He bent to retrieve her coat, keeping a careful arm-length between them.

She'd called around four. Kary could feel something solid moving up and down in her throat, very lucky indeed. "Thank you for playing along. I owe you." She shivered a little without her coat on, an entire wall of the office was glass and she could feel the cold radiating in.

He was looking her over thoughtfully, clinically appraising. Whatever act he'd just put on for the police, it was obvious from this cool gaze that it was exactly that: an act. Kary shifted under his eyes. "Yes, you do." Was he really gonna call her in? Right now? Seconds after she said it? Could he *do* that? Call favors in immediately?

She resisted the urge to hug her coat or cross her arms over her chest. "Um…" This was Adamant, she could trust him. She just *really* wanted to put on her coat and zip it up until he quit looking at her like he was calculating something. "So if there's anything I can do…"

His tone was peculiar as he sat back behind his desk. "Two things, actually." Forget trust, she was going to regret this.

"The first is simple, we should go to dinner."

Dinner? That wasn't what she'd expected. He must've seen it on her face. "The press has sources within the CPD, if we go on the record as—" he coughed into his fist and it sounded staged, "—dating then we'll need to go on a few dates."

Kary Dogg didn't date. "Do the press really care…"

"Reclusive billionaire playboy who's never given an interview that wasn't scripted is dating a college undergrad? Yes, they care."

Since when was he a recluse? She'd read the gossip about his eligible bachelor status, but did that *really* translate to playboy? Kary flopped into the deep leather of the chair across from his desk. "This is gonna be a headache, isn't it?"

"Adamant and Aspect and Adamant Girl will smash a few buildings soon enough and take the cameras elsewhere but until then it might be a little hairy for you." Hairy? Hairy press killed a princess and made pop stars shave their heads. She didn't want to deal with *hairy*.

"When can we stage our breakup?" Was she at least going to get to throw wine in his face at an expensive restaurant?

"I was thinking of having my people leak it quietly instead of us staging a scene."

Was thinking? He'd had *maybe* an hour to collect himself and handle the cops since she called and thrust this gig on him. Just how much *thinking* could he've done? "No wine to the face?" She tried not to sound disappointed. She'd never cared enough about a guy, nor dated one long enough to justify throwing things at him and wanted to try it at least once.

"We could, but then they might think you're *interesting*. The press *loves* interesting people." Oh yeah, hadn't she decided a long time ago that she didn't want press because of the supers? Something about a TV deal...

"Makes sense." Damn him and his logic. "So we go to supper a few times, what's part two?"

"I need you and Audra to be friends." He wanted her to babysit his niece? "She's not a child, you don't need to babysit her. Just… befriend her."

"Did I say that out loud?"

"You did. Like I said, not *babysit*, friends. You could pick her up from school tomorrow and hang out, do whatever it is girls do…" 'Cause she knew what girls did? Kary had one girl friend and half of their relationship was built on a mutual appreciation for getting hammered.

"She's not talking to you, is she?" Kary remembered her own teenage years and the rows she'd had with Rodney over her brother's schedule.

"Kary, are you okay?"

She put her fingers to her face. It was wet. "Yeah, fine." She scrubbed her eyes. "So, you want me to make nice with Audra, why? 'Cause she's falling in with the wrong crowd at school?" The idea of a sidekick, especially a sidekick to a boyscout super like Adamant, falling in with the *wrong crowd* was laughable. Kary would've been considered the *wrong crowd* not long ago.

Had Adamant Girl even *been* to school yet?

"It's not that, it's just… Mynx. She's friends with Mynx."

Now the truth came out. "What's wrong with that? They're both supers. Why shouldn't they be friends?" He gave her a crossways glance and Kary shrugged. "I mean, *I* don't like Mynx but I'm not going to let my personal feelings dictate—" The hell she wasn't but she wanted Adamant to say it out loud.

"I don't want her picking up Mynx's attitude." His face was sour. He didn't want to admit what he was saying. "She's careless and disrespectful. Audra would benefit from a more *mature* female influence."

Mature. Twenty-two years young and Kary was being called *mature*. "What about her mom?" In books wasn't it always the mothers or aunts or grandmas who were the positive—

"Not an option." His elbows were on the desk; his hands fisted together under his chin to prop it up. Kary heard Adamant's knuckles crack when he spoke even though his voice never changed.

Kary looked at her own hands and then met his eyes again; she knew something about mothers who weren't options. "I'll pick her up tomorrow afternoon for a couple hours of girl time. No promises about the whole *befriending* thing." Teenaged Bruiser hadn't liked the assigned friends and babysitters she was given when Seth was on the road and she doubted a baby Adamant would be any more receptive.

"Thank you Kary, that's all I'm asking. Before you do this you'll need to know a few things…"

They stayed there for well over an hour. At one point Kary mentioned the cops' alleged connection between the fire and Bethanne's disappearance and Adam became pensive, pulling out a phone model she'd never seen and typing rapidly without saying a word. He was quiet long enough that Kary had to ask: "You don't think it has anything to do with the prostitute thing in Commonland, do you?" Surely not, they didn't have any evidence of this problem in other cities—that's what Johnnie had told her. Johnnie didn't lie. Kary didn't like to think about the fact that she couldn't say the same.

"I don't know Kary. Bethanne's vanishing would've been close to the beginning of the abductions and it's within a hundred miles. We'll look into it."

✦

When she finally stood to go, Adamant stood also. "I'll walk you out." He wasn't Adam, he had his serious super face on now, even without the mask. It would've been more intimidating if she hadn't watched him put away three slices of pumpkin pie in a row just a couple nights before.

"Oh, that's fine. You've got work and—"

"No, I insist." Odd. "I need to kiss you goodbye in front of the cameras that gathered on our front steps twenty minutes ago." What? "See for yourself." He spun the monitor of his computer around so she could see a surveillance feed of the front doors of the building.

Kary's stomach dropped. "*Already?*"

She didn't like how wicked his smile was. He was enjoying her discomfort and she didn't approve. Hadn't he been awkward back when they first met? Forever ago? "Come along *sugar plum*, we have to sell this."

Chapter 23

Kary parked in the lot across from Commonland High rather than driving through the line to pick Audra up. She was sitting on her car's hood thirty minutes after the final bell when the teen came sloping out the glass doors, her bag drooping from one shoulder. "Just 'cause you're boning my uncle doesn't mean you have to make nice with me." She told Kary, slinging herself into the front seat while Kary stayed crosslegged on the warm hood of her car. "Are you *coming*?"

Patient. *Patient.*

"You know Adam and I aren't dating, right? It's all a cover for where I was Thursday."

"What? My uncle not *good* enough for you?"

The girl was *looking* for a fight. "No, we just aren't like that. We're friends."

"Friends can have benefits."

Naïve, did Adam know his niece thought sex was that simple? If not Kary foresaw awkward conversations in his future. "That doesn't really *work*."

"Yeah it *does*. I know plenty—"

Kary's snort cut the girl off. The college student slid off the hood and walked around to lean through the open window on her driver's side door. "Let me tell you something that's going to be true for the rest of your life, *chica*—sex complicates *everything* and anyone who tells you otherwise is lying or trying to get in your pants."

She sounded like a mom from a sitcom and Audra didn't believe her. It was written all across her face but Kary let the topic go. The kid would learn, hopefully before she did anything stupid. "*Whatever.*" Kids still said whatever? Kary'd been sure that one went out with her generation.

"*Anyway,*" Kary slid behind the wheel and shut her door. "I thought we could hang out this afternoon." There was a whine in her engine that Kary wasn't sure of when she cranked it, probably the oil again.

"Liar, my *uncle* thought we could hang out this afternoon. You didn't *think* anything."

The older girl rolled up her window and laid her right hand behind the passenger headrest when she turned her body to watch as she backed out of the space. Naïve, stubborn, *and* clever. A stellar combination in a normal teenager, never mind one who could knock buildings down. "Think of it as training. I'm taking you to my gym and you're gonna pretend to be a real person."

They were turning out of the lot when Audra asked: "Why? The gym at the House is better."

And how would she know that? She'd never been to Jimmie's, probably never even *heard* of it. Though, she was right about the quality of the gear. "I told you, *training.* My friends at the gym are going to teach you some kickboxing and you're going to learn like a normal

179

girl. No super strength." They were only a few bocks away, if she'd been sure about the weather later this evening they might've walked instead of driving.

"I mastered a dozen different martial arts forms while training with the Recluse, *including* muay thai. This does me no good." The kid knew the root form of kickboxing, almost impressive.

"You mastered those without needing to pretend to be a real person. Now you have to blend in, this is an exercise in restraint, not power."

"*Whatever*, it's still pointless."

Kary parked outside the gym. "Say what you want but you're either coming in and sitting in a corner to watch or coming in and getting to play with the trainers and show me up on the canvas. You choose." The girl hadn't been friendly Thanksgiving night, but she hadn't been this hostile either. The fighter remembered her own mercurial teenage years and tried to keep her expression neutral. She half expected the baby Adamant to choose sitting in the corner out of protest.

"I don't have clothes."

"I have spares."

"Whatever." But she followed Kary all the same.

⁕

"Kary, you know we're closed today." Jimmie came out of his office when she came through the door past the deserted front desk. "All the gyms are closed this week." Until the funerals were done.

The college student had forgotten. "I know Jimmie but I wanted to show my friend Audra a thing or two on the reflex bag. She's been in a karate class these past few weeks but never worked with one." Kary could feel the girl's boredom behind her and kept her expression bland through the lies.

"Oh yeah? She any good?" He wanted a distraction. He wanted to watch them fight. With anyone else he might be angrier longer, but Kary could see an edge of fire in his eyes, he was as bored with the mourning game as she was. Even retired from the ring twenty years, he'd rather hit something to vent emotion and if he couldn't do that watching one of his favorites was almost as good.

"Not sure, lemme warm her up and we'll see."

"Do that." He stumped back into his office and Kary steered the young super into the dressing rooms to change.

+

"What are you *playing* at? My reflexes are ten times faster and I'm a thousand times stronger than you'll ever be *norm*." Audra sounded exactly like Mynx when she was calling Kary a norm. It was nostalgic the same way the last thing she ate before contracting a stomache bug was be nostalgic.

"Hold your strength back but not your reaction times. You can do that, *can't you*?"

The girl looked offended. "I once meditated for thirty-six hours straight sitting on the crest of a dune in the center of the Sahara."

Sandstorms and all? Kary tugged her sports bra, adjusting it roughly. "That doesn't tell me anything." Audra was changing with her back to the older girl. Something in the set of her shoulders told Kary she was uncomfortable with this conversation. Or maybe just that they were having it half dressed.

181

"It tells you that—"

"That you like to impress people with red herrings." The uncomfortable shoulders twitched. "Can you control yourself or do I need to tell Jimmie that you started your period and forgot tampons and we can't fight today?"

Audra turned to face her but avoided Kary's eyes. Naïve, uncomfortable, embarrassed. This bonding thing was going great. The girl didn't argue again.

The reflex bag hit Audra four times; three of those were a surprise to her but not to the older girl. Adam had told her that Audra would underestimate normal training techniques and that her reflexes weren't *actually* faster. *We're stronger than normal humans and with that strength comes speed but only after we've trained for it. Take her down a peg. Remind her to respect norms.*

"She's warm Jimmie, wanna come watch?"

Audra's eyes widened perceptibly. "*Now?*"

"Come on kiddo, not *scared* are you?" She was baiting a sidekick. Last time she did this she hadn't felt comfortable in her own gym for a week. Hadn't gone back to her bar for two.

"*No.* I just don't wanna hurt you."

"You're not used to kickboxing, so come at me with karate. And remember, this is *fun.*"

Kary kept her distance when Jimmie rang the bell for first bout. Hands up, she watched the sidekick narrowly, and waited. She didn't have long, the girl rushed in without guarding, sloppy. The fighter let her get in close and put her knee up under Audra's ribs, *hard*.

The girl lurched back, bent over coughing. She hadn't tightened her abdomen against the blow. Jimmie leaped onto the canvas with more agility than his Bruiser had seen on him in a long time. "You okay kid?" His hand was on Audra's shoulder. "What was *that*? You *know* knees aren't allowed." He was scolding Kary but it was Adamant's niece, not Audra the teenager, glaring up at the college student.

"Back away Jimmie, she's fine." The old trainer slid back out of the ring. Kary felt a low fizzle in the back of her skull, and an itch in her palms that had nothing to do with the quality of her gloves. She needed this. The sidekick might need the lesson, but Kary needed the brawl.

The bell rang again and Audra charged just a little faster than a real person should, the fighter stepped out of the way and brought her elbow down on the back of the girl's neck. She dropped like a stone.

"*Kary.*" He'd let them in to watch punches being traded, not to watch his fighter dissect the younger girl on the mat.

"Stay *out* of it Jimmie." Audra lunged at her ankles from where she'd fallen and Kary skipped back out of the way. "Stand up Audra. We're not done." The teen growled as she climbed to her feet. "*Good*, now focus."

The trainer's face was inscrutable but he kept his mouth shut, watching the girls in the ring. He could tell the teenager was not as trained as his Bruiser had said: her stance wasn't solid for one thing. For another, there wasn't a dojo in the area that would allow an ankle grab like that, there were other factors at play here.

Audra's hands were up in a guard but she was standing still. Planted. Kary bounced around her, jab-jab *punch* the hit connected with the teen's jaw. "Move your feet, you're standing like a tree. Trees get struck by lightning and cars all the time." She swung her foot in a kick. Audra threw up a clumsy block. "Good, learn to guard, always guard."

"Show her." Rocks cut Kary off and immediately the fighter dropped her stance and grabbed the other girl's arm, bracing her forearm up into the proper form, he continued speaking as she did: "Rememer what this feels like." Kary knew this routine and threw a slow punch without him asking, letting Audra brush it away. "Good. *Resume.*"

Kary stepped away and dropped into stance. She gave the sidekick a cut heartbeat to settle back in and then kept circling. Kept dancing. Kept punching and kicking and baiting the girl while Jimmie watched. He'd never seen her work with someone like this; she only sparred with his trainers or other gym regulars. Everyone knew his Bruiser didn't give advice often and never demonstrated like this.

This teenager was different, whatever the reason, so Jimmie bit his tongue when his fighter barked: "Up, Audra. Again." Dodge, dodge, jab, *elbow*. Elbow to the cheek, Kary knocked the girl's mouth guard out. "Get your guard. Can you continue?"

"You bet your ass I can *nor*—"

"Good, guard *up*."

✦

"Do you feel better?" There was an edge of disapproval in the question as Jimmie followed Kary around while she cleaned the equipment they had used in their session. The fighter had already sent the pride-sore teen to the showers. "You could've gone easier on her, Bruiser."

Now *that* was laughable. "It's none of your business Jimmie."

"Of course, it only took place on my canvas on the week when I'm closed for mourning. *None* of my business. Bruiser," He stopped her with a hand on her arm. "I'm worried about you and your brother—"

Kary shook him off. Brother? "Seth? Is he okay? How's he working out?"

"He's been calling me since he moved back, wanting to get training sessions in."

"Even though you're closed?" And he wasn't recovered. Seth should have at *least* another month of rehab scheduled before he could think about a full session.

"Didn't stop *you*."

"Yeah but I'm…" What? She was what? A paying member of the gym just like any other member and therefore not entitled to coming in on days when the gym was closed and certainly not welcome to bring guests without notifying Jimmie first. "I'm sorry." She hung her head and the shame wasn't faked. "I shouldn't have come today."

Jimmie thumped her back. "That kid needed a lesson, kinda like someone else I know." He tugged on Kary's braid and let go, walking toward his office. "Just remember to be nice, Bruiser. They're not all as tough as you were." He stopped at the door, "And tell your brother to chill. He needs to relax and enjoy his retirement a little."

185

◆

Audra leaned on the chest high divider between shower stalls while Kary began running water and testing the temperature. "I didn't spend a whole year with the Recluse."

Kary glanced at the girl, wrapped in one of the cheap towels the gym provided and looking abashed. She also looked refreshed from her shower, whereas Kary was going to need an ice soak and a long night's sleep after battering around a baby Adamant. The norm might've won in the ring this afternoon but it was the super who'd wake up smiling in the morning.

"I figured that." The college student turned off the water and leaned back against the divider across from Audra. She crossed her arms over her chest. "How long were you with him?"

"A couple months maybe? I couldn't *stand* it, all the meditation and breathing exercises and no *actual* combat training and Mynx was always saying how much *better* experience in the field was so I—"

"So you ran away from the Recluse, spent what? Ten months fighting small time crime in a ski mask before you came to Adamant and told him your training was done. That you were ready to be a real sidekick?"

The girl hung her head even lower than it already was. Much further and her cheek was going to be on the tile and then Kary was going to get the joy of explaining to Adam why his niece had staph infection on her face after just one afternoon of this dynamic duo he'd forced them into. Kary reached across and poked Audra's cheek a little so the girl raised her head away from the tiles. "You're gonna tell him, aren't you?" The

186

teen's voice was distorted with Kary's finger still jabbing her cheek.

The college student sighed before she answered. Sneaky Adam, there was no way he hadn't already known this. He'd wanted Kary to get it out of his niece to cement some sort of a bond. Or test his sidekick's friend. Maybe both. "Not if you don't want me to. But *you* should tell him. He needs to know so he can pick up training where you left off."

"But—"

"He's going to be trusting you with his life every night until you're ready to go on as a solo act. Even more so after Johnnie leaves in a few months, he needs to know *you* trust *him*." Audra nodded without meeting Kary's eyes. "Now scram." Audra was probably too shy to look, but the older girl didn't want her seeing the bruises she could already feel rising on her arms and legs. The girl dragged to the other section of the dressing rooms where dry clothes were waiting for her and Kary shrugged out of her gear, continuing to attempt to coax hot water from the stubborn pipes.

+

Dropping Audra off at the Adamson mansion was Kary's first time actually seeing the place. It was big and immaculate with wide granite steps sweeping up to the front entrance like it was some sort of old public building. A courthouse or a library, maybe. "So this is what I'm gold digging for." The press story she'd read that morning seemed plausible now that she was looking at a physical representation of the Adamson fortune.

It was almost a pity she *wasn't* getting more out of this deal than a free supper and a little newsprint in the gossip columns.

"Enter." Adam's voice was foreboding when it echoed through the heavy, brass studded doors to his study. The hall outside those doors was dark and some long dead Adamson ancestor was glaring at Kary and Audra from a gilt framed canvas hung at the far end of the corridor. There was a window at the near end but heavy velvet curtains were pulled shut over it, blocking the last of the afternoon light.

Audra shot Kary a look, as if hoping the older girl would change her mind and bar the door to keep the young sidekick from confessing her transgression. "Want me to come in with you?" Kary made the offer guessing that a proud Adamant wasn't going to take her up on it. She'd stiffen her lip and march in there chin up chest out before asking someone to hold her hand.

"Yes, please."

Oh.

Huh.

Wonders never ceased.

Chapter 24

"**So** how's it feel to be dating the most eligible bachelor in the city, if not the country?" Kary was digging through her closet while Johnnie lounged on her bed, a textbook open and ignored beside him.

"Like he needs to learn how to pick a better restaurant." She pulled out a cocktail dress and held it against herself, turning for her friend to see. Tonight was going to be the first, and last, staged date Adam was taking her on. They'd originally thought to play this thing a little longer, but impending exams made the college student cut plans short. Sometime early next week his publicist would leak that they were breaking up and hopefully the press would be mostly gone in time for Kary to knuckle down and study for finals the week after.

"Nope, too short." Audra was in the doorway shaking her head.

"Welcome back *chica*, you done with practice?" It was the Friday after their girls' afternoon at the gym. Since the teenager's confession to her uncle she'd been training intensively in the House every second she wasn't at school or sleeping.

"Uncle gave me an hour off to help you get ready."

"Tell him I'm not going. I've got *nothing* to wear." Kary made the second sentence as melodramatic as she could, throwing the cocktail dress, which really was too short and too sparkly for the swanky resrautant in question, and herself on the foot of her bed in a fit of fake tears.

"Figured that, I ordered you a few things."

"*I ordered you a few things.*" Kary parrotted from where she was still prostrate. Johnnie was poking her side with his toe experimentally. "What is this, a Victorian novel?"

"Just try them on?" She tossed a pile of bagged dresses across the older girl's back. "We can't have you shaming my uncle in *public.*"

"Only in private then." Kary rolled off the end of the bed with her feet under her and the dresses in her arms. "Do I wanna know how you guessed my sizes?" She called through the mostly closed door of her bathroom.

It was Johnnie who answered, not Audra. "I borrowed from Mathlete a few years back, got his ability to calculate sizes, speeds, and trajectories based on surrounding objects."

"Mathlete?" Kary poked her head out the door and squinted at him. "Should I know that name?"

"Mathlete's what we call him, norms call him Algorythm."

The super calculator. He hadn't been a major player in the super game in *ages*. "Well then I'm going to thank you for guessing right and *not* find this creepy, even though it *is*." Johnnie shrugged, unembarrassed. "Audra, come zip me."

190

+

"*Audra?*" Kary turned in her bathroom mirror to see the last dress at all angles. "Just how old do you think I am?" There were three, each fit perfectly and each more matronly than the last.

"I dunno, thirty something?"

Kary thumped her forehead on the door in frustration. Teenagers, anyone older than them was *old*. "I'm twenty-two, *kid*."

"Oh."

Johnnie was squirming on her bed to keep quiet at the chunky sweater sewn to the current dress in six different spots. Kary had attempted to snip it off at the attaching threads with a pair of nail clippers but that only made the seams pucker in weird places. "I'm wearing my dress." Kary scooped up the original discard from the bed while both sidekicks shook with giggles. "I'm a slut anyway." If she'd read the tabloids right. One, industrious reporter had even dug up Johnny and gotten a slew of juicy, inaccurate, details on Kary's preferences from the night in Marshal.

Audra laughed again and Johnnie didn't say anything, he hadn't commented on her sex life since their row the day after her brother's last fight. Kary hadn't taken the time to indulge in a one-night stand since the night before Seth's injury.

+

Kary did let Audra talk her into a fur coat, though it felt out of place wrapped around a dress she'd bought on sale for a party her freshman year—back when she

191

thought college parties looked like they did in the movies. It wasn't a long coat, but the dress was even shorter, and it left a dusting of red glitter in the satin lining. When Adam picked her up in a car that was low, quiet, and Italian, he looked pleased. He pressed his lips to the corner of her mouth for the sake of a camera man crouched in the bushes of the apartment building next to hers. "Glad Audra couldn't get you to into one of the dresses she bought."

"You *knew?*" Kary kept smiling like she wasn't fuming at him for not giving her a heads up. Or helped his niece with her choices. "Those dresses were hideous and probably expensive."

"Oh they were. Special order from France using my card three nights ago. She had them airlifted in."

"*You* bought them?" He had better taste than that. She *knew* he had better taste. The car said *that* much. "But Audra—"

"Audra thought she was being sneaky when she took the card from my office and used one of the secure computers in the House. I'm sneakier."

During dinner they talked about bland things and played footsie for the cell phone camera two tables over. Kary's dress was indeed cheaper, and shorter than any other in the restaurant but her fur was also nicer and her date richer. When she complained about the tiny portions of artisan food they were being served Adam called a waiter back over with the menus and they ordered again. And again. And then they ordered all five desserts, each as expensive as an entrée and almost as tiny.

The other patrons shot them looks around champagne glasses that weren't topped off as often as Kary and Adam's glasses but the couple didn't pay them any mind. Kary had gotten onto the subject of her misdeeds among the other young toughs she ran with while her brother was just starting the circuit. Adam was responding with stories of his own escapades in college when he had been too young, his father too rich, and his friends too clever for anyone's good.

Kary studied the man across from her. Strong with clear, dark eyes and thick blond hair combed neatly back away from his face. He didn't *look* like the sort of person he was describing but he was describing too well to be lying. Then again, being a Register super with an inherited name probably meant he was at least as good as she was at turning a phrase.

He read her face. "You don't believe me." It was a statement, not a question.

"You're a boy scout." She leaned back to tip her glass to her lips. "Irresponsibility, even past irresponsibility, doesn't suit you."

"A boy scout on a date with a girl ten years his junior."

She raised the glass a fraction in toast before setting it down. "What *would* your parent's think?" A tease, a light one from some TV show sometime, Kary didn't know much about parents who thought.

His eyes lost their mischief for a second but his smile didn't move. "My father would be thrilled that the *phase* was over." There was a bitter note in his words.

Kary felt a pang. *Bearkat.* "Does it really matter that much?"

Adam's smiling mask was better than hers. "The family name has to be passed down." He raised his glass and drained it. "Here's to many more Adamsons to come."

Kary finished her glass, unsure how to answer that.

Adam waved away the waiter rushing forward with the towel wrapped bottle. "Are you ready to go?"

His fingers trailed across on the back of her hand, reminding her that they were still on stage, Kary pulled out her widest grin and tried it on for size. "Oh *darling*, dessert again?" There was a couple sitting two tables over that had shared the cheapest entrée on the menu, drunk only water, and were leaning toward Kary and Adam. "You *bad* boy."

He stood and offered her a hand up, kissing her finger tips as she rose out of her chair. "Oh my dear Kary, you have *no* idea." The look he was sending her over her knuckles made her cheeks, already warm from the wine, burn.

As per the plan, Kary was to spend the night at the Adamson mansion. There was a spare room and an overnight bag waiting on her. The bag she'd packed and given to the sidekicks before leaving her apartment, the room had been prepared by them after the mansion's staff left for the weekend. There was a fire burning on the hearth when she finally got there and kicked off her heels. "Johnnie, did you light this?" Kary was drowning in the comfort of the armchair by the hearth.

He came out of the shadows. "How'd you know I was here?"

Her eyeballs felt heavy. "Figured you would be." It seemed like he always was when she wanted him. "The fire?"

"Yeah, that was me. How'd it go?"

"Good food." She briefly considered changing clothes while Johnnie was in the room and decided getting up and digging for her pjs was too much effort. "Good wine. Had to play footsie all night so the cameras got something."

"Oh? Think there'll be a second date?" There was a tease in his voice like he knew something she didn't. Kary wondered idly why he'd never come out and told her about Adam and Bearkat.

"Not sure I'm his type."

Johnnie laughed and sat on the wide, cushioned arm of her chair. "You know, I think you're right." Besides, there was that line she'd told Audra about friends having sex. The fighter curled deeper into her chair while Johnnie continued: "So you're breaking up next week?"

"Whenever the publicist says. 'm just a pawn." She was tipsy enough to be the cuddly kind of sleepy that had gotten her into trouble at houseparties before. Waking up with a hangover was bad enough, waking up with a hangover in some else's bed could be murder. Good thing Johnnie was here to keep her out of trou—

He derailed her train of thought. "Says the girl who told a billionaire she was dating him and *then* gave him a lead that cracked his case wide open."

Que? Kary jerked up, sleep and cuddles forgotten. "The Coliseum fire? Bethanne? Were they really connected to the prostitution thing?"

"We think so. Did you know there was a sub-level beneath the stadium floor—"

Everyone knew that. "Well *duh*, the dressing rooms." Kary cut him off louder than she'd meant to and then shrank a little when he glared at her. "*Sorry,*" she muttered while he continued, brushing clumsy fingers across her lips to mime zipping them shut.

"Anyway, it looks like they were being used to store the same stuff they use to knock out their abductees in crates of industrial sized sponges but that wasn't all, there were also barrels and barrels of something else."

Kary forgot her zipped lip. "The brainwashing stuff?"

"The samples we got were highly corrupted by the fire but that's the working theory. I'm breaking it down in the lab. Within the next couple of days I'll figure out the compound and we'll know *exactly* what we're dealing with."

"And Bethanne?"

"Once we knew where to look we found out there *were* disappearances in Marshal City before they started here. It's just that the ones who went missing were mostly runaways or homeless to begin with so no one but other street people knew they were gone and police don't take reports like that seriously."

Now *that* was heartbreaking. "How many?"

"How many what?"

"Runaways, how many runaways do you think are missing?"

"Twelve that we know of in Marshal, plus Bethanne." Plus the fire victims, but he didn't say that out loud and neither did she. "But there's something weird, they stopped about a month ago. Bethanne Rogers was the last disappearance in Marshal City."

"And they started in Commonland right after?"

"We started working street contacts here, turns out our runaways have been disappearing too. The same time as the Marshal abductions but you're right. The ones in Commonland became more frequent after the ones in Marshal stopped. We're looking at upwards of thirty missing within Commonland city-limits, almost fifty all told."

How did that many people go missing in two cities and no one notice? "And they destroyed whatever stock they had in Marshal, meaning the operation is either entirely here…"

"Or has moved to another city."

"But you don't think that."

"No, not with the number of girls that are still disappearing and the local availability of the ingredients used in that knockout juice."

"So it's up to you and Adamant."

"And Adamant Girl once she's cleared to go in the field again."

"When do you think that'll be?" She paused, something tickling her mildly muddled memory. "Didn't you say something about her being *hot*? Like *way* back when—" Kary must have drunk more than she thought if she was bouncing subjects like this.

"That was 'cause you were—" He was flustered, she could see his blush. "It was a joke." He was cute when he was embarrassed, she almost said it out loud but snatched the words back before he could hear them. "I dunno when she'll be cleared." He spoke fast, like he wanted her to drop it. "Adamant actually wanted to talk to you about that, something about you training with her? A better female influence?"

She'd pick it up another time, when there wasn't expensive wine fuddling her head. "He does know I have finals coming up, right? Besides, Audra's all buddy-buddy with Mynx and Mynx is a *super*, shouldn't she be Audra's—" There was a single word for what she wanted but Kary couldn't find it. "—guiding female light?"

197

"Mynx has been banned from the mansion and is only allowed in the House when supervised by Bearkat. Even on the case, she and Bearkat are just auxiliary."

Oh? "News to me." Kary hid her not-so-secret glee by standing and walking to her bed to burrow through the overnight bag. When she stepped the air around her head swooped and her legs wobbled a hair. She knew she was doing a poor job faking indifference to this latest development in Adam's disapproval of his niece's friend.

"Something about her being a bad influence on impressionable young sidekicks. He wouldn't tell me details."

Kary tried on her innocent mask and found that it fit a little funny. "Well that's a huge surprise, I had no idea—" She abandoned that line when she saw he wasn't buying. "But why should *I* be his first choice for his niece's... person?" What was the word she wanted? "I'm just a norm."

"You're milking this." Even if it was true, was rude of him to say it. "He heard about your gym session with her and liked the results. He wants you to do meditation and tai chi with her. If someone else does lessons with her then he thinks she'll be more..." He trailed off looking for the word and shrugged.

Kary tried to raise an eyebrow but was pretty sure she just wrinkled her forehead funny instead. "You know she's not a kid, right? She's not gonna fall for that."

Johnnie shrugged. "Maybe, maybe not. Can't hurt to try." Said the super to the real person about learning a martial art with another super. "Gotta go patrol." He was trying to escape this convesation, *cabrón*. He needed to stay with her so Kary could berate him fully. And so she could figure out what that damn word was. It was right *there*, it was…

"Might hurt *me*—I don't know either of those." Who meditated anymore, anyway? Besides generic Asian monks in generic kung fu movies.

"That's the beauty of *learning* Miss mentor." He closed her door before she could argue.

Mentor.

That was the word that'd slipped her mind. He wanted her to be a *mentor*.

Holy piss.

Chapter 25

Kary woke up slowly, pleasantly, luxuriating in an excellent mattress and fine linens. It would be worth following this charade if she could continue sleeping in beds like these. Kary rolled over, balling her covers up against her face to slide back into her warm doze, ignoring the buzz from her bedside table. Whoever was calling could wait until the afternoon.

The cell phone vibrated again, Kary rolled across the bed, as far from her device as possible without rolling off.

The drone turned into a ring mid-buzz. A ring far louder than any setting Kary would leave her phone at. When she peeked over her shoulder at the upturned screen it was pulsing like a bad rave.

She answered with a name and a hunch. "Adam?"

"I'm in the study, we should talk."

"How'd you change the settings on my—"

He cut her off. "Our technology makes hacking a cell phone, even remotely, simple. Join me in the study, there's coffee."

Kary groaned. "Sure, just gimme an hour to clean up and—"

"Now, Kary. We need to talk about Audra."

They did, but she wanted another half hour of sleep. "But—"

"You don't need to make yourself decent, *sugar*, so come get coffee, please."

Bastardo. The word ran through her mind but there wasn't much venom. "Be there in ten." Just as soon as she figured out where the study was.

She slid her feet onto the floor and shivered a little at the cold floorboards. A robe was hanging on the back of her bathroom door and Kary swung it on, tying the belt firmly against the fall chill and her own sleepiness.

When she opened the bedroom door, there was a map of the house taped to the back, Adam's study circled in green. Kary raised an eyebrow at someone's forethought and dutifully set off.

✦

The study was just as big as Kary remembered it from the night of Audra's confession but less foreboding with sunlight streaming through the floor to ceiling windows in one wall. "Did you sleep well? Coffee?" It seemed Adam had a thing for working under windows he could fly a small plane through; at some point she'd ask him about that.

"Thank you" Kary took the china cup he offered.

"Sugar? Cream? There's American or Irish, whichever you prefer."

Kary quirked a smile and poured a dram of Bailey's into her coffee. "Isn't it a little early for this?"

Adam added a drop to his own cup and Kary saw at a glance that it was already very pale. "Not for a Sunday." He led her to the fireplace at the far end of the study and waved for her to sit in yet another, impossibly comfortable fireside chair. The windows behind them gave great natural light and an impressive view of the grounds but the cold was also pressing through like water through a rag.

"So," he returned to his first question, "Did you sleep well in Casa Adamson?"

She laughed a little; the coffee was helping her forgive the morning hour. "Very well, could've slept all day." She meant the second part as a dig and from the twitch in the corner of his mouth she knew the super caught it.

"Excellent. Johnnie tells me you are up to speed on current progress."

"About how the fire and Bethanne and your case are connected? Just happy I could help."

"That, and the other thing?"

"Other thing?" She was feigning ignorance and he knew it and she knew he knew.

"You will be taking lessons in yoga, tai chi and other forms of martial and meditative arts with Audra from now on. She needs a positive female influence in her life and you've proven yourself an able instructor." One sparring session and he was ready for Kary to do this full time?

"I have my own studying Adam and a job that I have to show up for. Finals are coming up and—"

"This might be the only way to get Audra to take her training seriously."

"*Have you* asked *her*?" The cup rattled in her hand, the words had come out louder than she'd meant. "I mean come *on*, she's not much younger than Johnnie, surely between you and him and Bearkat you can instill *some* sense of how important *training* is." Had none of them dealt with difficult teens before? Surely, they'd heard and given more pep talks and work ethic lectures than Kary.

Adam sipped his coffee, composed. "Bearkat's free time is spent *instilling* other lessons into his own sidekick. Johnnie is busy in the lab working on the compound we found under the Coliseum and an antidote that doesn't involve concussing a person to entirely reprogram them back to who they were before they were abducted."

"And you? Why can't Audra's uncle be her lone mentor?" He'd been Johnnie's only mentor, why couldn't he be there for his own niece?

"Oh I will be her mentor—" The look he'd given her while he kissed her hand was back only this time, coffee notwithstanding, Kary felt chills. "—and yours too. Someone has to teach the lessons."

"KaryKaryKary, how'd it go?" Audra was bouncing on the bed in the guest room when Kary came back from the study.

"Good?" The older girl wasn't sure what she was answering for. The date or the fact that she was about to stop sleeping entirely because her friendship with supers was now translating to keeping their hours and training schedules.

Kary crossed to the bathroom and turned on the tap, taking a long draught straight from the stream. "So it's true? We'll be training together?" The younger girl wasn't asking about the date.

Kary stepped out of the bathroom, scrubbing drips from her mouth with the back of her fist. "Yeah, when I can. You'll probably think I'm the slowest person *ever* though." She sat crosslegged on the bed next to her young friend. "And Adam's going to be the one teaching us, so it'll be tough."

"Nah, uncle's nice. It'll be fun."

Fun. "I'm sure."

Johnnie poked his head in the door. "I brought breakfast. I can take you home after we eat."

"Goody, bring it here." The three of them ate folded up on her bed, heedless of the crumbs they were scattering and the greasy spots their fingers left on the covers.

Kary stumbled out of the back seat of the sedan in the dress she'd worn the night before, Johnnie was behind the wheel in a chauffeur's uniform trying to hide his laughter. The older girl hadn't showered and she'd let Audra go to town on her hair with a teasing comb before leaving the mansion. She looked disreputable and that was the point. This was the last scene of the play that she would act in. By Monday there would be rumors flying about her breakup and with any luck by Friday she'd be able to stop worrying about the smattering of paparazzo's she'd had on her tail for a week now.

Her overnight bag was waiting on the bed in her apartment when she got in but neither of the sidekicks were waiting with it. That was a little unexpected, she'd grown accustomed to them being around. Shrugging, Kary stepped into her bathroom to yank the dress off and climb into a shower.

✦

"What's this I hear bout you dating some rich-boy?" Seth was watching her work the speed bag at Jimmie's that afternoon when he asked.

Kary tried to be glad that her brother was around and not annoyed that he was hovering. "Not for much longer, he's an ass."

"But a rich ass."

"So?" Talking was disrupting her rhythm, she stepped away from the bag and someone else rushed in to claim it immediately. This was the first day any of the gyms had been open since Thanksgiving and the floor was *packed*.

"*So?* You can put up with a lot of assery for that kinda scratch."

He knew she wouldn't do that, why would he even make the joke? "*You* date him then."

Seth uncapped her water and took a swig without asking if she minded. "Think he'd go for me?" His face was wide and earnest, Kary punched his shoulder at the tease. He didn't flinch even though it was his bad shoulder.

"I don't think you're his type." Why hadn't he flinched when she hit his injury? "How's the arm? Shouldn't it be in a sling?" Anything to get him off of Adam.

They were at a rack of free weights now. Kary snagged a bench, bracing one hand on it and raising that leg until a flat line ran from her neck, to her back,

205

to her ankle. With her free hand she lifted a dumbell from the extension of her arm to even with her ribs and back down again, keeping the pace measured.

Seth watched her form without commenting on it, answering her questions instead. "Doc said I was healed up and could start using it normally again." The weight stilled, tucked up against her while Kary absorbed that. He was lying. The doctors in Marshal had said it'd be Christmas before he'd have full use of that shoulder again. She'd called and checked after the funeral, after he'd gritted his teeth and helped carry Rodney when they both knew he shouldn't.

"What about rehab?" She lowered the dumbbell again, slowly, cautiously.

"Done, clean bill of health."

She raised and lowered the weight another three cycles, considering that. Docs said he'd be doing rehab for months before he had full range of motion and even then he'd never have the same strength as before. She answered him while she switched sides. "That's *really* fast. Like, I don't *believe* you fast." Her braced arm shook a little with the effort of holding everything in check.

"Relax Bruiser, I got in on this new drug program and they healed me right up."

New program? She laid the weight on the floor, slowly standing so they were as close to eye level as they would ever be standing on level ground. "You never *told* me you were taking different meds." He rolled his head away from her at her tone, "You said you were just on *pain* meds." Which was a separate worry, but not the main issue at the moment. She put the dumbbell down. "Seth? What was it?"

"Nothing—just a new treatment thing. I didn't wanna worry you 'cause it's not FDA certified yet and—"

"Not *approved* yet? You mean it's not *safe* yet?" She'd seen and heard way too much about crazy drugs in the past few weeks to be any kind of comfortable with—

"Simmer down Bruiser, you're making a scene. How was I supposed to take care of you if—" He was doing that deep, calm voice thing he did. Only this time it wasn't going to work, not on her.

Hadn't they gone over this? She didn't *want* to be taken care of. "Making a *scene?* Says the guy who's taking meds that aren't *tested?* Says the guy who doesn't tell his own *sister* that his ex is *missing?* Says the guy who thinks—"

"How'd you know about Bethanne?" There was something dangerous in his calm now that normally would've made her back down. Today it made her boil.

"*Que?* The fucking *fuzz* ambushed me after Rodney's funeral. *That's* how. And then they had to interview my *boyfriend* for an alibi—" *ex*, she should've thrown ex in there in front of boyfriend.

"Oh, *I'm* keeping secrets? Who dates a *millionaire*—" Billionaire "—without telling their *brother?* Cameras following you to his house and… *Es nauseabundo*, Bruiser."

"Oh *I'm* disgusting? I'm the disgusting one when you made it a *habit* of fucking— Did Bethanne even *know*—"

"Says the girl who hooked up with one of *my* sponsors at *my* party and then didn't even *try* to use her cunt to save my endorsement—"

"Now I'm supposed to be *whoring* for your *career?* I *knew* you were getting old in the fight game but would you even make an *effort* at getting long term contracts? No you just—"

"*Effort?* Says the weekend warrior who got her *ass* handed to her by some nobody off the *street?*"

"You wanna see a weekend *warrior?* Strap up Mad Dogg, I'll show you a *weekend* warrior." The gym was frozen, watching them.

✦

Kary shoved in her mouth guard, waiting on the canvas on dancing toes. The entire gym crowded around the ring, staring as her brother wrapped his hands and pulled on his gloves with deliberate calm that betrayed his fury. Someone laced the gloves for him and helped the Mad Dogg with his own guard. Seth threw two test punches and faced her, mitts up.

The younger Dogg retreated to some small, still part of her brain. He still outweighed, out reached, and out classed her by a lot. But he'd also been loafing for over a month and had a recovering shoulder. His kicks had never been as sure as hers, and he'd want to hold back. Even wearing helmets and looking like rage in bare feet, he wouldn't come after her with *everything*. Her brother would never try to hurt her, and that was going to be his—

He was moving before someone rang the bell. Surging across the canvas like a hurricane or a wildfire or a falling mountain. Kary barely got her guard up in time for her forearms to take the brunt of one of his cannon punches.

She danced back. The corner, she was almost in the corner. If he hemmed her in he'd… she slipped around and delivered two fast jabs over his bad shoulder into

Seth's jaw. He turned his head and grinned around his mouth guard like the mad dog they called him. Kary danced back, away. She needed to get awayawayaway.

This wasn't right.

He was light on his feet, following while she danced. Her last sparring match had been the lesson with Audra and she'd let that stoke her ego too much. She'd come into this too confident.

Kary sensed the hook coming, felt it in the rhythm of his step and the angle of his breath but even with the sense, she didn't get her fist tucked behind her skull in time for a full block and his glove landed *hard*. Light and dark flashed as she jabbed him back, her punches landing on his guard but not doing any damage.

She couldn't see. Kary danced away again, trusting long instinct to keep her off the ropes. She blinked at the blazes of flame and shadow that still licked across her eyes. Somewhere far away someone called for him to stop so someone could check her.

Aguas-aguas-aguas.

The blazes were clearing and her brother was there, a mass of something solid between the dancing lights. She ducked under his one-two and her fist connected with the point of his chin but she had to jerk back without a full follow-through. She was too close. She needed *space*. The girl kicked desperately under his ribs. She just needed to wind him and get him to back away. She just needed to—

Her leg was hard, strong, and trapped. He had it pinned between his arm and his side. He was raising his free hand. This wasn't her brother. This was the way he would— He was looking at her knee. His fist was still in the air. He'd made his point why was he— He was—

"*Enough.*"

209

Jimmie.

Chapter 26

Seth went still but he didn't let go. Kary bounced on the ball of her free foot to keep her balance. He was squeezing too tight, hurting her ankle. A bruise would be rising there in a few hours if he didn't let her go soon. She squirmed in his grip and he only clenched tighter. "*Drop her.*" He didn't let go. Why wasn't he letting go? She wouldn't whimper. She wouldn't. *She wouldn't.* "Seth, *put* Bruiser *down.*" She wouldn't. She wouldn't. She wouldn't. "Garth?"

Garth climbed into the ring and laid a hand on her brother's arm. "Hey man, let 'er go." His voice was soft but it carried in across the ring. "Seth, man." Garth's hand was tightening on her brother's bicep. Kary could see their friend's knuckles going white with pressure. "You're *hurting* her."

Letgoletgoletgoletgoletgo.

Seth's eyes rolled in their sockets like an animal. Kary could see every cord in his neck pulled tight and every crease on his chest clenched down. "Seth, put me down." He blinked at her voice and his hold on her leg loosened a fraction.

Kary ripped away, dancing back fast when he surged at her sudden movement. But Garth was between them, Seth's equal in size even if he couldn't match his skill. He wrapped her brother in a bear hug and held him there while the last of the gym goers were sent out. She hadn't even noticed Jimmie and the other staff directing them towards the doors, she'd been so wrappedup in the tense universe on the canvas she hadn't seen the world outside it.

Seth wrenched away from Garth but stayed on the far side of the ring from Kary, pacing like a caged animal.

"I'm ashamed of you both." Jimmie was standing in the center between the siblings, Garth at his shoulder between the old fighter and the new trainer. Kary was watching her brother pace and keeping weight off her bad leg. Her cheeks were burning now that the fire was gone from her head. "Seth, hit the showers. I'll talk to you when your temper's cool. Bruiser— my office." Kary ducked through the ropes and didn't look back to watch Garth lead her brother to the dressing rooms like his arm was a leash.

+

"What was *that*?" Jimmie was scraping at the accumulated frost in his mini freezer with a pocket knife, collecting the shavings in a ziplock.

"Private argument, I'm sorry we had it here."

"Sit down Bruiser, prop that leg up." Kary sank onto the cracked seat of the chair across from his desk and raised her foot to rest on a short file cabinet. Jimmie slapped the half-full bag of ice shavings on her ankle and told her to keep it there.

212

"That was quite a domestic you staged. Anything I should be worried about?"

"Nothing Jimmie."

"Everyone knows there's only one person the Mad Dogg won't bite and that's his kid sister. Any idea what changed that?"

"I baited him too far. He's under a lot of stress these days."

"It have anything to do with the disappearance of his girlfriend? Or maybe the drug trial he took part in? Or maybe it's something to do with *your* choices." The last wasn't a question.

Kary winced, so he'd heard everything? "Like I said, it's private."

"Kary, I'm family." He was, or as close to family as she had besides Seth and Rod—. Not Rodney, not anymore. "You can tell me."

She could. She could admit everything to him and he'd listen and give her a drink and some half decent advice before she left. He was also her brother's employer. If Jimmie fired Seth she wasn't sure he'd be able to find another job—at least not one where he'd be surrounded by people who could watch his back like they did here.

"We haven't fought in a long time Jimmie, we were due a blow up. I'm sorry it was here."

He knew, or guessed she was lying. She could tell from his face. "Bruiser, I—"

"Seth's just stressed. I'll have a beer with him tonight and we'll talk it out and we'll be good." He still didn't believe her. "Can I go? I've got an appointment I'm late for." He waved vaguely toward the door and she hobbled out. She didn't look at him so she didn't have to see the disappointment on his face.

213

✦

"Bruiser, you know this is the guys' showers, right?" Garth was barring her way to the dressing room.

"Move Garth, I need to see my brother."

"No Kary, you don't."

"*Garth.*" She made her voice a warning. She might've lost to Seth, but Garth didn't dance near as fast as she could, even with a gimpy ankle.

"Bruiser, go home. Cool your jets. Let him cool his."

"He's my—"

"He's not your brother right now Kary. I don't know who he is but I've never seen him like this and frankly I'm not—"

She cut him off. "Then you need my—"

He sliced back in. "No, I don't need your help. I need you to go away so he doesn't see you and go off again."

"But—" *he's my hermano.*

"No buts Bruiser. For once listen, please?"

Seth. "Tell him I'll call and check in tonight."

Brother.

✦

"Audra said you were hurt." Johnnie was sitting on her counter when she unlocked the front door and limped into her apartment.

"Oh?"

"One of her assignments today, following you without you knowing as stealth training."

"In broad daylight? What if she was caught?"

"We figured you'd probably cover for her. Can I see your ankle?"

No. "It just needs ice." She stiffened her lip and walked past him to put her bag in her room, careful not to favor one leg while he watched.

214

"You gonna *seriously* be up for starting tai chi tonight?" She shouldn't have been surprised Audra was waiting around the corner in her bedroom. Not with Johnnie on the counter in her kitchen. "'Cause we can totally reschedule."

"I'll be ready. Can someone pick me up at midnight?" Kary flopped on her stomach on the bed. Something cold pressed to her ankle, when she craned her neck to see around her shoulder Johnnie was there holding a bag of frozen peas. "Thanks."

"No prob, so what happened?"

"Stupid argument with Seth. He was in some medical experiment for his shoulder and 'cause of you guys investigating mystery drugs I freaked and then he was shouting about me dating Adam and I couldn't explain that that wasn't really dating and... it was ugly."

"I'll say, she got her *butt* kicked." Audra had stolen one of the spare pillows and was hugging it to her chest. "And that's saying something 'cause she kicked *my* butt."

"You're strong but you're not trained. There's always a way to beat someone who hasn't been trained. And this was *different*."

"How so?"

"He wasn't supposed to be... like that."

"You challenged your pro-fighter brother because you thought he was still injured and you could beat him?" Johnnie was saying things she didn't want to admit again. "Or did you think he'd take it easy on you even when he was angry?"

"I was mad. I wasn't being *reasonable*." Her face was in the pillow and her voice muffled.

"Yes you were. You were using logic."

"*Cállate*, Johnnie."

Audra was the one who kept talking when the older sidekick clammed up. "But it's *true*. There isn't anything on the market that would've put him back to fighting fit a month after an injury like his."

Why was Audra chiming in? She hadn't even been *around* when Seth got hurt. "He's in excellent shape, even after downtime. And instinct counts for a lot. He's trained so long and so hard he probably—" Kary sounded like she was making excuses.

"The instinct to harm his family?"

"I said shut *up*, sidekick."

"*I'm* just saying, whatever he took, our computers couldn't find it mentioned in any database which means it's not a sanctioned FDA trial, or sanctioned by any *other* agency on the planet for that matter."

She didn't like them. They were making her feel small and her brother look bad and she didn't like these clever, logical sidekicks at *all*. She wanted them to go away so she could call Seth and bring over a sixer to share while they watched football and bitched about bad ref calls even though they knew next to nothing about the sport. But Adamant told her she was a mentor and mentors didn't do things like curse at teenagers for being right.

Even when they wanted to.

Kary stayed facedown on her pillow rather than look at her friends and risk saying something else she might regret. "Can I get a nap guys? I'll see you tonight." She didn't watch as they left. She was doing a lot of that today, not looking at the people she loved while they moved further and further away.

Chapter 27

Kary called her brother twice that afternoon. She bought a six pack and drove to his house in time for the evening game but the windows were dark. She parked on the curb and sat in her car to call him one last time, listening to it ring until the beep for voicemail. *"Hey Seth, just thought we might hang out. Call me back. Love you."*

When she got back to her apartment it was barely eight. She considered watching movies until midnight or downing the sixer by herself and not worrying about the stupid tai chi, yoga, whatever lesson she was supposed to be having tonight with Audra and Adamant. She could do that and go to bed and forget that today'd ever happened.

It'd be easy. And if she let them down once then they'd quit expecting things from her. She'd be able to slip out of their lives same as she'd slipped into them. Without worrying about keeping the supers' secrets she could focus on her brother and everything he was working through. She could focus on her studies. She could go out with her real friends, the ones she actually had things in common with. She could quit being a role model. She could—

She lit a candle and put it on the windowsill in the living room before going back to her bedroom to pack a bag. By the time she'd gathered everything she would need for an evening workout and re-wrapped her weak ankle with athletic tape Johnnie had slid open the glass and swung through the living room window to wait on her couch. The jet was waiting, hovering, camoflauged over the apartment building on engines so quiet they blended with the highway noise. He was already in uniform.

✦

Audra fussed that Kary was early but she didn't sound like she meant it. Adam looked pleased too. "You're early. The kids told me not to expect you until later."

Both sidekicks made disgusted noises at being called kids but those didn't sound like real complaints either. "What's got everyone so cheerful?"

"Aspect didn't tell you?" Audra was beaming up at him and Adamant was looking particularly proud and mildly fatherly.

"Tell me what?"

"That my sweets figured out the ingredients to the brainwipe drug and will have an antidote in a matter of *days*." Mynx slid down from nowhere on a chain that didn't seem to have any real purpose, kissing Johnnie's cheek when she was level with it.

"Congrats. So we're that much closer to me jogging on my own after dark again?" She wanted to be excited but not with Mynx watching her through narrow, suspicious eyes. This was her first time seeing the lady

218

sidekick in weeks and it wasn't a streak the fighter was happy to have broken.

"Thanks." He looked pleased. Kary hoped her friend understood how proud of him she was. Johnnie shifted under their eyes and glanced at his mentor. "Adamant, should we…?"

"Go. Call if you need backup."

Kary let out a very quiet breath when they left to patrol. Adam was watching her. "I warned her to be on her best behavior but I can't keep her out. She and Aspect will be partners soon, protecting a city of their own. They *need* to work together."

"You talk like I care." She did care. Mynx got under her skin and left rot. "Is there somewhere I can change?" He was already in drawstring linen pants and a cotton tank top, his niece was dressed the same.

"Audra will show you. I'll be setting up in the gym."

"And extend your arms, grow through your palms and out across your fingers…" They'd been at this for over an hour, *after* spending an hour learning how to meditate. Breathing and stretching and 'growing through their toes' and fingers and ears and hair follicles and every other extremity Adam could think of. Sitting straight and square, whatever *that* meant, enlongating their spines as they inhaled— Kary understood why an impressionable young super might run away from an instructer who emphasized this stuff. "Good, now we're going to embrace the tiger and— *Adamant, go.*" His voice lost the dream blur it had contained for the entire lesson. "Understood, on my way."

"Are we going?" Audra wasn't nodding off anymore. Her eyes were bright, clear.

"I'm going. You two are going to sit down and meditate for at least another half hour. Then Kary's going to teach you... Kary what are you going to teach her?"

"Teach?" She was here to be a learner in this snore fest. Not a teacher. Adam was giving her an Adamant look. "Yes, teach, we'll be working on kicks? And... strength control?" It all sounded like questions. Audra didn't look impressed.

Neither did Adam. "You'll be busy until we get back." He gave them both a no-nonsense look that quelled rebellious thoughts and made Kary sit down crosslegged with a huff. Mentor. She was here to act as a *mentor*.

"*Seriously?*" Audra sat across from her heavily.

"Seriously. Straighten your posture and square up your sitbones."

The college student tried to clear her mind. To fit her thoughts neatly away and feel oneness with the world. She really did try. But when she sneezed and peeked at her watch less than ten minutes had passed. She settled back on her pelvis and drew her spine skyward, this was going to be a *long* half hour.

But even long half hours pass eventually, and pass it did. Audra was standing and stamping her feet to wake them up even as Kary's watch was beeping the end of their meditation. Cracks radiated across the floor from where the teen stomped. Kary had noticed spiderwebs of cracks in the House floor, so *this* was what caused them. "Alright, five-minute pee break then we get to kickboxing."

"*Seriously?*"

"Seriously."

✦

"Remember: *accuracy*. Speed can be added later." She was holding the boxing pads at her hip for the younger girl. "Good, balls of your feet, open those hips *up*." She braced back a step against the kick. "Not bad but you need to square your stance. *Again*."

"Are you sure? Am I hurting you?" The fighter was wearing every piece of protective gear they could find, Audra was holding herself in remarkable check and still the college student was getting banged up.

"I'm fine." No, she wasn't. She was sore and tired and starving but they'd been kickboxing for hours and Audra was finally getting the kind of accuracy Kary had been hoping to see. She'd just need to bathe in that orange ointment after this. "*Again*."

Adamant and Bearkat came back after midnight to find them still working the one kick at hip height; Aspect and Mynxweren't far behind. "She can already kick that high, why is the *norm* making her continue? Can she teach her *nothing* else?" Mynx's mutter carried across the gym.

Kary wiped sweat and raised her other glove. "Left foot, twenty kicks."

"But Kary, you *heard* her—"

"Is Mynx your instructor, or me? Twenty on my hip Audra." The girl planted her foot and swung up in the beautiful, controled pivot she'd been developing through her hip all night. 20—19—18 "I'm proud of

221

you, you're doing really well. But we're doing this *properly*." 13—12—11 this was killing her. "We're not practicing 'til you get it *right*." 8—7—6 "We're practicing until you *can't* get it wrong." 2—1. "Good job, take five."

Kary shucked the pads off her hands and pulled the helmet from her head. She was sticky. There were lumps rising up and down her where Audra misjudged her strength or missed her target. Her ankle was still sore from the fight with Seth.

Bearkat came over while the older girl leaned on a rack of weights and poured water over her head. It felt great until the liquid trickled under the kendo armor she'd found to protect her chest. Then the college student felt even stickier. "You should drink that, not waste it."

"Drinking now'll make me puke." Kary dragged a clammy fist across her mouth.

"You are a normal human, yet you do not care for your body as a normal human does." His voice had a musicality to it at odds with the ferocity of his appearance.

He was right. She wasn't being responsible about her health but she tried to bluff through anyway. "Her progress is more important, any good trainer would tell you that." Rodney, at least, would say that.

"How is her progress, in your opinion?"

The question was genuine, coming from a super who had a martial arts background far beyond anything Kary would ever accumulate. The younger fighter was flattered and tried answer as eloquently as she could after the grueling session.

"*Es bien*. She probably doesn't realize it but for the past hour I've been moving her targets even as she starts her kick. Raising or lowering, backing the pad up or angling it different, she still hits the mark most of the time." Then there were times she missed the mark and left Kary with a fractured rib or three. "That's what I like to see."

"At the expense of your wellbeing."

"I'll recover." Audra was coming back and she still hadn't said anything to Bearkat about the thing with Adam. She opened her mouth: "I'm sorry about the—"

He raised a hand that was almost as broad as the boxing pads she'd been wearing all night. "Never apologize for the job, little one. We all do the work the best way we can."

Kary nodded slowly, that was that. It was't a perfect apology, but there wasn't time for anything more. She leaned off the weights as Audra joined them: "Break's over, *chica*, back on the mat." Audra changed trajectory, "And thanks for worrying 'bout me, Bearkat." He patted her shoulder as she passed and Kary almost buckled with the weight of his hand.

She walked back toward where her pads and helmet were. "Audra, one last set of twenty-five each foot and we'll call it a night *if* you don't miss any. Miss and we start count over from the top."

They only had to restart once.

"Good work kiddo. Hit the showers." Kary made sure her student and spectators were well out of the room before she began removing the chest plate. She couldn't let Audra see her injuries after what had been for the young super a long and technically challenging, but not physically punishing workout.

223

Her shirt was soaked through. Wincing, the girl peeled it up to look at the dark green that was spreading along the side of her ribs.

"*Kary.* Why did you—"

Mierda. She'd thought everyone was gone. "It's nothing the magic orange goop won't fix Johnnie."

"You're a *norm* you *idiot.* Why'd you let her—"

Kary let her shirt drop back down. "Go get the ointment or leave me *alone.*" She wasn't in the mood for a lecture over something that she knowingly let happen. She wanted to sleep. And eat. And bathe.

She wanted to fall asleep in a bath while eating—as long as she could be sure she wouldn't drown that way. As long as she didn't fall asleep like in that one movie with the girl in the tub and the dream and the hand coming out of the water to… "Kary—*Kary* stay awake. *Damnit.*" Hands coming out of the water and catching her, holding her like she was small and still had to be held gently. There was a warm wall pressing against her side and it felt nice even as her ribs jangled against each other, Kary curled into the heat and the pain and let her mind quit for a little while.

Chapter 28

Kary woke up immersed to the neck in a tub of the orange healing goop. "I wake up in your sick bay a lot." Johnnie's head was propped on his fist where he dozed beside her.

He opened his eyes slowly at the sound of her voice. "Well if you'd stop getting into fist fights with supers…" Kary was disappointed, she'd hoped he was sleeping deeply enough to startle.

"Last time wasn't a fight with supers." She pulled her hand up out of the goo with a sucking sound, turning her palm down to watch the orange slide away.

"No, just twenty other norms. You're lucky we've been stockpiling supplies since the time we ran out 'cause at this rate you're gonna get yourself—"

Kary cut him off: "It was only thirteen. Can I get out yet?"

He looked exasperated, but reached down, sinking his arms deep in the tub to cradle under her legs and behind her back. She didn't stuggle as he dragged her from the ointment and carried her to the decontamination shower in the corner. "It's *cold*." She barked when he stood her up between the pressure sprayers.

"*Good.*"

"Heartless."

He turned a tap and the water stopped. Kary shook her knotted hair, she was still tired and hungry but her injuries were almost gone. How long had she been soaking? "You know Audra'll kill you."

"Hm?" She was poking at the dusky spot across her side that still twinged a little when she probed it.

"On accident and she'll feel terrible."

"I'm sure." Healing ointment, not magic goo.

"And join the Enlisted."

"Wouldn't that be something?" Now Kary was picking at the orange cakes under her nails.

"And destroy the planet all because *you* wouldn't take care of yourself."

"Does she know?"

"Know what?" He was thrown by her question.

"How bad it was?"

"No, only Adamant knows and let me tell you he was not—"

"Good." She patted his cheek like a movie mob boss. "Let's keep it that way."

"*Kary.*" He made her name a reprimand as she made her beeline for the kitchen. It was time to carb up.

They gave her a room in the House to sleep through the meager hours left until daylight, when Johnnie drove her home in a taxi that was a part of the House's fleet. "You know I don't like you training Audra like this? I'm serious Kary, we're too strong. We're dangerous."

Generic danger warning? That didn't even work in the movies. "She'll be even more dangerous if she can't pretend to be a real person. She's learning control. *You* need to find me better body armor."

Adamant was on her side with this, she'd heard him and Johnnie arguing about it in the computer room after she ate. His niece would become a public figure in Adamson Industries at some point, like her uncle, she'd need to learn how to maintain a persona as a real person. Adam said training with Kary was going to be integral to that.

The only thing Johnnie could do was express how unhappy he was, he didn't have any real power in this. If Adamant had actually seen the extent of her injuries pre-healing he might have felt differently but as it was, he only had her and Johnnie's conflicting descriptions of the severity of her injuries and was inclined to believe his sidekick overreacted.

There were three messages on her voicemail when Kary got back to her phone.

Hey Sis, you're right, we really do need to hang out. Call when you get this, we'll do lunch or something.

Bruiser, it's Garth, listen, don't blow up but Jimmie's seriously thinking about firing Seth. You need to talk to your brother. I can't get through to him.

Hey girl, we haven't hung out in forever. I'm on shift tonight at the winery and I bet I can talk the owner into putting the fight on the TV, come hang out. First round's on me.

Her friends, the real world, it was all far away. She only had two weeks left in the semester and she needed to get back into her studies. Her apartment was a steadily collecting mess that she needed to clean up. She'd neglected Garth and Diette, fought with her brother, even argued with Jimmie. It was a bright Sunday morning in late November; she needed to put her entire house in order.

✦

She met Seth for lunch at a restaurant on the trendy side of downtown. It wasn't somewhere she'd ever been but the waitstaff greeted her brother by name. "What is this place?" Kary asked, opening her menu and sucking in at the prices. "*Seth*, I can't pay for this." She kept her voice a low hiss. Wasn't lunch supposed to be the more affordable meal?

"No worries Bruiser, it's on me."

On what salary? She knew Jimmie couldn't afford to pay a new trainer much above minimum wage, especially if he wasn't sure he would keep said trainer. "Thanks, Bro." She was here to make peace, not interrogate.

"No problem, I want to apologize for the gym the other day." Yesterday, it had been *yesterday*. But his eyes were big and repentatent. "Kary, seriously, you know I'd never hurt you, right?"

He was stretching a hand across the table, asking her forgiveness. Her brother. Her best friend. Her *family*. She slid her fingers into his. "I wasn't exactly on point either, Seth. Forgive me?"

"*Always.*"

They ordered and ate and teased back and forth. Kary told him that she was doing a little training herself, private lessons for a friend. "We're working on kicks, the only problem is he's *strong,* doesn't know how to control it for training and I don't know enough about redirecting bad hits to keep from getting beat up when he misses the pad."

Silently she apologized to Audra for verbally turning her into a boy but Kary knew her brother would never accept that there was a girl out there strong enough to make his Bruiser whimper.

"Hmm." Kary half expected a sardonic question about this new *him* in her life, in the light of her rapid fall from Adam's grace but Seth was all business, asking about her drills and diving into a breakdown of blocks and manipulations that made his eyes spark and his voice animate. He was so *alive* when he talked tactics.

This was why he had been such a great fighter. Because of the way he could watch hours of footage and balance out his opponents like they were an equation. Because of those instincts he'd honed for so *long.* Ten thousand hours and more spent making himself into the perfect fighter. Fast, strong, smart, fearless—

Brutal.

The word came unbidden. It wasn't a nice word. Brutal was how the papers described murders. Brutal was the word used when discussing the fighters who took roids until they weren't good for anything but guarding the warehouses where the gangs stored drugs…

Or girls. Was the prostitution ring using roid brutes? Brutes were difficult to make and easy to track if you knew who to ask. Surely the supers had some underworld connection who could tell them if someone was making a new batch of brutes for—"Bruiser? You listening?"

"Huh?" *Mierda*. "Sorry, I was just thinking about a project for class. Had an idea that my group might like to use." Another friend, another lie.

"Oh? What class?"

Damn. She needed details. "Spanish lit, we're working on this translation and writing an alternate telling of *Don Quixote* and my partners..." She droned on. She hadn't spun a lie like this for Seth in a *long* time. He hadn't been around enough for her to need to spin a lie for him in a long time.

Finally he stopped her. "That's awesome Sis. You know how proud I am at how serious you take this, right? *Always* knew you were the smart one."

Something guilty spasmed in her cheek. "We can't all live off our looks, Seth." It was one of their old jokes, something Kary would tell him after a bad fight beat up his face. "Not like you."

It wasn't enough to make him laugh but he did crack a smile. "Well you *did* make a decent try, dating Adamson and all. How'd you two meet anyway?"

Well how was she going to spin this one? "Mutual friend." She sipped her water as a stall tactic.

"*You* have a mutual friend with a telecom mogul?"

Since when did Seth do know the Who's Who of the telecom world? Kary fidgeted, she should practice looking embarrassed. It was a skill she needed if the last few days were anything to go off of. "His son comes into the tutor center pretty regular." How bad was she going to make herself look? "I *may* have *hinted* how much I'd like to meet his dad."

"Adamson has a kid in *college*?" Seth sounded impressed, probably because Adam was just barely thirty and having a son in college now would mean he fathered the boy when he was… Kary quit doing the math and focused on her answers.

"Adopted son, some sort of kid genius distant cousin he wanted to train as an heir. All very hush-hush." Now she was just lying again. Lying was fine, it was the acting that got tricky.

"Wow, that's like some Dungeons and Dragons shit." She didn't think the game included adopted heirs, but that wasn't her scene. "The kid have an arranged marriage too?" He was laughing at his own jibe, like he'd ever been in the same room as a D&D game.

The college student tried for a mocking smile to keep him from seeing how close he'd come to the truth. "Dunno. I wasn't around long enough to hear *all* the family dirt."

"You okay? You look tense."

She couldn't look away. He'd recognize avoidance. "Nothing, just still sore about some of the stuff he said Friday."

Her brother's eyes were suddenly colder than she'd seen in years. His face was hard, the way it'd been the first time he saw her with a black eye back when she was still brawling in alleys while he was on the road with Rodney. "Need me to pay him a visit, Bruiser?" That wasn't a joke. Why didn't it sound like a joke?

Kary crinkled her eyes to try and make her smile look more natural. "No thanks, I'll handle him if he needs it." She made her voice as playfully menacing as she could. Seth eased back in his seat, relaxed again. He didn't look like someone who'd just seriously offered to go drag an internationally known billionaire down a dark alley. Maybe she'd just imagined the threat.

Kary leaned back too and took another sip of her water.

✦

"What do you *mean* you *can't* keep him on?" After lunch with her brother, Kary visited the gym and asked Jimmie if the rumor was true.

"I *mean* he's picked fights with two patrons *besides* you, both of which *would've* ended in shouting matches or worse if Garth and the others hadn't stepped in."

"But we only argued *yesterday* and you sent him *home*." What other trouble could he've gotten into? Jimmie had kicked everyone out and probably hadn't let anyone back in after their spat.

"*Oh* no." He drew the two syllables out long. "This was Saturday morning, *before* you got here. He's too volatile for me to have him on staff."

Kary flared at her mentor. "Too *volatile*? He's been the coolest head around this gym for *years*. And you're just gonna—"

"Bruiser, I have enough hot heads paying me to sling *my* iron around and get on *my* canvas." Kary winced, she probably counted as one of those hot heads. "The trainers are out there to keep everyone kosher, I can't afford to employ a wildcard."

"*But*—"

"*But nothing.*"

"He's *family*, you can't turn him out. What's he gonna do? There won't be another gym in the city who'll take'im if word gets out *Jimmie* fired'im."

"No Bruiser, *you're* family. *He's* been gone so long I don't even recognize the kid anymore." Liar. He'd been happy enough to claim Seth while her brother was winning every week on the circuit.

"*Rocks.*"

"And after what he did to *you.*"

Oh, because she was a *girl?* "How is that any different from what *I* did the day after Rodney's funeral?" The day she brought Audra to the gym. Or her string of fights the night after Seth's injury, for that matter.

"That was *different.*"

"*How so?*"

"You didn't *hurt* her." She'd put Audra on the ground almost a dozen times.

"*Perdóname*, Jimmie, that—"

"Oh *hush*, you think I don't know that girl walked away with only injured pride? Gimme a little credit Bruiser, you were just trainin' her. What your brother did, *that* wasn't a lesson."

Jimmie knew or guessed Audra was... "How 'd you know he wasn't teaching me anything? We're just two Doggs in—"

"In a pit, yes, I know what you call yourselves." He snorted when he said it. "That doesn't change the fact that until Seth gets his head on straight, I won't have him back in my gym."

That wasn't an end all ban. "You mean he can come back when he's better?"

"Did I stutter?"

She could hug him. She wouldn't, because that would be weird for both of them but she *could*. Seth would be fine, he just needed a little more time to figure himself out.

✦

She took Diette up on that drink, one glass of wine while her friend wiped the bar and got ready to open for the Sunday evening crowd. "You *sure* you can't stay? Garth'll be here in an hour or so and we haven't hung out in *forever*."

Kary finished her glass, "Sorry, but I've got work at eight tomorrow and homework to get through tonight." Diette pouted dramatically, until Kary stretched across the counter and hugged her. "Thanks for worrying 'bout me Die, sorry I haven't been around."

"You owe me a *proper* girls night."

"Soon... after finals."

"Two *weeks*? Gotta give me more than that."

"We'll stay in and drink wine, watch romcoms and eat chocolate chip pizza—my buy on everything."

"Chocolate chip *and* bacon?"

"Did I have to say it?"

Diette swatted at her with the rag she was using. "Go, I'll see you around."

Kary left just as the first patrons were coming in, tearing out of the winery's drive in her rush to get home and wait for her ride to the House.

Chapter 29

Meditating with Audra and Adam was easier the second night. After the first night's practice Kary was able to slip into stillness that at least mimicked what Adam was trying to demonstrate. She still wasn't getting the whole mind clearing thing down but at least she'd figured out what *sitting square* meant, and her feet locked into lotus position across her thighs more naturally this time.

Doing tai chi with an uninjured ankle was relaxing. The entire practice was built on control and controlling her movements was much, *much* easier with stable joints.

Audra watched her: Kary could feel it all through the warm-up breathing exercises, looking for signs that the older girl was bored. Kary ignored Audra's preoccupation and focused instead on Adam's instructions.

When they broke for water the older girl mentioned being excited to see how all the extra training helped her fighting. Audra didn't comment back but her eyes were thoughtful and she didn't complain when Adam called them in for the next part of their lesson.

Aspect and Mynx left to patrol somewhere in the middle of their second round of meditation. Adamant left shortly after that to conduct his own business in the city and Bearkat took over teaching the two girls. Bearkat continued with tai chi but instead of breathing and body movements, he started showing them the basics of its use as a martial art.

Audra perked up tremendously when she thought they would be fighting and didn't wilt when she realized that Bearkat was only teaching one strike and the block used in response that night. She was narrow, focused, and careful with her strength when she swung her slow, loose fist in towards Kary.

The fighter in turn reacted with smooth forearm blocks that slid Audra's hand away and made Bearkat nod his approval at both of them. He came over to Kary while they took water again. She was fairly sure the supers were fine to work without pause all night and that these water breaks were in deference to her as a norm. Whatever the reason, she was grateful. "I was impressed with your training philosophy last night."

What training philosophy? "Thank you, just something a coach told me when I was young." It was probably true, whatever doggerel she'd spat out in the fourth hour of training with a super who had the stamina of a demi god had likely been instilled by either Jimmie or Seth or Garth at some point early on.

"You are an excellent liar."

Huh? "I don't know what you're talking about." Her poker face fluttered.

"I do not know why you lie but you are. I hear your heart." Kary gave him her best puzzled look. The

236

craggy face smiled around the edges and he reached up to touch one of his gently tapered ears. "Your pulse speeds when you lie. Your's not so much as most humans but enough for my ears." His eyes were gray-blue and steady on her when he repeated: "You lie well."

The first time she had been caught in a lie in months and it was over something she honestly didn't remember saying. "Honestly, I don't know what I said last night toward the end of training. I wasn't... well."

"Are you well now?"

"Yes." If he didn't call her on it, it was the truth. "Could you tell me what I said?"

"That you did not intend to practice until Audra could perform the action, you intended to practice until she could not get it wrong."

Rodney, that was one of Rodney's favorites. She smiled at him with a tight throat, "Thank you."

✦

They finished that night with meditation again, concluding the four-hour session just before two in the morning. If Kary'd had the energy, she might've been upset that she didn't get the chance to use her brother's tips teaching Audra. As it was she slept hard enough in the back seat of the jet that she needn't have bothered with the blindfold when Johnnie took her home.

He tried twice very gently to shake her awake and then gave up. The fighter woke the next morning tucked neatly in her own bed with no recollection of how she got there.

✦

"Aspect and Mynx are *totally* the next power couple on the Register." Was how Jason greeted her Monday morning when she dragged in still feeling the pleasant kind of stretchy-tired that came from hours spent working on muscle control.

"Oh?" She thumped into her chair and began pecking at the keyboard. "What makes you say that?" Hadn't they already established this?

"'Cause they were seen *all* over this weekend in Commonland and Marshal, even as far east as Lake Alexandria and as far south as Andersonville. Beating up baddies and stopping plots and being all around *awesome*."

Kary wished she could share Jason's fanboy moments with her friends at the House, they'd get a kick out of his enthusiasm. "Careful, you'll drool on the hardware."

"But it's just so *cool*. Them teaming up like this without Bearkat and Adamant probably means they're about to go on the Register as full supers and partners, it'll be *historic*. Like, in *textbooks* someday historic."

"Uh-huh." She pulled up her email and winced at a hasty note from her research professor asking for her final report on the diary.

"*And* that means Bearkat and Adamant'll be taking on new sidekicks soon. I can't *wait* to see the next generation. For a little while there Adamant had a girl helping him and Aspect but she didn't last long..." Kary tuned him out, instead imagining Audra's reaction to being told she didn't 'last long' as her uncle's sidekick. "—Are you even listening?"

"Nope." She deleted some spam and opened a university wide notice about a snow forecast for the week.

"You *should.*"

"Why?"

"You should know everything you can about the brave men women and otherwise that defend our planet from all invaders."

"Is it my civic duty?"

"Yes."

"The same way I'm supposed to have… what was it?" She made air quotes with her fingers, "*pride in humanity* at supers making babies?" If he didn't remember the conversation she was referencing she was about to feel very stupid.

"We *should.* It's the only way we'll know there'll be supers to—"

"Keep your fanboy shipping to yourself."

"It's not shipping if they're a real couple."

"Still creepy." She made her tone light; she was harder on Jason than she should be.

He fired back with a classic: "Your mom's cr—"

"Excuse me—"

"*Buenas dias señor Foxx*, Spanish homework?"

She waved Johnnie over towards her desk, unembarrassed at the conversation he'd interupted. By now he'd walked in on her talking supers with Jason so many times she'd quit caring what he overheard. "Our Mynpect debate isn't over Dogg." Jason said as Johnnie sat at her desk.

Mynpect? "Your misunderstanding of the word *debate* is sad, like your fanboy lifestyle." Johnnie chuckled while he dug for the homework and Jason swung back to his computer, grumbling.

"*Mynpect?*" Kary muttered when he spun the crumpled sheet on the desk to face her.

"What the fanfics call Mynx and I." He breathed, making a show of gesturing to a question at random.

Kary squinted at his correct answer. "*Fanfics?* As in fan*fiction?* Oh I have *got* to see this."

"There's some half decent art out there too, they always make my suit much more flattering than it really is."

"Oh?"

"I'm always *cut*, even though you can't see my abs in the real uniform."

Couldn't see his abs in the civvies he wore either. The loose hoodies and jeans of warmer months now had a heavy coat and scarf layered on top. Only someone who looked *really* close might notice that the scarf was designer, or that the coat was tailored to fit awkwardly. "And Mynx?"

"They make her… chest bigger and if she's pictured with me she's *usually* naked or almost. Generally looks kinda helpless." No surprises there, not if the art was catering to fanboys like Jason. "It ever creep you out? That people idealize you like that?" Or idolize.

"Nah, the people who matter know the truth."

He was sending her a look with enough heat in it to make her shiver. Where'd the kid learn *that* trick? Had Adam been giving him pointers? Kary slid her hands away from his when he reached for his paper. "Looks good Mr. Foxx. Now you know we'll be closed next week, correct?"

"Yes, for finals week, right?"

"Yes." She stood to shake the hand he offered. "Good luck on your tests Mr. Foxx and have an excellent break if I don't see you again between now and then."

240

"You as well, Miss Dogg." His fingers were hot around hers, since when did she notice things like that on *Johnnie?*

✦

She took Audra to Jimmie's gym that evening. It was after nine and Kary knew the floor would be almost empty, so she decided to risk it. "Karissa Dogg and guest." She told the girl at the front desk, the first time she'd had to talk to anyone about her comings and goings to the gym in *ages*. Jimmie kept headshots of his favorite regulars behind the front desk so they never had to bother with checking in with his desk girls.

"Why're we here again?"

"'Cause I want to see if you can blend in with real people in a setting like this now that you've had a little more training."

"*Seriously?*"

"Yes, seriously. How're you handling gym class in school?" She raised a hand to wave at Garth as they edged around the floor to the dressing rooms.

"With a doctor's note."

"Smartass."

"Better than a dumbass."

"*Language.*"

"Hypocrite."

Yes. "Get your gear on, I'm gonna show you a real punch today." As opposed to the loose fingered, twisty wrist punches that came with tai chi.

"Shouldn't we keep up with kicks?"

Probably. "Let's do that when you're tearing up your uncle's equipment, not Jimmie's."

241

✦

Garth came over while Kary was standing behind Audra hands on the girl's shoulders, shifting them into position. "Who's this Bruiser?"

"*Bruiser?*" Audra widened her eyes over her shoulder at Kary. Had the baby super not heard her nickname yet?

"This is Audra Nicklson, she's a friend." Audra twitched when the older girl gave an invented last name but didn't contradict her.

"Pleased to meet you Audra, welcome to Jimmie's."

"Audra, this is Garth. One of my best sparring partners."

Garth scoffed. "One of? Try only." He was right, there weren't many regulars who were still willing to crawl in the ring with her.

"Really? Can I watch?"

"Watch what? Square your shoulders and jab the bag."

She jabbed. "You spar with Garth. I've never seen you spar with another... with someone else." Kary breathed a prayer that Garth wouldn't ask what Audra had meant to say before catching herself.

"Remember jab *up*. As a girl you'll probably be shorter than whoever you're punching so don't forget to angle up. And move your feet." Not true necessarily if Audra was a norm in a circuit where she'd only be fighting other girls, then punching up wouldn't be so vital but Garth didn't call Kary on the height thing. Audra jabbed again. "Better, now jab twice with the left and punch with right." Audra did as told and the bag didn't split open and spill its sand. Her control was getting better. "Good, again, switch hands."

She swapped her stance and jabbed with the right, landed with the left. "If I do it again will you spar Garth?" He was getting tickled just listening to them. If they did spar Kary'd have to remind him she wasn't going soft.

"How old are you, six?"

"*Please?*" She drew the word out long and threw pleading eyes over her shoulder at the older girl while landing a punch just to right of the target.

The fighter sighed deeply. "Hey Garth, *if* Audra gets thirty sets perfect on each hand would you spar with me?"

"Thirty sets? Isn't that a little much?" Audra looked like a skinny teenager. Kary forgot that sometimes.

"Um, *yeah.*" *Mierda*, "Sorry Audra, you learn so fast I forget you don't have those muscles built up. Ten each." Kary said it and shot the girl a look that said she'd finish those reps and more at the House later.

"Spar now?" Audra asked as she turned away from the bag, her reps finished.

"You just wanna sit down for a while." Kary was pulling her mouth guard from where she kept it wedged under the strap of her sports bra.

Audra smiled sheepishly. "*Yeah.*" Liar. It was a good one though, Kary was proud. Adam claimed he could go a week without sleep, longer if he had to. The baby Adamant just had top ractice and she would match him. Her uncle had told them both that Audra's final test as a sidekick would likely be a race across North America without rest, to see if she could stay awake and moving that long. Kary had laughed like it was a joke but Audra looked thoughtful.

Garth slapped his friend's back with a *smack* that made a lifter across the floor look up. "Grab the popcorn kid, you're in for a show."

Chapter 30

"**That** was *awesome.*" Audra was gushing in the dressing room while they bundled up to go out in the cold. "I mean he's so much *bigger* but you were right in there like *pow-pow* and—"

Kary shouldn't be milking this but she was. She hadn't won in the ring since the night she fought at the bar and the crushing defeat from Mynx immediately after had drained any sweetness from *that* victory. "Thanks, it was good to win on the canvas again."

"You won against me."

That wasn't a real match. "You hadn't been trained at that point. No victory in beating a novice."

"*Novice?*" She looked ready to argue long and loud but there were a few other late-night gym patrons just over the partition in the showers, so instead the girl clamped down and didn't say anything. Kary could see the angry hamster running fast inside Audra's head; she needed to do something to win the girl back.

"Let's stop for ice cream on the way back, my treat." Ice cream? It was barely above freezing out there. *No way* the young super was going for a carrot like that.

"Sounds great." Kary should've expected that.

✦

"How was the gym?" Johnnie found her working on her final report on the translation surrounded by a half circle of books at one of the wide worktables in the House library around midnight. Because of their evening training, Bearkat let the girls out earlier than usual. Kary suspected Audra would have some sort of morning workout tomorrow but at the moment she needed to focus on her studies more than worry about a high schooler getting up early to make up for missed reps.

"Not bad. She's getting better at controlling her strength, didn't break any of Jimmie's equipment."

"That's good, would've been hard to explain."

Understatement. "Mhm." Kary flipped a page in one book and underlined something in another. "Does Mynpect have patrols tonight?"

"Monday's are always quiet, Aspect told us to get some rest unless anything comes over the scanner."

"So naturally you're in the library after midnight on a school night." She made a note in her spiral, lifting the book she referenced over her head to read the title and make note of it without losing her page.

He sat on top of the table across from hers, folding his legs into a pretzel and elongating his spine to perfect posture. "Well yeah, you're here."

"Late night library rendezvous with an unknown woman; do I smell trouble for the Mynpect shippers?" She gave the super her best impression of staring him down over the rims of her glasses without actually wearing glasses.

"Mynpect shippers don't know the half of it. There's *always* trouble."

Did Kary sense the impending baring of souls and hearts and sappy stuff? "Oh?"

"Yeah." Johnnie scratched his head but stayed perfectly upright. "She's just *difficult*, you know?"

Yes, she knew. "Every woman's gonna be difficult about *something*, Johnnie." Even the one settling down to listen to his sob-fest. "If she's not, she's probably too boring to worry over."

There was a smile at the corner of his mouth. "Well she's certainly not *boring*."

"Okay, so what is she?" Kary began marking her places in the books with slips of paper and dogears, closing them to keep from being distracted while he spoke.

"We were raised together, trained with Recluse together, and our mentors have been together for *years*." Kary wondered briefly how that worked, with Bearkat and Mynx spending most of their time traveling between cities while Adam stayed here in Commonland, but Johnnie was on a role.

"We go on joint missions and now these joint patrols..." backstory, always nice to get context, "and all that time we've been told that we'll be partners once we're on the Register." All that time? No way, 'cause that'd mean— "I told you I went to the Recluse when I was six, so I've, *we've*, spent two thirds of our lives preparing to fight crime *together*."

"And your engagement?"

"Sensible. We know each other, we have compatible genetics, and if we were married we wouldn't need to worry about secret identities or maintaining cover in our home." He sounded like he was reciting a grocery list.

"You say sensible. I say cold." Seth was right, this whole concept was antiquated.

"What's the alternative? There are only so many eligible supers on the Register in the right age bracket. We could both marry norms and *either* tell them our secrets and worry about them telling someone else, *or* not tell them and worry that they'll find out. Both of those options come with complimentary worry about spouse's safety and elaborate cover stories."

Logic was stupid. "What about love? Or are you going all Victorian on me and shooting for *fondness*?" She was here to be a calm sounding board, she needed to remember that.

"But I do... love her. She's my partner, my friend, the super I trust most in the world besides Adamant. When we're fighting it's like... a dance or something." He was embarrassed, his perfect posture sagged.

"What about talking to her? If you two become partners on the field and off you'll need more than fighting compatibility to be happy. Are you willing to eat breakfast with her every morning for the rest of your life? What about kids?" For like six minutes until the Register snapped any child they had away to be trained and turned into the next generation of super.

"Mynx isn't exactly the *nurturing* type."

His mouth was wry. Kary had climbed onto her table to sit cross legged on the top, same as her friend. Their eyes were on a level when they sat like this. "Around *me* maybe, but what about around you? She befriended Audra, I know that."

"She's nice to me." Nice? *That's* how he described his prescribed bride? How vanilla could he get? "I mean

248

she's funny and smart and a *hell* of a tactician and she's got this *amazing* sense of where she needs to be in a fight and she's *always* there. Always on point. Always focused. Always objective. Always—"

"Unless she's harassing me." Kary kept her voice low, not sure if she really wanted him to hear her.

"Huh?" Her quiet interruption threw him for a loop.

This really wasn't her business. "She's never been focused or objective when she bullies me." Bullies? Karissa Dogg had never been bullied in her life. She *did* the bullying. *Fuerte.* She was the—"She's... childish."

"She was jealous." Was? Past tense? "She thought you'd come between us and she was..."

"What? Trying to prove something by doodling on my posters? What about the fight at Jimmie's? What about Audra 's training? You can't put that on me 'cause I wasn't—" She needed to pull it back. Simmer down. This wasn't about her. It was about Johnnie.

"What training?" His eyes were sharp when he cut her off. "Adamant won't tell me why Audra's so behind. Only that she wasn't with the Recluse as long as she should've. Does Mynx have something to do with that?"

She shouldn't tell him. Not if Adamant wasn't telling him. It wasn't any of Aspect's business. It was between Mynx and Adamant Girl. His eyes were bright and hard, like two blue stones. She couldn't lie to him. "While Audra was with the Recluse, Mynx told her that real world experience was better than training. Audra was only there a couple months before she ran away." Why did they trust her? She was awful at this secrets thing.

"*What?*" He sounded dangerous.

"Ask her, ask any one of them. You already know I'm training with Audra so she has a *mentor*—" She spat the word. "—because Mynx wasn't that for her."

"But *why?*" His logical mind couldn't cope with it. Kary could see the cogs getting stuck.

'Cause she's a possessive bitch. "Hell if I know, but it's something you should talk about if you're going to be in each other's pockets for the rest of your lives."

"I—" He looked lost; the way most kids his age were but wouldn't admit it. "What do I do?"

Run away fast, crazy wasn't worth it. But she didn't say it out loud. Instead she felt for one of the books behind her, "You read poetry to me."

"What?"

"Poetry, great for getting you out of your head, especially if you're reading out loud 'cause then you can't think about anything else too hard. *Catch.*" A thick paperback spun through the air between them and landed neatly in his lap. Kary glanced at the syllabus lying on the table beside her. "Page 347 first."

Dutifully he flipped the pages. "Invictus: The Unconquerable." His eyes flicked up at her over the pages, she gestured for him to continue.

"*Out of the night that covers me*
  Black as the Pit from pole to pole—"

She cut in.

"*I thank whatever gods may be,*
  For my unconquerable soul."

250

He shot her a glare for the interuption, and continued without missing a beat, finishing on her second favorite pair of lines from her Poetry post-1800 class.

".... I am the master of my fate:
I am the captain of my soul."

Kary applauded. "Beautiful, were you taught recitation? Next up is page 214."

He didn't complain, already thumbing toward her requested page, Kipling.

"I keep six honest serving-men, (they taught me all I knew)
their names are What and Why and When..."

"Okay, one more." Kary paused after he finished, ticking her fingers, "War poetry, since you are a soldier of sorts." She smiled wickedly, "Wilfred Owen "Dulce et Decorum Est," should be about 485?" There was a scrawl on the syllabus where she'd made some note and scratched it out, obscuring part of the number.

He strummed through the pages. "486." He corrected her.

"Bent double, like old beggers under sacks..."

"What was the real reason you made me do that?" He asked while he helped her gather the books and tuck them into her backpack or stow them away on a shelf for easy finding later.

"Performing like that clears the head. Rhythmic words are soothing to humans. There's a whole lot of wisdom in poetry. I like watching you fumble up the cadences, take your pick."

"But you *chose* each of those."

"They're things you need to hear." And she had an exam coming up on those three and wanted to hear them read by someone else.

"I—thanks, Kary."

"*De nada.* Now am I sleeping here tonight or is someone gonna take me home?"

Kary spent hours at the House every night that week. She meditated and trained with Audra and Adam. She listened to Johnnie fret over when he was going to confront Mynx. She studied in the House library and read the books she found while browsing when she needed to break from everything. There were entire shelves devoted to journals kept by all of the Adamants, dating back to the original Adamant, the one who had helped found the Register with the other Firsts.

The fighter had known Adam wasn't the first to wear the red and white tights, she hadn't realized he was the seventh; that the men of his family had been donning masks to protect real people since they discovered that their line carried this inherent gift.

Johnnie told her once that some supers were like the Adamants, born with an ability that had sprung from their DNA long ago, meta-genes, scientists called them. Some weren't human, either newer arrivals as earth extended cautious treaties and trade negotiations across the cosmos, or species that had existed in near perfect seclusion since Pangea split, as in the case of Bearkat and Mynx's clan. Kary had wanted to ask more about the feline-esque tribe, but Johnnie hadn't given her time to interject. More still were engineered in a lab, or the byproducts of experiments gone very wrong or very right. Many of his generation, were born from super couplings, making their powers combinations of their parentage, or sometimes entirely new.

And your parents? She'd asked him when he trailed off. A super and a scientist, he'd mentioned that once, now with the talk of experiments and accidents she wondered...

He'd smiled at her and it was tight around the edges. *They wanted me to be powerful and didn't really care how that power manifested, so now I can have all the powers.*

He'd changed the subject then and Kary had never brought it up again. It wasn't the type of thing she felt like she could ask about.

According to the journals there was an active debate in the upper eschelons of the Register as to whether powers were being diluted down the generations or strengthened by the different genetic combinations. The Adamants, it seemed, didn't hold with the idea of knowingly mixing their line with that of another super family. They actively looked for wives among the norm population and kept having children until another Adamant was born. As far as she could tell from the sixth's journal, Audra was the first girl born into the Adamson family with super strength. There wasn't much about her father, Adam's older brother, in the journal. Only that he had been born without the gift and, in later pages, the sixth Adamant's despair that their legacy would end with him since his gifted son was impotent.

Impotent. The sixth Adamant left a record that his younger son was incapable of having children, instead of admitting in writing that he was gay. It was a hateful, hurtful idea.

Kary flipped to the end of the journal, to a single entry in Adam's hand that his father died courageously in the field and that his life had been an example and a beacon to all. He hadn't lived to see Audra's birth.

✦

The weekend came and Diette begged Kary for a night out. Garth begged her to talk sense into her brother. Her boss begged her to cover the closedown shift Saturday when every session for the semester was cataloged before they shut doors until spring semester. Audra begged her to talk Adamant into giving them a night off. And Kary begged everyone else to leave her alone; she had a final every day but Friday next week and needed to study.

✦

She arrived at the House early Friday afternoon with a bag packed to stay until Sunday and the intention of camping in the library and ignoring the world except for meals and training sessions with Audra. Johnnie defended her stance, probably because he had tests of his own and spent almost as much time holed up in the House library studying as she did. Their quiet hours and soft conversations were soothing, cloistered away in the massive room where no one dared disturb them.

Johnnie had been watching her study for months now and didn't judge Kary when she sat on tables or under tables or on the thick hearth rug surrounded by her perpetual circle of books. He didn't comment when she

254

recited facts, poets, birth dates, death dates, translations, summaries, creative movements, and gibberish in two languages at the walls. Nor did he comment when she napped curled into knots in the leather armchairs for brief increments before jerking awake and continuing whatever sentence she'd been on when she drifted off.

Kary tolerated his pacing with books in front of his nose and incessant need to teach her whatever he was studying. She nodded and paid attention to his theoretical physics lessons and asked questions from the study guides he handed her. She butchered her summaries of the theorems he explained. She watched as he scrawled out improbable combinations of letters and numbers and geometric figures on chalk boards and she checked them against a cheat sheet he copied down for her to use while he wrote from memory.

Sometime around noon on Saturday she asked why he needed to study at all. "Couldn't you just use your powers and get the test questions and answers from your professors?"

He was laying on top of the bookshelves twenty feet over her head, having flown up there on a circle of black, runic writing, theoretically to nap but really to grumble over inconsistencies in a set of class notes he'd copied from someone. "I could but I need skin to skin contact to borrow and I can only borrow one thing per person."

"Only one *ever?*" She found the ladder hooked onto a shelf on the far end and began climbing up to peer onto the top of the shelves, to see if hanging out up there was worth the dust.

"Mhm, and I have to know what I'm borrowing before I can have it. So if you had some awesome super

255

power I didn't know about when we met, I couldn't get it now 'cause I've already borrowed from you. And they all take practice, I've only just gotten the flying thing down these past few days and I've had it since we fought Tituba."

Huh. She dragged herself onto the broad top of the shelves. The ceiling was high enough that she could walk to the end where Johnnie was still sprawled without stooping. "Well good to know you've got *some* limits, Mr. Ultimate Super."

He craned his head up and looked at her down the length of his body. "Don't know about *ultimate* but I'll take the compliment."

She wasn't sure she'd given him a compliment. "So this is what you see when you perch on gargoyles and watch cities by night." She was crouched on the end staring out at the library spread below.

"We don't *all* do that. Moonwatch was always a bit weird. Standing on buildings hundreds of feet above the city does *no* good when looking for crime."

"But there's that photo, the one they always show in the lists of most iconic pics ever taken."

"So? It's impractical, cruising in the jet with all of the sensors out is how you patrol."

"You mean to tell me you've *never* perched on a gargoyle over Commonland and watched the lights and felt full of yourself?" She'd seen the gargoyles on Adamson Tower and had a sneaking suspicion that they weren't there for practical reasons.

"Now I never said—"

"But you *said* it's not practical, and aren't you all about *practicality?*"

He sounded sheepish, "*Okay*, only once."

"Liar, I bet you do it at least once a week."

256

"Shush norm, I'm protecting my city."

"By imitating a decades old photo?" She turned a little to see him, shuffling on her toes where she was still perched.

"Hey, be careful, the—" Too late, Kary was falling.

Chapter 31

"*Uk.*" Johnnie caught her before she'd fallen half way, "What've you been *eating?*"

"Say that again when we're on solid ground and I'll black your eye, *compañero.*"

"*Sí, señorita, lo siento señorita, nunca más, señorita.*" Spanish, more accurately, *her* Spanish. Kary recognized her accent, the accent of her neighborhood and of the little mixed girl whose fighter big brother got her out just a few years ago, in his tone. He really had copied *all* of her Spanish.

She patted his cheek and he set her down. "That's what I like to hear." His hands were lingering on her waist.

"Well *that* was smooth." Audra was grinning in the doorway.

"That's just how it goes." Kary tossed her head out of habit and felt her braid swing. "Time for another session?"

"Nope, Adamant wants to brief everyone on something." When the older girl moved to sit back in the center of her circle of books Audra stopped her. "You too, he says you're part of the team."

✦

Adamant had them gather in the sickbay around a stranger who stared at the ceiling without blinking. The girl was strapped to the gurney with wide, leather bands but didn't twitch when everyone piled in around her bed or respond when Mynx snapped fingers in her ears.

Oh *now* they had leather restraints? There was a joke she'd make if everyone wasn't so serious. "Who is she?" Kary asked the room at large, the girl was dressed in a hospital gown but the fighter could see a pile of slinky cloth on one of the counters that didn't belong.

"We picked her up last night, according to her finger prints she's Rachel Baker, one of the missing girls." Adamant's tone was delicate and Kary didn't appreciate it. He showed her a photo, a driver's license shot or something similar. If she hadn't been told they were the same woman, Kary wouldn't have believed that Rachel Baker's face belonged to the wasted creature on the bed.

"She's one of the brainwashed hookers." She'd been locked in this oversized cave for almost twenty-four hours now, how did they sneak this around her? "I didn't know you'd caught one." The girl's face was thin like she hadn't been eating, but familiar from somewhere. Was she a student at the university?

"Catching them isn't the problem, they're as easy to find as any prostitute in this city." Kary raised her eyebrows at Adamant. Did he have much *experience* finding prostitutes in this city? "The problem was that any girl we took back would be replaced within a matter of days by a new one and the only way we could find to wake them up was beat them over the head until their synapses started working overtime and fried away the brainwashing drug."

That didn't sound like a real thing. Science and skulls and medicine didn't work that way. "So rather than concuss a bunch of girls and risk more being forced into sex work, you what? Left them as is and started working on a reversal drug?"

"Exactly." That was right? Either supers were getting predictable, or she was spending too much time with them. "If it works, the antidote we've developed will not only wake her from this state but retain her memories of her time in captivity."

"Meaning we'll be able to question her and finally figure out who's behind this." Audra was excited with her deduction.

Adamant clapped his niece on the shoulder. "We wanted everyone here to watch and help record the process. Bearkat, would you do the honors?"

Bearkat was already holding a thick syringe of something pink, tipped with the wickedest needle Kary had ever seen. "Um…" She cut in as he was reaching for the girl's IV line. "Should we *really* all be in here?"

"Why shouldn't we, *norm*?" Mynx purred in her ear and Kary resisted the urge to swat at the lady sidekick like a mosquito.

"I'm just saying, if this works she's gonna have her memories right?" Adamant nodded slowly. "And she's just gonna wake up and suddenly be here, without explanation?" They all still looked bemused, except Mynx who just looked disgusted. Were supers always this *dense*? "God only knows what her… keepers and clients made her do while she was brainwashed and you're gonna wake her up to a crowd of masked *strangers*?" There was a light dawning. "She's gonna be terrified."

"Perhaps in our haste we did not consider the patient." Bearkat was looking at the syringe thoughtfully. "Maybe we should observe from outside the sickbay." His voice was always so calm and measured, she liked that about Bearkat, he never said unreasonable— "Kary, you should be here when she wakes."

Wait *what*? "I'm no shrink or doctor or super or *anything*. I shouldn't even be—" Never mind, Bearkat was the most unreasonable of them all.

Adamant cut her off. "You're the only one who thought of the victim's wellbeing before the case."

So? Didn't mean she was the best person to be there when the girl woke up from some sort of crazy brainwashed walking around *coma*. "Kary, please?" Why was Johnnie pleading with her? "I've been synthesizing this thing for *ages*, it *has* to work."

So that's what he worked on while she trained with Audra. "If it's your project, you should administer it." The performance of his drug shouldn't hinge on who watched it take effect.

"They say that women who've been attacked by men sexually won't feel safe around other men. Just *seeing* me might continue the trauma." He wasn't a man, he was a boy. Okay, *legally* a man. Still a boy. If he knew that factoid, why hadn't he pulled it out earlier?

"I'm *really* not sure…"

"Who else then? Audra? A teenager? Mynx?" Adamant had a point, neither had anything the fighter would call bedside manner and Johnnie'd already ruled out the guys.

She shouldn't do this. It was ludicrous. She'd end up doing more harm than good. She'd end up— "I'll stay but someone else do the injecting. I don't do needles."

✦

Johnnie held the syringe needle inserted to the IV's injecton port. Kary was sitting on the girl's other side; everyone else was watching from the next room via an inconspicuous camera in a corner of the ceiling. "Ready?" Johnnie's hand was steady but he looked apprehensive. He'd put so many hours in at the lab for this investigation, Kary just hoped she wasn't about to screw this up.

No. She exhaled slowly. "Yes."

His thumb was smooth as it pushed the plunger, adding the serum to Rachel Baker's IV. "She should be waking up within the next few minutes but she'll be groggy for a while after that. Be patient and no matter what happens *stay calm*. We're right here with you." He pulled the empty syringe from the IV line and laid it on a counter. "Anything else you need?"

The college student stroked the leather cover of a book of poetry she'd found in the library during one of her breaks. She liked the weight of it, the years she could feel when she hefted it on her palm. "I'm good, go Aspect." He gave her a salute with two fingers and the sliding doors of the sickbay closed after him with a pneumatic hiss.

Kary opened the book to a poem at random, Dylan Thomas, serendipity had good taste. She parted her lips and channeled her brother for the calm he radiated before going into the ring. The calm he *used* to radiate: *"And death shall have no dominion…"*

Two poems later the girl's eyes were starting to flutter. Kary kept the calm in her voice and kept reading. She had moved on to Kipling out of habit. Kipling had become a friend in her freshman Colonial Lit class:

> *But the she-bear thus accosted rends the peasant tooth and nail.*
> *For the female of the species is more deadly than the male..."*

Kary flipped through the book, stopping at pages randomly and reading a verse, a line, a single phrase before moving on. It was as close as she could get to pacing without actually leaving her chair. She couldn't leave the chair. Leaving the chair meant she wasn't calm enough to stay in the chair and he'd told her no matter what she had to be *tranquila*.

So instead of pacing the room or running away to work the heavy bag or the reflex bag or *anything* else to take her mind off the *stupid* logic the supers had used to leave her alone with a girl who was about to wake up from a living nightmare, Kary kept holding the book. She kept thumbing through and reading and stopping and flipping pages to keep her hands and mind busy until, finally, Rachel Baker made a small noise that wasn't from sleep.

"Where'm I?" The girl's voice was soft, broken.

Tranquilidad. She closed the book slowly. "You're safe, my name is Kary. I'm a friend. Can you tell me your name?" She was careful not to let the pages slap when she laid it on the floor under her chair

"Rachel...water please?"

"Excellent Rachel, give me one second." The fighter stood, making her movements as slow and smooth as possible, the way she'd been told to act around a skittish animal. "Rachel, can you tell me the last thing you remember?" Name repetition created a bond; it helped to reassure someone that you thought of them as a person. At least that's what that one psych prof said one time in that one class she'd mostly slept through.

There are clean cups in the second cabinet on your left. Johnnie buzzed through the earwig they'd given her, reminding Kary that she wasn't alone.

"Where'm I?"

She set the water on a table and pressed a button to raise the head of the gurney until Rachel was sitting up. "You're with friends." She steadied the cup against the girl's lips. "Here."

Rachel drank slowly. "They're supers, aren't they? The ones who saved me."

"Yes, my friends."

"Are they here?"

"They're close."

"Who are they? Can I see them?" *Ask what she remembers.*

"They're away right now but I'll ask them to drop in when they get back. Can you tell me what you remember about your rescue?" *Do you always lie that smooth?* Caught twice in one week. Her friends weren't going to keep trusting her if they realized how often she told little lies.

"I was on my corner and then I wasn't. Everything went blurry and dark and loud." But the jet wasn't loud. *I flew with her until the sedative we used kicked in. Then we brought her here.*

"That's very good Rachel. Can you tell me why you were on that street corner?" Rachel reached toward the water and the fighter helped steady her hands again. This whole thing was going much better than Kary had expected. She felt a nervous little knot behind her jaw start to unclench.

264

"S'where I was told to be." *Good, press that.*

Kary shifted forward, she could hear the tension in Johnnie's voice. "Who told you to be there, Rachel? Do you know their name?"

"No." the girl was stiff on her bed.

"Could you describe them?"

"No."

She was lying. Kary could see it in the way the girl's hands twitched around the empty cup. The knowledge set her itching. "Did they have an alias or nickname, like the supers?"

"*No.*" The cup fell when her arms spasmed. *Lie.*

If she could just— *Kary...* He drew her name out like a warning inside her brain.

She bent down to retrieve the cup, hissing: "*I've got this.*" without thinking. Rachel's eyes widened.

"Who're you talking to?" Kary stood slowly, putting the cup behind her on the counter and raising her palms to placate the girl. Rachel forged ahead. "It's *him*, isn't it? He's watching us. He's here. He's watching me—he's always watching—"

"Rachel, *Rachel*," *Mierda* "please, it's no one." She didn't have this. "It's *just* my friends, the ones who saved you. See—see?" She dug the tiny bud from her ear and held it for the other girl to see. "They didn't want to overwhelm you so they put an earwig on me and—"

"You said they weren't here. You said they were out. You said—you *lied*—"

Lie again? Fess up? Lie again? Fess up? She wished she could put the earwig back in or tag out. She could feel the bud vibrating on her palm like someone was yelling into it even though they knew she couldn't hear.

Rachel snatched it, cramming the device into her own ear much rougher than Johnnie had inserted it into his friend's. "You're watching aren't you? Hello? Take me *back*. Take me home. *Take me home*." She was getting hysterical. Kary held out her hands again, not sure what she was reaching for but Rachel slapped them away. "No—*No*. I *won't*—don't make me— *won't*— *No*."

"Rachel? Rachel? What'she saying? Rachel?" Kary sent a glare back at the camera over her shoulder. "Rachel, breathe, he can't get you. *Rachel*?" What was she supposed to do? In the movies this was always the point when someone got jabbed with a tranq and the camera went black. In the books this was always where someone fainted. In stories this was always where the narrator glossed over and got to the good part.

She wasn't ready. She wasn't prepared. She couldn't do this. She shouldn't be—

"Rachel? My name is Adamant, I'm a friend." His voice was low, cutting across the panic that had collected between them like a gas in the room. "Rachel? Can you hear me?" He was familiar, standing there in the doorway. Like a family member who was talked about but never seen except in pictures. Seven generations had defended this city in that suit, just *seeing* him seemed to soothe the girl in the bed.

But not enough. "No—No, I won't, don't, can't, ask no *please*?" She was whimpering, her fingers to her face and her nails digging in. Kary reached towards her again and the girl threw an arm out, catching Kary under the chin and sending her back into the counter with more force than the fighter expected.

"Rachel, I'm going to give you a sedative, do you understand me?" She was shaking her head. Kary stayed pressed back against the counter and cabinets, out of

266

the way. "Something to calm you down. When you wake up this'll be over." He injected fluid into her IV line while she clutched at him and shook her head. "It's okay Rachel. Kary, hold her hand."

The fighter came forward and took the girl's hand, holding the squirming fingers until they stilled. "I'm sorry Adamant, I should've been—" Should've *what*? Kary told them from the beginning she wasn't equipped for this. *They* should be apologizing, not her.

"You were right, we let our ambition get ahead of what this girl needs." That didn't sound like an apology. "Aspect will transfer her to St. Michaels," the hospital nearest the university, "she'll be cared for and the psychologist there can be convinced to keep us updated on anything she says." That still wasn't an apology. He was gently removing the earbud from the other girl's ear and re-taping her IV.

The college student walked out before she said something she'd regret.

✦

"What's eating you?" Johnnie caught up with her in the library an hour later. She was sitting above the room on top of the bookshelves, the book of poetry open beside her. He sat on the shelf opposite her. "Meditating outside practice?"

"Can't a girl meditate in peace?" Kary was folded into her lotus with her palms down on her knees for grounding. She wanted to feel solid again.

The book rose from beside her on a circle of black fire and floated across to his hand without losing her page. She'd seen more of his powers the past couple of days than she had in the months they had been friends.

267

"Not when you're reading this, *Wasteland*? *The Hollowmen*? What is this stuff?"

"T.S. Eliot, gimme back my book."

"This is the way the world ends,
not with a bang but a whimper?"

He laid the book aside. "Yeah, you're reading *that* 'cause you're at peace."

"If you're gonna be like that I'm going somewhere else." She unfolded and turned toward the ladder.

"Stop that, Kary. Seriously, what's wrong? I dropped Rachel off at St. Michaels, she'll wake up any minute now and there's a shrink waiting with her. What're you worried about?"

"Not worried, *tonto*." She fisted her hands against the wood of the shelf before pushing up to stand. "Why wasn't that the plan from the *start*? You had no *right* to put me—*her* through that."

"We told you—the cure and she needed—*Kary*?"

Kary took a half step start and flung herself across empty air, landing with a teeter on the shelves beside him. "*Ow.*" punching his face broke the calluses on her knuckles open like they were day-old blisters. Johnnie just looked concerned.

"Kary?" He wasn't even *red* where her fist landed. What was he *made* of?

She heel kicked his gut. "*Apologize.*" At least he staggered back and looked winded after that one.

"For *what*?"

She advanced on him, lacing her fingers and slinging her doubled fists up across his chin like a club. "For putting me *in* that—" There would be bruises on her thumbs. "—For not *thinking*." She brought her clubbing fists back down to hit the other side of his jaw.

"*Kary.*"

"*What?*" She thwacked him over the skull with a beautiful roundhouse that didn't even move his head and would've sent her falling off the shelves again if he hadn't caught her calf and steadied her.

"I'm sorry."

If Audra noticed the marks on the older girl's hands when she came into the library to get Kary for their next training session, she didn't say anything. If Kary hurt when she wrapped her hands for the boxing pads she held for the young super, she didn't say anything. If Johnnie ever explained to Adam why Kary's knuckles were bruised and bleeding, the older super didn't say anything. If Bearkat thought the other frequents of the House were acting strangely around each other for the remainder of the weekend, he didn't say anything either.

Chapter 32

There was a voicemail waiting for her when she returned to her apartment, and her cell phone, late Sunday evening. Hey Bruiser, just wanted to say good luck with finals, I know you'll be awesome. *Call after your last test and we'll go eat, on me.*

Seth. He'd been doing this since she was a teenager, calling and leaving messages before major tests. He never forgot her, never doubted her, never got angry... *he did once*, never stayed angry, always forgave her. *Seth.*

Kary went to sleep before midnight for the first time in weeks. That night she dreamed with her cell phone, and her brother's voice, lying on the bed beside her pillow like a talisman against all the ills of the world.

She didn't see Johnnie on campus at all that week, and only saw him briefly at the House. His patrol schedule had been modified to allow for continued study time and she was on a lighter training regime. Audra focused on her lessons now without Kary needing to drop encouragements during breaks. She was growing more interested in the arts of controlling and honing her powers rather than the simple art of punching through walls.

Now that Audra was getting the basics of kickboxing and tai chi as a martial art as well as a meditative exercise she was allowed sparring matches against her uncle. The spars were rewards for her patience with training and the only time she could use her full strength. Kary didn't understand how this was a reward when Adam made the announcement to the two girls early Tuesday evening. In response she was told to strap into the jet and she'd see exactly why it would be such a treat for the young super.

The match wouldn't be held in the gym of the House but instead in a clearing at the center of the national forest preserve south of Commonland. Kary asked why they needed such absolute isolation as the three of them flew to the center of the thousands of acres of deserted woodland.

"We get a bit rowdy." Adam spoke into their headsets from his place in the pilot's seat. It was the first time Kary had let herself actually see when she left the House and even with landmarks like roads and rivers she was lost from the air. Audra was strapped in behind the older girl and so excited she wasn't even pouting about not being allowed to pilot the plane.

The moon was massive overhead when they finally landed several minutes after seeing the last light or road or other sign of civilization. Kary shivered in her coat while Adam and his niece stripped down to the barest fight gear. They weren't wearing gloves, or shoes, or tape. "Kary, count us down." Audra called, tossing her thick, blond braid over her shoulder and standing opposite her uncle on the rocky ground.

There was an element of theatricality to this moonlight brawl in an isolated clearing peopled by the only humans for what felt like hundreds of miles. Kary threw her arms out and embraced the moment. "Ladies and gentlemen *welcome* to the *Frost-Bound Throwdown.*" Terrible excuse of a rhyme but she gave herself leeway for spontaneity. "In the west corner—" She picked a compass point at random; no one here was going to correct her. "—weighing in at *much* bigger than me we have the champion the one, the only, the undefeated, *Ad*-a-*man*-t."

She circled between the poised fighters, listening to her imaginary crowd. "And in the east corner, standing a *little* shorter than me we have the challenger, the young, the *hungry,* the protégé *Ad*-a-*man*-t *Girrrrrl.*" Kary beckoned them both in toward her, taking their fists in her cold hands and holding them almost touching before her. "Now I want a good clean fight." She had no concept of what constituted a clean fight on a winter night between two supers in lonely forests but Kary wanted it. "Bump fists and back to your corners." They did as told. "Judges ready?" She paused for a signal from her imaginary judges. "*And,*" she drew the word out long, dropping one hand in a chopping motion: "*Fight.*"

Kary skipped back as far from the pair of juggernauts as the rim of trees would let her. They were already slamming against each other, feet plowing furrows in the ground when their hands came together. Two titans shoving mountains. Audra threw her uncle to the side where he left an imprint in the dirt like a child falling into deep snow.

He was dragging out of the hole before Audra could even turn, grabbing her around the waist and flinging her fifty feet away into an old growth pine. The trunk split where she hit with a sound that shook Kary's teeth. When the tree toppled, it fell like the death of a nation. The young super shoved the trunk pieces and branches away, grinning as she dragged the stump and all its accompanying roots and clinging earth from the ground; throwing it across the clearing at her laughing uncle.

This was what Adam meant.

The college student climbed a granite scree under the shelter of the forest edge, perching there to watch as Audra dashed across the clearing. The high-schooler was dragging a root as big around as Kary's bicep from the ground while she ran. When she had ten feet of it she broke her piece from the rest and whipped it at her uncle. Adam dodged the first strike but not the backlash Audra put on it, staggering a fraction, giving his niece a heartbeat to get in close, leap high and bring her doubled fists down on his head like something out of an overly CGI'd movie.

These were her friends.

This was the man she'd entrusted herself to when the cops knocked on her door and requested an alibi. This was the girl she'd been training with for weeks now; the girl she'd taken to Jimmie's to teach a lesson about respect.

Holy piss. That could've been bad. That could've been bad to the umpteenth degree. That day could've been the end of her and Jimmie and the gym and almost everything she loved in this world.

Holy piss.

Hindsight *sucked*.

Adam caught his niece's hands before they made contact, gripping them tight and swinging her like a baseball bat before letting go and sending her flying again. He ran after her, coming down on her almost as fast as she landed, and was sent flying in turn when, from flat on her back, Audra thrust up with both hands and feet against his tackle. The seventh Adamant flew twenty feet in the air before crashing to earth in the center of a crater like he was a meteor from space.

Savage. They were forces of nature caged inside human skins. They were animals who never tired. They were terrible and beautiful in their dirt and blood and clothing ripped to shreds that barely hung against them.

What material were supers' uniforms made of that it didn't get torn to pieces every time they went out to fight? What material were supers made of that they destroyed trees and rocks and ground and things but only sustained bloody lips and even then Kary wasn't sure she was seeing right. The moon was bright but the light it cast made details vague. The dust they were raising with every earth-breaking step they made didn't help.

Assume the port of Mars; and at his heels, Leash'd in like hounds, stood famine, sword and fire Crouched for employment.

It was a verse from one of the Shakespeare plays she'd read last semester, a shameless boast made in *Henry V* by the chorus early in the play as a herald to the bloodshed that could be wrought by one man.

Famine, sword and fire, they could do it. Her friends. They could render countries, continents, to dust with strength like this. They could commit genocide. They could destroy cities. They could be as merciless as they chose and no one would stop them. No one would dream of trying. No real person or super or combination thereof.

Johnnie would. Aspect *would.*

The cold was starting to sit under her skin. The rock was leeching heat even through her layers, and tired was starting to tug at her bones. It was Tuesday night, her Wednesday test wasn't until the afternoon but that didn't mean she needed to stay out until frosty dawn drove supers back into their guises as real people.

"You ready to go?" His voice was low and warm behind her.

Johnnie: thinking of devils and calling them up. "Yeah," She didn't look away from Adam and his niece. How long had she been watching? Time didn't feel real. "Looks like they'll be here all night." Nothing felt real.

"They might. When I was young, Adamant and I would train out here for days on end while Bearkat covered patrols in Commonland."

What had that been like? Johnnie, even skinnier and shorter than he was now, throwing down with the strongest super on the Register. His child's wits and whatever accumulated powers he had at that point pitted against Adam's experience and extensive training. It would've been something to see. "Maybe if it was warmer but tonight I wanna go home and find something hot to drink."

He flew her home with no sign of strain in his arms. Kary guessed that made sense, if he really was as strong as Adamant. When he slid her through her bedroom window she asked if he needed coffee for the road.

Johnnie shook his head ruefully, his breath coming in little steaming puffs as he perched on her windowsill in a convenient shadow. "Tonight I'm going to bed before 11." She glanced at her clock, it really was only 10:30, she hadn't realized.

"Good for you, me too. *Lagarse*." He scrammed and Kary slid her window closed, retreating to her bathroom for a shower hot enough to boil the shakes out of her cold bones.

Her last test was Thursday at noon. She called Seth as she walked out of the exam. "Hey Bro, just wanted to say that your Bruiser just *killed* her Spanish lit final, killed it in the good way—not the bad way. Anyway, call me, love you lots." She hung up before the voicemail could cut her off and hustled to her car, she needed to escape the campus. Retreat to the warmth and comfort of her apartment where she would have the privilege and the pleasure of not thinking for the next eighteen to twenty-four hours at *least*.

She'd told the supers they were not to contact her tonight unless the world was absolutely ending. Diette deserved a proper girls' night in without a secret friendship with supers making Kary weird and that was exactly what she was going to get, just as soon as Kary took down her ruined posters and hung up the replacements she'd bought online with Adam's credit card and blessing.

"So I *know* you said you'd bring wine, but bossman ordered a case too many and isn't going to notice, so…" Diette pulled a bottle from her purse. "It's that Cabernet *Sauvignon,*" she over pronounced the French through her nose to make Kary smile, "that you like when someone else's buying."

Kary took the bottle from her friend eyeing it suspiciously, "Not when *you're* buying, just everyone else." The Cab was too expensive for her to let a friend who basically lived on tips buy for her. "What's the catch?" There had to be a catch, there was no *way* the winery just let overstocked bottles walk off in the oversized purses of their employees.

"None, unless you count helping finish *both* bottles a catch." Diette pulled a second bottle of the same wine from her purse. "It's a sixteen-year vintage Kary, come *on.*"

Wine drunk. They were getting *really* wine drunk tonight. Her hangover was going to be as earth shattering as any force the Adamants could conjure up. "Guess I'd better put the cork back in my bottles then." They were cheap anyway.

Diette helped her with the corks and berated Kary for the umpteenth time on her lack of a proper wine rack in her apartment. "You shouldn't keep wine upright on top of the fridge like common *liquor,* you *know* that. Air gets in through the cork—"

"If the wine's not pressing on it like a seal all the magic… yeah-yeah. Are we gonna watch *Titanic* or not?" Diette shut up and got the wine glasses down without being reminded what cabinet they were stored in.

✦

They ate dessert pizza and drank wine and watched movies until they passed out on the selection screen of the fourth or fifth romcom of the night. It was always romcoms with Diette, or crying movies with sappy endings. No action or explosions or dramatic reveals of dastardly plans any heavier than one woman trying to ruin another's wedding.

That was one of the nice things about her relationship with the one woman, roughly her own age she was friends with: with Diette things could be as simple as Kary wanted them to be. No jealousy or rigorous training or suspicion of manipulation involved. No alibis or secret hideouts required. No need to worry about Diette accidentally killing her if she sneezed too hard. Nothing that might end with someone's feelings hurt or a city torn up.

This was what she'd been missing. This relaxation. The simplicity. The ability to get absolutely *shitty* on wine that was far too good for that purpose and not need to worry about accidentally ruining someone else's life. The... "*Bored.*"

"Wha was'at?" Diette slurred from beside her on the pile of couch cushions they'd been nesting in on the floor since they'd given up on using glasses and started drinking straight from the bottles. She checked Kary's phone because it was beside her and tossed it across the room. "No'nes lookin for you."

"*Nada.*" Kary growled, hauling her carcass like it had no bones inside it up against the cheap entertainment system that came with her apartment. "sup next?" The DVD cases fell from her hands without her telling them

278

to. "huh." She bent at the waist to pick them up, pitched forward and remembered nothing.

✦

Buzzing, screaming, roaring… phone. Her phone. That was her phone. Over…*there*, why was her phone over *there*? Kary dragged herself toward the noise. Her arms were weird and shaky or maybe her brain was weird and shaky. Maybe her tummy? Maybe—oh *god*.

Her chest slammed into the toilet bowl because she couldn't stop herself in time. The seat banged down on her head as she emptied and emptied and emptied until there wasn't anything left inside. Her guts and lungs and uterus were all in the toilet. Her bones and blood and eyeballs and everything else inside was now outside and being flushed away by reeking water.

The phone in her hand buzzed again. She didn't remember grabbing it.

"*Hello?*" She answered without checking the number.

"Kary?"

Johnnie? Since when did he have her number? She'd never given it to him. Or gotten his. That had been a problem once but now talking was a problem. And sitting up. And light. And living. "Kary?"

Had she not answered? "Yeah?"

"We've got a plan, when can I pick you up?"

279

Chapter 33

Kary drank a Gatorade and swallowed three aspirin before driving Diette home. She wore her darkest sunglasses and kept the radio turned down to a low hum.

"But my car…" Diette was confused, mostly asleep, and still drunk. Kary was probably still drunk too but there wasn't time for that to stop her.

"Garth can bring you back for it, I just… gotta go do something and I'm not sure when I'll be home." If she could be sure of his whereabouts, she'd use her brother as an excuse for this unceremonious morning, but that wouldn't work. Seth was so erratic these days she couldn't be sure any alibi involving him wouldn't fall apart.

"*Pero cruda.*" Raw was right, but there wasn't time to let their hangovers wear off naturally. Typically they recovered from expansive nights in together in whoever's apartment played host to their Bachanalia. Sipping sports drinks instead of wine and crunching pain killers like hard candy were their longstanding traditions.

"Nex'time Die, I promise."

"*Y'always* promise." Her friend muttered and slept the rest of the drive.

✦

Johnnie was on her couch when Kary got back from dropping Diette off. "Good night?" He rolled one of the empty bottles on her coffee table with his foot while she slumped against the counter. He was in uniform and mask; had she ever seen him in uniform during the day?

"Can you be quieter?"

"*This good*?"

It was only the memory of last time she hit him that kept her from trying again. She sloped toward her room, muttering at him over her shoulder. "Gimme twenty to clean up."

✦

"You look *dead*." Audra was bouncing a lot for it being before noon on a …

"You look like you should be in school." It was Friday, Kary was *not* hungover enough that she'd forgotten what day it was. Nor had she drunk enough to lose a day somewhere. Surreptitiously she checked the date on her watch. *Definitely* still Friday. The high schools wouldn't be out for winter break for another week at least.

"She'll be taking a leave of absence." Adamant was typing at the main console in the computer room where they had gathered. He didn't turn around to answer the fighter's question. "She has an assignment."

281

Assignment? Did that mean— "You're going out in the field?" No wonder the girl was bouncing, Kary raised her hand for a high five. "Bad *ass*, congrats." Audra grinned and slapped her hand hard enough to make the older girl hold it down against her leg so no one could see how red her palm was. "So what is it? Johnnie said we had a plan."

"*Yeah*, I'm going..." She paused for effect, "*undercover.*"

"*Sweet*, watch out super spy Audra coming through." Adam was making his niece a *spy*? "Where're you undercovering?"

"With the prostitution ring, can you believe it? My first solo mission and it's gonna be seriously—" *No.* "—awesome, we're gonna crack this thing wide—" No. "—open. Dunno why we didn't think of this—" *No.* "—earlier, I mean it makes *total* sense—"

"*No.*" Adam and Johnnie were staring her down with grim, hard-lensed eyes, Bearkat and Mynx were impassive behind their masks. "You are *not* agreeing to this." They weren't. They couldn't. "You *can't.*"

"She's aware of the risks Kary."

"The *risks?*" Something like hysteria was edging the hangover to her peripherals. "She's aware of the *risks?* We are talking about the same thing, *right?* You're sending a *kid* out to be *abducted* and brainwashed and *whored* to the highest bidder for what?" She swept all of them with her eyes. "For your *case?* Because you're *stuck?* You—"

"Kary, it's my *first* assignment. Why can't you be happy?" Audra looked hurt, like the child she was. "It was my decision."

"You're *decision?*" She shouldn't get a vote in this. She shouldn't *have* to. "You're just a—"

"I've been trained, I'm ready—"

"To be *raped*?" They were all very still. "This isn't people *shooting* at you, Audra. This isn't something where you'll get to punch through *walls* or juggle *cars* or whatever you do." The young super was growing pale. "You're gonna have to do what*ever* you're told by *whoever* tells you no matter what you want and—"

"Enough, you're scaring her." Adam wasn't Adam when he glared at her like that. He was Adamant, from the posture to the eyes, flat black framed by a white mask that had been protecting her home city for decades.

"*Good.*" Her temper was too far gone for his words or stern looks to have any affect. "*Someone* should be talking sense to her."

"Norm, why're you—"

"And *you.*" Kary rounded on Mynx, "Why're you even *here* if you're not gonna at least *share* the danger this *child*—"

"I am *not* a child." Audra sounded low and angry and suspiciously like her uncle. "And you are *not* my mot—"

"You're mother? No, I'm not." There was a bad taste in her mouth. She was going to say something she'd regret. Something worse than she already had. "I'm *just*—" Kary choked on the words, she wouldn't say it. She couldn't tell them. Not that. "—know what I'm talking about." She shoved blindly past Johnnie and Bearkat, through the door and out into the spine of the House, already running.

Already escaping.

She needed to hit something.

He found her in the gym, the second place he looked. "Audra needs you."

Kary was bare handing the heavy-bag. The pain in her knuckles, still sore and broken open from hitting him a week ago, helped keep her numb. She needed to not feel anything except her hands. Not her anger at Adamant for sending a child in for a job no adult should. Not her helplessness in the face of this situation. Not even the meek logic-place in the back of her head that whispered that girls were being abducted, girls were being hurt, girls were *dying* and this might be the only way to stop it.

"*No.*" She rolled her leg high in a kick that made the untethered bag swing like the pendulum on a clock. "Audra—needs—a—guardian—" She punched every time it swung past her, punctuating her words by making the bag jostle and its arc unsteady. "who—won't—send—her—out—like—meat—for"   she stepped back "*dogs.*" Her second kick countered the momentum of the swinging bag, stopping it dead.

"Kary, she's terrified."

"Good." She should be. "She shouldn't be doing this."

"You think we have other options?"

Jab-jab *punch* jab-jab *punch*. "Why can't Mynx go?"

"The antidote won't work on her. Her DNA's not human enough."

"So?"

"So? We can't *fix* her. Civilian hospitals don't do supers like Mynx much good. Only the healers in her clan-lands can deal with something like that and we couldn't get her there in time. If she went down she might not ever get up."

"So?"

284

"The Register doesn't like risking irreparable supers when they have reparable ones waiting to be tested in the field."

The *Register*? "You little *puppet*." When she finally faced him her fists were bleeding. "She's a *child*. You're *all children*. Why are you *doing* this? Why are your *guardians*—" She stopped. She was raging about children doing work of their elders… "Send me."

"What? *No*."

"I'm not some kid. I'm stronger than most civilians. I'm perfect."

"*No*."

"Why not?"

"'Cause you're not a super. You're not strong enough to—"

"To *what*?" She narrowed her eyes and grabbed him by the collar of his uniform, dragging his face close to hers. "To deal with the things you're going to send a *child* in to deal with? *What* am I not strong enough for?"

"I'll talk to Adamant about it." He shifted his blue eyes away from hers. "But you *have* to talk to Audra. She was thrilled for her first op and now you've scared her. Just… answer her questions, please? While I bring it up with Adamant."

Kary released his collar and he fell back onto flat feet, she hadn't realized she was lifting him. "Where is she?" There were wet smears on his uniform where her knuckles had pressed the fabric.

"Her room." He still wasn't looking at her. Kary left the gym without bothering to bandage her hands allowing the drips of blood to follow her out unheeded.

✦

285

"Audra?" She knocked on the door of the spartan little room the teen slept in when she stayed in the House. "You wanted to see me?"

The young super was sitting on her bed, looking at her hands. "Does sex hurt?" She didn't raise her head to look at Kary but the college student could see that her cheeks were pink.

Poor, scared kid. "Yes, the first time..." honestly? "and sometimes the next few times after that, it does hurt. You'll bleed."

"*Seriously?*" Her voice was a whisper. Why weren't there any women in this girl's life? She needed someone maternal to have these conversations with. Someone besides a college student with bleeding knuckles.

"Yeah, it's stupid. But it won't be... sex," certainly not on this op. "it'll be, something else. Same mechanics... different... other things." She didn't have words, she couldn't explain this properly. Not here, not now, not *ever*.

"So what do I—"

The fighter's gut clenched down. Now or never. "*You* stay here. Johnnie—I mean *Aspect's* seeing if I can go in for this one."

"What? But it's *my* op."

Kary poked the girl and she rolled to the side before rolling back to sitting upright. "Listen here, you're first op is going to be *perfect*. It'll be storming some secret base where you get to throw dozens of heavily armed men through doors and disarm nukes before they destroy third world nations—*that's* going to be your first op."

"Sounds like a movie."

"*Exactly.*" Audra was smiling a little over her knees, Kary could see it. "None of this infiltrating the sex trade stuff." Not while she was too young to get a drink to deal with it afterward. "Let me handle this one, it feels like a job for a norm."

"But you don't know my—"

"I can memorize orders just as well as you can kiddo." She poked the girl again. This time when Audra rolled away and back the young woman wrapped an arm around the balled-up girl. "*You* just need to have my back when I panic the first five minutes in and blow cover and need to be rescued."

The girl giggled under her arm. "Can't imagine *you* panicking."

Kary gave her friend a playful shake. "I wish I was that brave but the idea of you going out and… that had me pretty damn panicked."

"Seriously?"

"*Seriously.*" Adam and Johnnie came in then, Kary looked up at them. "So? She's not going right? What do I need to kno…" Johnnie slapped an adhesive patch on the exposed skin of her neck and Kary's words slurred away.

The last thing she remembered was that he still wouldn't look her in the eyes, even as she fell.

Bearkat was the one sitting with her when she dragged back into consciousness, still laying on Audra's bed in the House. He wasn't wearing his mask and his pale eyes were sad when they settled on hers. "I am sorry."

Kary closed her eyes against the world. "She's gone, isn't she?"

"The A's are with her. She is jogging the same trail you and Aspect ran the night you were attacked. They expect her to be picked up soon."

Like a rabbit for a greyhound. "Why did they…"

"This is her op, Kary. Her first. You cannot understand how important that is to a young super."

"So you'd just *let* her go out there and—"

"We explained the risks. She understood and agreed."

"But how could *you* agree? I watched my moth—" *No.* She hadn't meant to mention her mother. Whatever knocked her out must still be in her system.

"We know about your mother."

Kary went quiet. No one knew about her mother. Even Seth didn't know his sister had watched it happen. Had watched their mother twitch with that needle in her arm while her dealer ran away. He'd been one of the ones who paid in product instead of cash, a regular, but Kary told the cops she didn't recognize him. Even then, she'd understood that her and her brother's lives would be difficult enough without tangling up a dealer and running foul of his protection.

But Seth didn't know that. *No one* knew that.

"Adamant found the sealed records. The officers on scene speculated that you did more than find the body, that you knew who gave her tainted ice."

"You knew that and *still…*" *Ruthless.* She didn't want her friends to be ruthless. That didn't mean they weren't.

"Audra wanted you to have this." Bearkat pressed something the size of a pill into Kary's hand. An earbud. "She has an implant in her ear, a permanent earpiece. She can hear anything you say while wearing this, and you will hear whatever she says."

Kary held it tight. "Aspect? Adamant? Do they have…?"

"You have the only one. She wanted *you* to be the voice in her ear. Her way back."

The fighter fitted the bud into place. Once in she could feel it mold to fit her ear canal. "Audra? You there, *chica*?"

"Kary?" There was a bounce in her voice, an unevenness that told the older girl she was still jogging.

"I'm here. I'll be here the whole time."

"Kary? I think I see him."

Aguas-aguas-aguas.

She couldn't do this. "Just breathe Audra, our superspy." She'd panicked over a *stranger* waking up in safety. "I'm here. I'm right here with you." There was no way she could listen to her *friend*—

There was an intake of breath like the girl ran into something. "Kar—" and a sigh like the tired dead.

"Audra? *Audra?*" She'd never forgive them. She was going to *kill* them—him. *Johnnie.* How could he do— She'd pull them to bleeding pieces with her hands and teeth. She'd tear them— "*Cuidate, chica.* I'll be here when you wake." She focused back in on Bearkat, her eyes dry. Hard. "She's in."

Chapter 34

Kary was told to sleep while Audra slept but she couldn't. The idea of catching a nap while her friend was drugged up and dragged off to god only knew where to have god only knew *what* done to her… Kary shuddered and cupped her hand over her ear protectively, as if she could reach through sound and hold her young friend safe.

"She's in a warehouse on 13th and Broad. Mynx is on surveillance duty." Johnnie was speaking to her dead eyes because the fighter didn't trust him with her back. "Before she left we inked Adamant Girl with a tattoo containing the anti-brainwashing serum. We also injected trackers into her bloodstream and gave her tracking patches to put on anyone she sees while undercover, girls, guards, handlers." He was explaining these things like they would make her feel better. "As long as the patches maintain skin contact for thirty seconds the person they're on will absorb enough of the agent for us to follow them anywhere in the city using our scanners. We're hoping that by following their movements we'll find some sort of nerve center where they manufacture the drugs and receive orders from the boss."

Hope? This entire, terrible, plan rested on *hope*? They were betting the wellbeing of Adamant's *niece* on—

There was a stirring in her ear. Audra was waking far away in the warehouse on the corner 13th and Broad. "*Hope is a thing with feathers…*" The college student began reciting the poem from memory, keeping a steady stream until Audra murmured a *thank you* that could only be for the older girl. "It's what I'm here for, *chica*. I'm not going anywhere."

🕂

Johnnie brought the clothes and books she listed from her apartment. He also brought her phone back with him, a flat beetle contraption clinched to its back. "It's a scrambler. Your signal can't be traced back to this location as long as you leave it attached."

Kary nodded and said something soothing to Audra. She'd quit speaking to the other residents of the House because it confused the girl on the other end of her earwig. Instead she carried paper and a pen, scrawling notes when hand gestures failed. She tried to say something every five minutes, something calm, something warm, something telling the girl she had a reason to fight her way out and come home.

It wasn't easy. The fighter sat through every conversation the girl had. She listened to her whimper in her sleep. She heard her ask the other girls what they knew. She heard her answers when she was asked questions.

The day after Audra was taken she was interrogated. Kary heard the water and the gasps and the wet slap of

291

a rag and Audra's small screech when she could speak again. "Calm, calm, you *can't* break cover." Water boarding, they were water boarding her. "Audra? Audra I'm here, *chica*. I'm with you. You can do this. You can—" They'd seen her face. She couldn't bull her way out of this using super strength. Anyone who saw her face, found out she was a super, and walked away from this with memory intact was a—

I am Audra Nickleson. Not Sinamen.

Nickleson. The alias Kary had given her the last time they were at Jimmie's. They were trying to rename her. Rachel Baker's psychologist had told them about this part, the kidnappers renamed the girls to make sure their brainwashing drugs had taken full effect. If the girls accepted the new names over their birth names, something so integral to their previous lives, then the handlers knew they had them completely.

A hot spot formed under the college student's collarbone. Shame at letting the younger girl carry this burden alone. "No Audra, let them think you agree. The quicker you agree the sooner they stop."

No.

"Okay *chica*, I'm here. I'm here." She was so full of *shit*. She wasn't there. She was safe. Tucked away in a super's bunker, hidden away from the rest of the world. She yanked at the pad of paper, scrawling across the sheet *Get eyes on her now!*

There was a wet gurgle in her ear. "*Audra.*" God help her, if she was— "You'd best be about to come back to us *chica*. I've run out of proper sparring partners in this pit." Light. She needed to distract the girl. The sodden girl on the other end of her hearing. "You'd think your uncle'd put up more of a fight but—"

NO.

292

It was a scream like a baby bird made before being crushed. She was being crushed. She was being... why wasn't Mynx dragging her out of there? That was Mynx's job, to keep eyes on Audra in shifts with Johnnie and Bearkat. Even Mynx couldn't be so negligent that— "Audra, we're going to get you—" Johnnie was waving at her to cut off. *Que?*

He read her scrawl and wrote his own under it. *She can handle it. She'll be okay.*

"—you out of there as soon as we can. Just hold on Audra, a few more days, a little longer, and we'll get you out of there and I *promise* your next op's gonna be something out of an action movie. Explosions and all the door breaking you want. Just hold on Audra. Can you do that for me? Can you be brave and—"

Promise?

It was a gasp that grated through Kary's soft inside parts like a rusty spike. What air had the word cost her? There was a thud like a head being slammed against something it shouldn't be slammed against. "I promise." She couldn't promise that. She had no power here. Not even the power to be awake when they took a teenager off to endure *this*. "You listen to me Audra. I *promise* that I'll get you out of there. You just need to trust me and do what they say. Cooperate and it'll go-"

Sinamen. I'm Sinamen. Sinamen.

A wet spot leaked from the corner of Kary's eye. "Good girl. It'll be over soon. I promise." She kept whispering promises she couldn't keep until her voice was worn to a dry hiss and her face felt like it'd never be dry again.

✦

When Audra murmured a request for Kary to sing her to sleep, the young woman did. She didn't know any lullabies so instead she sang the old rock ballads that played over the speakers in the gym. She sang about drunk men and lost love and the way fame corrupts until she could hear the soft sounds that meant the girl had finally tripped into fitful slumber.

What did she dream of? According to Mynx and Johnnie she and three other girls were kept in a shipping container in one corner of the warehouse. Other girls, ones who acted like they had been fed the brainwashing drug until they didn't know up from down, were pinned loosely in another third of the warehouse floorspace. The rest of it was taken up with quarters for the guards, a dressing room for the girls who went out at night and an office where the warehouse's manager stayed and the intitiations were conducted.

They said it looked like Audra and the others in the shipping container were being kept in relatively good condition. That they were being water boarded only when ordered by someone who never left the office. That they weren't being abused sexually. Johnnie didn't say *not yet* but the fighter heard it nonetheless.

What did kidnapped girls dream from behind the steel gates of shipping containers?

Kary was lying on top of the bookshelves again, the shelves against the wall furthest from the door. She'd made herself a nest of blankets, cushions, and books on the corner where the shelves they butted into the wall in two places. It made her feel protected, having two solid walls to curl against. Being this high meant she could watch who was coming. Being in the library meant that people rarely came. It seemed to be a side effect of Audra being in constant danger that Kary needed to create a fortification for herself.

She checked her phone from habit. No one had texted her since Audra was sent off some thirty hours ago and at this point Kary had no idea how she'd handle a phone call. By ignoring it probably. No one was important enough for her to answer their call right now. Not until Audra was home safe.

1 new message.

Who? Diette was probably still angry at her and the only other regular correspondent she had was... Seth? She hadn't heard from him since his voicemail wishing her luck on finals. Had he finally—

Garth. Why was Garth texting her?

Hey Bruiser, have you heard from Seth? I called him every day this week and he never answered.

Heard from Seth? No, she hadn't heard from him since Sunday. Kary shot her brother a note telling him to respond if he was breathing and laid her phone aside without turning the ringer on, leaning back on her hoarded nest of pillows and blankets. Audra would be sleeping for the next few hours which meant she could catch just a little—

The doors of the library opened and closed. She cracked her eyes and shut them again; any conversation between Mynx and Johnnie was not a conversation Kary wanted to hear. "I'm just asking; why would you *encourage* her to leave the Recluse? You *know* how important our training—"

"Guess I just wanted to see if she was that *gullible*, darling. I was only *playing*."

"That's not an answer Mynx."

"But *isn't* it? What are others for if not to be—" She paused circling him and breathed against his ear. "*played with?*"

He sounded tired when he answered. "*My*nx," he dragged her name out, "you *really* need to learn to respect—"

"Respect *who*, darling? I only respect my betters and there aren't many *better* than me."

"You respect me."

"*You*, sweets?" She was trailing herself around him again. "*You* are the most powerful super the Register has even *seen*." She lifted her legs until they were wrapped around his waist, until she was held up against him by her strength alone. "And you're *mine*. Why shouldn't I *respect* you?"

Johnnie lifted her off his hips and back to her own feet. "That's it? My powers, not me?"

"Your powers *are* you." She was stroking his face. "You and I are the same Johnnie dearling." She whispered against his face. "We are what we were *made* to be. We're stronger than the rest. We could watch the world burn or save it for ourselves and we *choose*." She pulled away, cold. "*That* is true power."

"So you're never going to really respect Audra or Adam or Kary or any of the norms, are you? Your reason for not taking point this op yourself was flimsy to start and—" So Kary wasn't the only one to think that.

The lady sidekick made a sound like a cat when it crossed a scent marker it didn't recognize. "*Norms?* They would see me and mine in a *cage* for their whelplings to stare at." She was sitting on the back of one of the leather chairs. Kary pressed further into her corner, making herself as small and still as possible. "I will save their hides and know they deserve less from *me*."

"Mynx, it's been centuries, they're not all like—"

"Your people have short memories." She flipped so smoothly off the chair that it didn't look like a flip at all. "Mine are not so fortunate."

"They've changed."

"Don't care." She laid her hand on his cheek and leaned in, kissing her partner. "*Won't* care."

Johnnie hadn't responded to her lips. When she pulled back, he spoke slowly. "If you don't care about the people we protect then—" He was struggling, was he *finally* going to think for himself? "I *can't* care about you."

"Care about me, oh *sweets*." She was patronizing him, she stalked away and back toward the younger super with all the natural grace of a pacing predator. "You don't need to *care* about me, per se. We can build a partnership on *other* things." Her hands were on his chest and sliding lower. "We already *know* how well you and I *fit* together."

"There's gotta be more than sex Mynx, there *has* to be." He almost sounded like he was trying to convince himself. Brave little puppet, cutting his strings.

"Like what you have with your *pet*? She'll never see you as a man dearling but I *know* what you can—"

"Get out Mynx." He was finally angry, a chilly kind of angry that Kary had never heard from him. She wasn't sure she'd ever heard him angry at all.

"Temper-*temper*." The lady super was walking away like she knew she was being watched. "You're only angry because you *know* it's *true*."

"*Out*." The door swung closed behind her and the sound made Johnnie deflate into one of the leather chairs, staring at the embers of the fire. Realizing he wasn't going to move anytime soon and not wanting to be caught as a witness, Kary lowered back against her pillows to doze restlessly until Audra cried out in her sleep, waking the college student with a start. Johnnie was gone and Audra whimpering in her ear. The fighter hummed a song about wasted love until the other end of her earpiece was quiet again.

After four days of listening helplessly, Audra whispered something to Kary that made her heart fall. She was in her nest on top of the shelves and then she wasn't. She was flying down the ladder and running through the halls of the House until she found Adamant aimlessly cleaning the spotless kitchen. He looked like he'd slept even less than Kary.

"Adam." She croaked; her voice spent down to whisps. "She's working tonight."

Kary was wrapped in the fur again and in the back seat of one of the House's fleet of unmarked limos. She was scrubbed down and dolled up, but pale and strained from days of little sleep or food. She knew her shakes were enough to make her look every inch the eclectic socialite with morally ambiguous tastes. Johnnie was in the driver's seat, Adam tucked away inside the limo out of sight. They'd discussed this, even out of uniform the older super was too recognizable and Johnnie too young to be believable hiring a hooker.

It had to be Kary who hired the youngest super to keep her safe for the night. "Audra, this is me in the limo." She murmured to her earpiece. "I'm gonna hire you for the night. Breathe *chica*, we're right here." The car rolled to an idle on the curb and Kary scrolled down the window at the street corner where Audra and two others lounged, cigarettes in their fingers. Audra's wasn't lit but the other girls didn't seem to notice.

There was a shaking breath on the other end of the connection. One of the other girls leaned down to look Kary in the eyes. "You lookin' to party tonight?" The line was like something out of every crime show cliché Kary'd ever seen but the girl's eyes were blank when she said them. Like she didn't understand her own words.

Why would she? She was brainwashed. They all were. Disguising herself and hiding Adam were unnecessary precautions, the dead heads wouldn't recognize him if he walked around with the issue of *People* that featured him on the cover. "You got it doll." Doll? No one said doll. "But not you." Kary pretended to consider the other girls, "You, skinny in the back."

"That's virgin tail, not cheap." The girl leaning over Kary didn't move. Adam handed over a roll of bills and Kary tossed it carelessly out the window.

The leaning girl scrambled after it on the dark sidewalk as Audra came forward to take her place to the window, her eyes were down. "Eyes up." There was hope gleaming in her face, the baby Adamant still had a long way to go in learning to mask her emotions. "You'll be with me tonight." As soon as she was in the car, Johnnie punched the gas, taking them all away from that place and those people.

✦

Audra was shaking when they parked in a lot just outside the city limits on a property owned by one of Adam's shell companies. "Don't make me go back." She was pleading with her uncle. "Don't—the others are drugged. They don't know what's happening. What they're *doing*. But I know. I know. *I know*." She was getting hysterical.

"Audra, Audra, listen to me." Adam was holding her, rocking her back and forth. "You're the next Adamant and *no* norm is going to break you. You are brave and strong and—"

"But he's *not* a norm." She whispered. "The one they call Slowburn, he is and he's not and he's *not like*... he *knows*." She pulled away from Adam to look at Kary. "He's not drugged, he's not brainwashed he's *just*..." she trailed off like she didn't have the words.

"Is he the boss?"

"No. He takes orders from someone on a cell phone."

Johnnie's mouth was a hard line in the rearview mirror. He was still in the driver's seat with the partition down between the front and back. "A lieutenant then, higher than anyone we've seen. Have you tagged him?"

Audra shook her head. Talking shop calmed her some. "He came out of the inner office late yesterday, after I'd used all my tags. Covered face, his fingerprints are burned smooth, nothing to identify except he's *big*." *Fingerprints*. Kary shivered. The men might not know how Audra knew he had no fingerprints but Kary did. Kary had listened, had *heard* him... Had spoken in the young super's ear through the entire ordeal. And covering his face even inside the warehouse, he was being far too cautious to be a deadhead.

300

Big did them no good. They needed something more to find this lieutenant with a covered face and burned fingers. Johnnie passed over what looked like a large Band-Aid. "This tracker emits a different signature than the others. We'll be able to follow without losing him among the other beacons."

"You're sending me *back*? Can't Mynx just follow him and…"

"Mynx hasn't seen anyone like you've described coming into or leaving the warehouse. And she can't be inside without people seeing her." No one but Kary seemed to hear the cold note at the back of Johnnie's throat when he talked about the lady super.

"*But*—"

"This is the only way Audra." Adam didn't look nearly as hard as he sounded. He looked like he was cracking inside.

"*Kary?*"

Don't. Don't. She couldn't. "Come here *chica*." Kary wrapped the girl in her arms. "Can you tell me exactly what you want to do to the people who're doing this?" She waved away Adam when he started to open his mouth.

"I want to *hurt* them. Tear them the way they tore…" She breathed like the air was burning her.

"It'd be easy for you. You could kill them all just as easy as you look at them or they look at you." Calm, stay calm. This took patience and careful wording. She hadn't led someone like this in a long time.

"But I can't."

"Why not?"

"'Cause then they'd know who I am and even if I killed everyone at that warehouse, there're others and we wouldn't and I'm not cleared for…" She trailed off and Kary laid the next step out for her.

"Go on."

"We wouldn't be able to complete the mission. We wouldn't get the mastermind and it'd keep going and spread to more cities and more girls would be taken and forced—"

"But what about torture? Surely someone there knows *something* that'd help us and all you'd need to do was make them *hurt*." Johnnie was looking at her in the mirror like she was a monster. He had no room to think that. Not after everything he and Adam put her through. "After what they've done surely it'd be *easy* to—"

"Torture doesn't work the way norms think it does. It's not reliable information. And everyone in there's as blank as it gets except Slowburn and he's… different."

"Different how?"

"*Bad.*"

"So torture's out, but we still need the info." Kary was cold with shame. She didn't like coaching her friends through a slipknot.

"Yes."

"Why?"

"'Cause of those girls. They're blank and empty and they're withering from the drugs. When one gets too shriveled they get rid of her." How? Had any bodies turned up? How many girls had died while this investigation dragged on? "I have to go back for them."

"Good girl. Sleep, we'll wake you when it's time for you to go back."

Chapter 35

Kary curled up in her nest over the library feeling unclean. She'd sent Audra back to that *place* just as surely as Adam sent her there the first time. Before shuddering her way out of the limo when they dropped her off back at the corner, Audra had whispered the knife through Kary's gut: *You were right.*

She didn't want to be right. She wanted to be wrong. She wanted Johnnie to quit staring at her. He wasn't even here but she wanted him to stop. She wanted to be told she was a child, to be cared for. To lay her burdens on someone else. Someone stronger than her. Someone wiser. Someone—*Seth*. She checked her phone; surely he'd texted back by now. They could make plans for Christmas. Plans for after. Plans for when she walked away and became a real person around real people again and quit needing to worry about *this*.

One of the girls said Audra was virgin tail and therefore more expensive. Kary knew how they knew the young super was a virgin. She'd been there, on the other end of the earwig, when they *checked*. When they...

"Audra, I'm still here *chica*. Remember, put the patch on him next time you see him and I'll extract you while the other's raid the warehouse and follow him to the... Audra? Are you there?"

Nothing but breathing. "It's okay *chica*, I'm right here. Pop your jaw if you're safe." There was a little click in her ear. "Good, you're doing great."

Sorry sir, just wanted wat—unh

A sound like meat hitting stone. "Stay down Audra. Keep your head. Pop your jaw once if this is Slowburn. Twice if not."

Pop-pop.

Damn. "Keep breathing kiddo. We'll get you out soon." Would they? What exactly would they be saving? By the time they got her out, how much of Audra would be left in her skull? "You're doing great." There was dragging and a sound like someone landing heavily on metal. The shipping container, she must be back in the shipping container. Kary read from the book of poetry until she was sure Audra was drifting toward sleep. High over the library, the older girl curled against her cushions and hummed her young friend a song worrying over a son in prison.

She was filthy. Doing this. Encouraging this. *Allowing* this. When Audra was back and safe she would walk away. She'd never come back. She'd spend the rest of her life being a norm and nothing else. She'd worry over her brother and fight in her gym and get her degree and be fucking respectable.

Seth still hadn't answered her text. It'd been days since Garth asked about him. He never took this long answering her messages. His phone lived in the ass

304

pocket of his jeans. She was pretty sure he slept with it in his hand. *What do you want for Christmas?* That'd get a response, surely.

There was a sound below her.

"Kary?" Johnnie. He was going to stare at her again, like he'd never seen anything like her. She thumped the shelf with her fist so he could find her without her stopping humming. "She sleeping?" Kary nodded. He stared at her mess of pillows and blankets and books. "What is this?" She trailed off in her humming to scratch something on her notepad. "*Querencia*? That's not a word I know." He would if he'd waited a few weeks to borrow her Spanish, it was a newer addition to her vocabulary. Kary scratched another word under it. "Nest? Well it looks like one."

Kary kept humming; Audra's breathing was getting deeper. "Listen, I just wanted to thank you for what you did back there, in the limo… that logic thing, Audra needed that." He didn't think… He wasn't horrified that she'd talked a girl into going back to that kind of— "I know you think it's terrible but Audra wouldn't forgive herself if she'd given up. She'd be sick over it the rest of her life. She picked you to be the voice in her head and you've been *perfect*. Usually voices just sit and take reports and offer advice but you've *been* there and she's—"

How do you know what she's thinking? I talked her in and left her there.

He read her message. "Where she is armed with her training and has the wisest person she knows in her ear whispering encouragement the whole time."

Just a norm.

"You're the only norm who's ever treated us like we're norms too. That's special Kary." The specialness

305

of normality; be still her beating heart. She wouldn't forgive any of them for putting her through this. "I just wanted you to hear that before you beat yourself up too much." Too late.

She should tell him she was going away. Tell him that as soon as Audra was back and safe she was going to walk away and never... He was already leaving. Why was he leaving? They never had conversations this short.

Kary let him go. She'd tell him later.

Kary was working the reflex bag listlessly that afternoon when Audra muttered in her ear. *I see him.*

Him. "Slowburn? Pop once for yes."

Pop.

"Good girl. Can you get to him?" Kary left the gym, jogging to the computer room.

Pop.

"Safely?"

Pop-pop.

Bearkat was at the main console, monitoring the moving green dots showing all the people Audra had tagged and the one blue dot that was Audra. "Don't take any crazy risks. Don't let this cloud your—" fast shallow breaths like a sprint. The blue dot was crossing the floor toward a loose circle of green dots. Toward the gap in the circle. "*Audra?*" The idiot. "*Audra?*" A slam like bones breaking and a body hitting pavement.

The blue dot bounced back. "Lie still Audra. It's planted, the signal's warming up." A dusky red dot was beginning to bloom where the empty spot had been. In twenty seconds it would be set, as long as he didn't....

While she talked Bearkat had been speaking in his com, telling Mynx to move in close and give status updates. Telling Johnnie to get the jet ready to fly them to town. Telling Adam to get a car ready in town for them to use since it was still afternoon and they couldn't risk witnesses to an air extraction. He was barking orders and Kary was pleading with Audra and then—

"Signal set, I'm on my way to get you out. Maintain cover. I repeat—*maintain cover.*" Kary was running down the hall toward the hangar, her gut getting heavier with every step.

Johnnie lobbed Kary like a football over the plane's wing and into her seat rather than wait for her to climb, banging her knee on the lip of the cockpit as she landed. Kary was fine with that, anything that got her there faster. "Two minutes to town. I'll drop you into the car, but we can't look like we're together so the jet's staying shielded. Adam's in a meeting at the company and can't leave.You'll be on your own on the ground."

"You hear that Audra?" She hadn't, couldn't have, but whatever. "Two minutes, we're two minutes out. I'll be out the front door in a car. All you have to do is run out when I tell you." Audra couldn't risk her identity being discovered if someone saw her using powers without a mask so they had to pull her out like she was just a scared girl running away. From the handheld monitor Bearkat had given her Kary saw the blue dot was almost hidden by a pile of green. There were grunts echoing in her ears: the sounds people made when they were kicked by hard-toed shoes. "We're coming. We're coming. Don't break cover, we're coming. Hold on, *chica*." Hold on to what?

Johnnie hovered the plane over a convertible with the top down and the keys in the ignition two deserted blocks from the warehouse. Kary slid down a rope from the cockpit to the driver's seat, ignoring the burn on her palms and the skin she left trapped in the cable fibers. "I'm almost there, Audra, just hold on." How was she going to get her out without blowing cover? If the handlers knew supers were on to them they might...

The car started with a purr and voices began squawking out of the dashboard, familiar voices. "Guys, that you?" She was hearing the coms everyone else was wearing.

"It's us Kary, Mynx, check in."

"She's *fine*." Mynx sounded way too calm for them being totally off-script. They hadn't planned an extraction beyond "hiring" Audra the night after she set the tracker and never bringing her back. "There's nothing a norm can do that'll—*oh*."

That wasn't good. "Audra? Audra what's happening?" *Gun*. She sounded like she was talking through a mouthful of broken teeth.

Shit. Audra might be sturdy enough to be thrown through walls, just like her uncle, but a bullet to the head would kill her just as fast as it would kill Kary. "I'm almost there. Mynx, get her *out*. Distract them—"

"I don't take orders from a—" *Chingao* she didn't have time for this.

"*Audra, I'm here, Broad Street entrance.*"

A gunshot. A scream. Kary's gut was a rock. "*Audra.*" The door was heavy, metal, the sort used to keep fires in one part of a building. The fighter vaulted from the car and slammed into it, rattling her head when it bounced against the metal. *Again.* She backed up and slammed again, there was a crunch in her arm that she felt in her teeth.

Again.

It gave, falling open with a screech that made the whole warehouse turn to face her. Audra was screaming on the ground, her leg bleeding from a black pit on the bend of her knee. *Never aim for your opponent's joints Bruiser. Damage to a knee or an elbow never heals right—takes 'em out of the ring permanent, and that's the cruelest thing you can do to a fighter.* Rodney told her that once, a long time ago, after they watched a fight where one man trapped the other's leg and brought his fist down on the knee just like Seth almost—

"*Get up.*" Kary was shrieking and no one was moving. "*Get up.*" Audra was dragging herself across the floor, tears and blood and dirt and—

The fighter shoved the first one that came at her, when he fell she kicked his head like a soccer ball and heard his neck crack. Punch, kick, *where were the supers?* She shoved back with the elbow of her crunched arm and broke the nose of a guy behind her. And then she had Audra's arm over her shoulder, the side she'd used to break down the door but she couldn't feel the pain. They were running, stumbling.

A burn through her side, a tunnel of burn. Like fire and ice and lead, Kary kept running, dragging without looking back. They were in the car, driving, driving *fast.* Faster than they should in the inner city. Faster than Kary'd ever driven.

The December air bit at their cheeks and made the fighter's eyes water but she didn't have the courage to look away from the road to figure out how to put the top up on the convertible. She pressed the pedal harder.

Audra was pale—*too* pale. "Heyheyhey—stay awake, you've gotta talk me back to the House." She slapped at Audra but her arm wasn't working quite right and the slap hit the girl's shoulder instead of her face. "Wake *up*."

She glanced at the dashboard; it had been quiet since they got back into the car. "*Adam?* How do I take her back to the House? Johnnie?" Nothing. She'd been spending more time there than her own apartment these past weeks and she still had no clue where the secret lair was.

Kary spun the wheel, Adamson Mansion instead.

The mansion was deserted when Kary dragged her young friend up the front stairs and into the foyer. The door was locked so Kary broke a window to get in, the alarms ringing in her head would tell the other's where they were. She took towels from the first bathroom she found but when she went to rip them into strips, she couldn't.

Her hands weren't gripping. She was getting fuzzy on the edges. Towels, she was using them for something.

Cleaning, towels were used in cleaning up... blood, so much blood. Blood at the source, clean up blood at the source to keep from cleaning it later. Press here on... girl...friend who was girl.

Hurt, her side was hurting. Blood was seeping down her side but the girl's leg hadn't been there. How could the blood be...?

Chapter 36

When Kary woke up the world was pain and she was pain and all was one in the softened edges of her understanding. "She's back." Adam was smiling at her from somewhere a million miles over her head. Johnnie was only a thousand away and looking worried.

Audra. "She's okay? We got her—"

"Audra's fine. She didn't lose near as much blood as you did." There was a red bag hanging beside his face. "We pulled the bullet from her knee but she'll need surgery to repair the damage. There's a surgeon the Register trusts being flown in, he and his team are accustomed to masked patients."

Kary's hand stretched to press at her side where a blunt throb was getting sharper. Johnnie caught her fingers before they got there. "Your bullet went all the way through and missed vital organs. Bloody, but you'll make a full recovery as long as you finish the transfusion and don't pop stitches."

"*Hurts.*"

"It should, we've held off on administering pain killers. The blood we stock is infused with agents that

311

speed healing and dull pain. You fractured your humerus but we injected it with some of our best stuff and bound it up." She broke her funny bone? Was he joking? "Your knee's kinda purple but we figured it could heal without meds. You'll be back to slamming down doors in no time." Johnnie squeezed her fingers, his hands were warm and she was cold. She wanted to sleep, but first…

"The boss?"

They exchanged a look she couldn't understand. "We got him and all his lieutenants. It went very fast after you got Audra out. Slowburn scrambled back to the mastermind in the panic, same as all the other pawns who weren't dead heads. I followed him with Mynx while the cops rounded up everyone in that warehouse and Bearkat took care of another den we found using Audra's tags. They cleaned out all six nests of girls and their handlers across the city while Mynx and I took down the boss and his three lieutenants and their center of operations where the drugs were made."

Good. "Adam?"

His face was rueful and he looked lighter now that the climax was over. "I couldn't get free until the cleanup, but I did help with transport after. We gave a vial of the antidote and its composition to a trusted chemist last week so the hospital was ready." *Good.* "Kary, there's something…" but she was already drifting back to a place that didn't hurt, leaving her friends hovering over her somewhere else.

✦

312

The second time she woke the fuzz at the edges was almost gone. Johnnie was still there, watching her. "Better?"

"How long?" She was better. The throb in her side was dim; the ache in her shoulder was all but gone. Even with all the supers' ridiculous healing tech she had to've been out a long time to be this much improved.

"Eight hours since the first time you woke up, fourteen since we found you in Adamson Mansion."

Less than a day *couldn't* be right. She'd confirm timelines later. "Audra? How's she?"

"Better than you. We heal fast even without all the extras in our meds. The Register's surgeon'll be here tomorrow and he's probably going to need Adamant to re-break her knee so his team can set it right." Good. She'd ask to see Audra for herself later but first—

"Food?" How long since she'd eaten properly? She'd had no appetite while her young friend was undercover. Now that they were on the down slope she was *famished*.

"Soup and bread first, you're still delicate." He pulled the silver dome off a dish she hadn't noticed with a flourish. "Ah-ah," he admonished when she reached toward it. "I'll feed you, oh fragile one."

"Come a little closer, call me delicate. *See* what happens." She growled but let him feed her one slow spoonful at a time. The soup had been sitting long enough to be cold.

"Kary?" He sounded apprehensive as he swiped the last of the bread around the bowl. "I have something to tell you."

"You're pregnant? Is Mynx the father?" She opened her mouth and let him put the torn chunk of crust on her tongue. Her humor was back but his mouth was pressing into a grim line. Once upon a time she had

313

been angry at him, now that everything was fixed and everyone was safe, she felt giddy.

"It's about your brother." There was a tremor in his hand when he pulled it away from her lips.

His shaking hand made her swallow down the quip that rose to her lips. "Seth? What's up?" Kary had no idea how she was going to explain her radio silence and new battle scars but nothing serious could've happened in less than a week. "He hasn't been answering my texts and I was getting a little—"

Johnnie looked ill when he cut in. "We found him."

The giddiness evaporated. Found him where? Oh hell. "He wasn't in the warehouse was he? One of the dead heads? I didn't even notice— *mierda*, Seth." There were crumbs in her throat and it hurt to swallow. She choked and coughed across the sheets.

Her friend pounded her back gently. "He wasn't brainwashed."

Good. "Was he out on the street? Don't know how I'm gonna talk my way out if he saw me driving Adam's car with an injured girl but we'll think of—"

"No Kary, he wasn't on the street. He didn't see you… or at least he didn't recognize you."

She didn't understand. "So where'd you find him then? If he wasn't in the ware—"

"He was in the warehouse."

"But you just *said* that he wasn't…"

"He was in the warehouse but he wasn't brainwashed." She couldn't hear him. "Kary, Seth is Slowburn." *No.* "He hurt Rachel, he shot Audra in the knee—" He *wouldn't* "—and he shot you through the side."

"*No.*"

"Kary—"

314

"He *wouldn't* you're *wrong.*"

"*Kary*—"

"You've never even *met* him so how'd you know? You *don't*. You're *lying*. You're—"

"Kary, I've seen your pictures of him."

"People *never* look in pictures like they do in life. You're wrong, you're wrongyou'rewroungyou're *Wrong.*"

"Kary—"

"*Prove it.* He's *not* my brother. *Show* me this guy. He's *not* my brother."

Johnnie sighed. He looked beaten down. Ashamed. He *should* look ashamed, accusing her brother like this. When she was healed up a little she'd punch the sidekick so hard he'd— "*Ha*, see, you *can't*. You're *lying*. He's not—"

He picked her up, sheets and all. Johnnie gave her time to unhook the IV bag to bring with them and didn't listen to Kary's tirade. "I can *walk* you *liar*. Put me *down*. Don't *touch* me. Don't call my *brother* a—and expect me to *let* you— *No*," they were in front of the interrogation room with the mirror wall between it and the rest of the House.

She struggled out of his arms, falling against the glass with a sound like a bell, making the man inside swivel to face what he could not see. *"No."* She dragged away from Johnnie, the IV bag fell from her hands; the needle broke inside her arm when she shook his hands off. "It can't—"

Adamant was in the box with him, asking questions that Kary couldn't hear and Seth wasn't answering. His arms were crossed, his smile was sardonic. She knew that look; he wouldn't say anything like this, not to a stranger.

Johnnie's hand was on her shoulder and he was telling her something. Telling her things that she didn't understand, like *come away*, and *you don't want to see this*.

Away where? *Want* what?

Don't you want to see Audra?

On the other side of the glass, Seth mimed zipping his mouth closed and locking it with a key. Something they'd done when she was a child and he wasn't much more than one, whenever their mom had tried to get one to incriminate the other. Kary didn't remember much from before their mother started bringing her johns to the house, but this little promise: *cerrado con llave*, she remembered this.

Kary? Audra? She's awake now, if you want to—

Audra? Little Adamant home from the war and so very, very far away. Baby Adament with the bullet hole to prove it. Bullet through the baby and the one who put it there was sitting across the table from Adamant wearing her brother's face.

She had to get in there; she had to ask him what this was. Why this was.

Kary?

"He won't talk."

The vague words, the dream words that he'd spoken came roaring back into her, making her lean against the glass to stay upright.

"*Kary?*"

Inside the room, Slowburn glanced at them again. Trying to see what kept hitting the other side of the mirror. Adamant asked another question and again he didn't answer.

"He won't talk to Adamant."

316

Johnnie's voice was a little sad. "They all talk to Adamant, in the end." Why would Johnnie be sad? She glanced at him and then back at the room.

Adamant had taken her brother's hand.

"Look away Kary, you don't want to see this."

How could she? She saw what was coming, even without the warning. The casual twitch of Adamant's hand, two of Seth's fingers bending upwards in broken crumples. Seth's face and the pain that flattened his smile into a hard line. The spasm in his arm and the hand that he couldn't pull out of Adamant's grip. The repeated question.

Audra had said torture didn't work. Her uncle, it seemed, had different opinions.

Still Seth didn't answer.

"I told you, he won't talk."

She couldn't see Adam's face from the way he'd angled his chair. Johnnie's eyes were inscrutable. "Why do you say that?"

His middle finger joined the outside two, standing upright and with too many little angles. Adamant spoke again.

"Because he locked his mouth."

"So?"

Cerrado con llave. "Closed with a key, Aspect. He won't open it no matter how many fingers Adament breaks."

"Then what will get him to talk?"

Kary shrugged away from him, towards the door to the interrogation room. "Me." The door opened when she turned the handle. When she staggered through to see him.

To face him.

✦

317

He smiled at her after Adamant left them alone. His grin every smile she remembered from their childhood battling together against the world. Every laugh they'd share over his victories in the ring. Over her victories in the ring. Over Rodney's fretting. Over Jimmie's training. Every time he'd ever told her how proud he was. Every phone call they'd ever shared. Every time she—

"Hey Bruiser, fancy seeing you here."

The fighter sat across from him, her hand cupped around the soft crease of her arm where it bled. She gripped the end of the broken needle between her forefinger and thumb, pulling it out without feeling the pain.

"He outside? The sidekick that got all scared when he pulled my mask off?"

"*How* could you?"

He kept talking like he hadn't heard her. "'Cause, now *that* was priceless. Hear you been spending a *lot* of time with kids these days. What'd Garth say 'bout you and some girl—"

"How *could* you?"

"Not that I blame you, I'm always partial to a tight—"

"How could *you*?"

"—cunt myself, I mean something about the younger—"

She punched him.

The powerful left hook she kept in reserve when fights were at their direst, a square hit to the side of his jaw. This was her best punch, the secret weapon Jimmie helped her cultivate for *years*. The southpaw that helped her put thirteen challengers down in one night. The—

318

Seth smiled indulgently, leaning back in towards her and Kary's gut sank. "You've gotten *weak* Bruiser. Time was that'd leave a mark." He put both hands on the table, palms down and three fingers still upright. Up close Kary could see the way the broken bones dimpled and distended the skin that held them.

Kary backed into her chair; it scraped on the stone floor sounding like an animal in pain. Why could he still talk? "What have you *done?*" Even with her arm still hurt from Audra's rescue, bare knuckles on his unprotected jaw meant it should've popped out of socket and left him speechless. Left him screaming. She sat heavily. Her hand throbbed.

"What'd they *do* to—"

"No one *did* anything to me Bruiser. You're not thinking." Kary was quiet. He sighed over-dramatically like they were teasing each other across the table. Like this was just one of a thousand and three play arguments they'd had as children. "All that schooling and *nada* to show? Should I write it down?" She still didn't say anything. "*Elegi esto.*"

"No, *no* you would never *choose*—"

"You said it yourself. I'm getting old for the ring; my career wasn't going to last forever."

"So *this?* Seth, your contracts, endorsement deals— you could've milked those for—"

"Ah, but I had to *win* first, didn't I?" Yes, but he'd always been the strongest, the fastest, the smartest the— "They found me last year after the championship, told me I looked pretty wore out."

No.

"Said they had something that'd make me fresh as teenager. Make me *hungry.*" He slapped the table with his uninjured hand on *hungry* and Kary flinched. He laughed and continued. "Make me solid as a rock and fast as a cat, make me the *best*—"

"*Juicing*?" Never. Jimmie raised— Rodney trained— "A *Brute*? Jimmie trained you better than *that*. Rodney never would've—"

"Yeah, Rodney didn't hold with it when he found out. Called my injury karma. He was gonna tell the league administrators at the Turkey Tourney and—"

Kary was cold and hot at the same time. She cut him off. "You *didn't. He was our family. He*—"

"He was going to have them strip *all* my titles." The ones he won without cheating. Seth didn't say it but the words hung there between them anyway. Her brother's good hand fisted around the bad one, forcing the broken fingers down until they curled back into a more natural curve. The anger was gone and he was calm, teasing again. "I *couldn't* let that happen and we *needed* to close up shop in Marshal anyway." His eyes were asking for her understanding like he was explaining away breaking something small. Something replaceable. "Besides, I needed to come take care of you."

Take care of—Kary couldn't finish that thought. "But you were *here*, you were—"

"Ask any of my overnight guests. They'll all tell you the girl… Rachel?… and I left the party early. Went upstairs, locked the door. She'll tell anyone I was with her all night, or she *would,* but she disappeared a while back. That was your lot, wasn't it?"

Rachel Baker. *He* was the one that left Rachel Baker in that *state*? "What about Bethanne?"

"What about her? She figured some things out and had to go away." It hurt Kary to see him so dismissive of the girl she'd been equally dismissive of just months before.

320

When she licked her lips there was no moisture on her tongue. "Hookers, Seth, even after Mom?"

"Wanna know why they call me Slowburn, eh Bruiser?"

"No. Why'd you—"

"'Cause it took me so long to get worked *into* the organization but once I did…" He trailed off and made a sound like an explosion, expanding his hands out from the table to demonstrate.

Kary didn't have patience for his theatrics. Not this time. "Seth, *what about Mom?* You *know* how I—"

"She was never our Mom, Bruiser. She was just *there.*"

"Seth you *killed*—"

"Yep."

"And *kidnapped* and *raped* and—" She gulped, she didn't want to say it. "and you almost killed *me.*" Everything he'd done to other people, Rachel and her sisters in wasting, Rodney and the other fire victems, *Audra,* and still shooting her was his biggest betrayal. Her fingers traced the rough place where she'd been sewn back together. She could feel the ridges like a growth on her abdomen through the thin shirt someone had put her in.

"But wasn't I clever *not* to? Through and through like that? You'll be back in the ring in *no time* Bruiser, I was careful. You *know* I'd never hurt *you.*" He held his hand across to her just like he had the day after their fight in Jimmie's. His eyes were wide and his grin was confident like he was asking her help nicking an extra cookie on free sample day.

Everyone knows there's only one person the Mad Dogg won't bite and that's his kid sister. Kary stood and turned to go. She'd heard enough, the lock on his lips was gone, the supers and the cops could deal with the rest. "*Hey,* don't you *walk away* from me Bruiser. I'm the man of this family and I—" She flipped him off over her shoulder, the same response she'd been giving him since she was thirteen and he declared she needed to heel to his every word 'cause he was the adult in the family now.

Scrapes and thumps and growls. He was lunging at her, the table and chairs crumpling out of his way and he reached— Her leg swung up, fierce and strong, every muscle, every ounce and pound and tendon and bone slammed across the side of his head in the beautiful roundhouse Rodney gave her.

The mirror wall cracked in a crooked spiderweb where he landed against it, groaning a little before grinning up at her with his good hand feeling behind his ear where her foot landed. "Not bad baby Bruiser. You've been taking them too, haven't you?" His bad hand hung limp at his side.

She stared at him. He was climbing back to a stand, wobbling on his joints. "I'm not the only one who's been taking juicers." His words were sing-song.

No. It wasn't the *same.*

"We're still the same." He was on his feet, walking toward her slowly. "All these years and we're still just two Doggs in a pit. Still don't know anything but the ring." He reached for her face with a slow hand and she flinched away. "Just because your drugs came from one side and mine came from the other doesn't make us—"

"*No.*" She laced her fists together and clocked him under the jaw with a wide swing that made him stagger back into the wreckage of a chair. She slammed him again with the roundhouse and returned to stance, fists out and waiting. This time when Seth fell, he stayed down. She dropped her arms, panting. "No Seth, it's not the same."

Kary left him there among the broken furniture, her hand on her side to hold in the blood where she'd ripped her stitches.

Chapter 37

Kary had to be at home when they dropped her brother off at the police station. She needed to be findable when they sent officers to inform her that Seth was in custody and to ask if she knew anything about his recent activities. When she answered her door early that afternoon it was the same two cops who'd questioned her the day of Rodney's funeral.

This time she invited them inside.

Returning to school for the spring semester was difficult.

All her professors and coworkers in the tutor center and friends from class and strangers on the quad knew what her brother had done. Even Dr. C, her research professor from the fall, quit looking her in the eye when he spoke to her. If he spoke to her.

People whispered around her and edged away when she sat near them or they were overly sympathetic and nosey. Wanting the gossip the newspapers didn't have.

Johnnie treated her the same way he always had on campus but he only saw her when she was at work. He was the only person who even pretended that he came to her for actual class help any more.

He told her that supers had it easy; they weren't followed by whispers about their escapades when they were in day-life. He told her he'd always be there for her, that she deserved better than the treatment she was getting from people who'd never given her a second thought before the events of Christmas break.

Once upon a time she'd been angry at him. Furious over the manipulation she'd endured, the stress and worry and fear and suffering that came with being a part of the super's circle of friends. The anger wasn't easy to get through. The therapist had suggested honest converstations; she hadn't said the circumstances they needed to be under.

+

"Why are we in your gym?" It was empty. After Seth's taint reached Jimmie's name, people quit coming to Rock's gym and after a few months of that he'd been forced to let his trainers go. He'd given Kary and Garth keys because they and Diette were the only ones who wanted to come by and keeping regular opening hours for three customers—only one of whom was actually paying, wasn't worth it. Kary had brought Johnnie to the gym on a night when she'd been assured that Adamant and the newly, publically debuted Adamant Girl could handle the mean streets of Commonland. "There's better equipment at the House."

The House had a hundred survelleince devices and supers in every corner; Jimmie's had one broken security camera on the door. "Because we need to talk." Kary shrugged out of her top layers there on the gym floor rather than retreating to the dressing room.

Johnnie watched her bend first one leg and then the other up behind her back in a stretch. "You mean train?" He too began stripping down to his shorts and tank top.

"Shrink didn't say anything about training." Kary climbed into the ring, rolling her shoulders and head with audible clicks. She threw a couple of test punches as he climbed up to join her.

Johnnie began his own cautious stretches, pulling one arm across his body and holding it there with the crook of his other arm. Kary was sliding on the fingerless gloves she used for training on the bags, not the heavy boxing gloves she usually sparred with. He relaxed a fraction when he saw that. He didn't see her slip the mouthguard between her teeth.

Johnnie bent at the waist, laying his hands flat on the mat without bending his knees. "Good because it kinda looks like *uk*—" her foot landed in vulnerable crease behind his knees, pitching the sidekick forward.

His hands already on the ground, Johnnie turned the fall into a smooth forward roll and was back on his feet, pivoting to face her in stance. "Thought we were talking?"

Kary danced in and jabbed twice at his guard to test him. "We are." Her words were garbled around the mouthguard.

Johnnie watched her between his forearms and bounced forward, mirroring her jabs with two of his own. They'd never properly sparred like this and he wanted to make sure he knew what his range looked like against her. He didn't want to hurt his norm friend,

326

no matter how tough he knew she was. "So what are we talking about?"

Kary had no such compunctions, her foot swung up again, forcing him to dance further back rather than catch it under his ribs. "*Feelings.*"

"Feelings?" He dropped stance to look at her face properly.

Kary dropped stance too, long enough to shrug. "Shrink says I gotta. *Think-fast.*" Her leg swung up all the way this time, catching his ear. Johnnie moved with the kick, taking some of the force but not all of it. He circled and Kary mirrored.

"And what feelings are those?"

His hook came towards her left ear. She tucked her arm up in a block and crossed with her right, landing on the point of his unguarded chin. Johnnie wasn't wearing a mouthguard. He grinned at her with blood in his teeth from where they'd cut his gums.

Kary shook her head against the ringing in her ears. Her braided pony tail thumped against her shoulders. "Anger." She danced in jab-jab *hook*.

He took the hook to his jaw and heel kicked up into her stomache. Kary danced back, unwinded because she'd learned long ago to keep her tummy tight. "Oh yeah? What else?"

When his fist came she slid it away with one of Bearkat's blocks. "Frustration." Blocking like that got her in close and Kary pistoned two underhand punches into his ribs. His arm snaked back around her neck, pinning her against his chest.

She'd managed to turn her back to him before the hold tightened; his next words were directly into her ear. "Anything else?"

"*Betrayed.*" She leaped, both feet in the air, her momentum forcing him to bend forward a fraction as she landed, giving her just enough slack in his body to heave the sidekick off.

He landed on his side and climbed slowly to his feet. He turned his face away from her to spit blood and wiped his mouth with his hand. He didn't return to stance and Kary relaxed hers. "I'm sorry you've had our lives put on you like this, it wasn't right."

No, it wasn't. Kary waited for him to continue.

"We just—there aren't many unRegistered out there that we can trust, so when Foretoken said you'd never betray us that night I just… I pulled you in and never asked if you wanted in and that was a—" He looked lost, young. She seemed to forget how young he was a lot. "a violation, and I'm sorry. I'm sorry I dragged you in and I'm sorry that you and Audra—" She held up a hand to break off that thread and he picked up a different one. "I'm sorry our lives aren't as shiny as a movie would make them."

He was quiet then, meeting her eyes and looking away and meeting them again cautiously. She broke the silence between them. "There aren't any supers in movies."

He looked hopeful, taking a step towards her. "Yeah, but if there were…"

Kary's southpaw made him reel back, hand clamped to his jaw. Rubbing it, he stood straight, this time keeping his distance. "Do you feel better?"

Kary dropped her hips, back into stance. "Getting there."

+

It took several more long talks and longer sparring sessions, mostly at Jimmie's but a few in the House before she forgave him but forgive him she did. In the end she was grateful for everything he and the other supers did for her in the aftermath.

For their steadfastness.

Kary ignored the stare mongers at school, spending more time than ever at the gym either with Johnnie for her venting sessions, or with Garth and Diette during the day-lit hours. Jimmie had to know that she was bringing someone else to his gym at night; she knew that they weren't replacing all of the equipment exactly, but he never mentioned it to her. The old fighter was just happy to have the three friends around; to watch his two fighters spar and their friend begin to learn. Diette's lessons were more to amuse Jimmie and give her friends an excuse to have her in the gym. Rocks had always maintained a strict no spectators policy in his gym and even now, with everyone gone, the three of them didn't want to violate his rule. Besides, he liked offering advice, and watching the three of them, the way they laughed together like they weren't worried about the future.

They were good actors.

✦

People still came to the bar, but it was never as packed as it had once been. Kary fought every Friday night once she'd healed up enough to put on a show. She used her infamy as the Mad Dogg's sister to drum up curiosity seekers and opponents. For a while it worked but the gawkers who came to see the convict's sister began to trickle off, no matter how good she made the fights.

She had to slow down for whoever it was that Jimmie threw in the ring with her. Even the men he found weren't as fast or as strong as she was after spending all winter recovering from a gunshot using meta-meds and training with supers.

We're still the same.

No.

She dulled her reaction time to keep the fights from being two second KOs every match. She let easy hits through her guard, so the spectators could bay over her blood. She used only one hand and one leg to deliver her blows. She wore outlandish costumes like something from the back of an old super's wardrobe, from the time before their uniforms were as functional as they were recognizable. She did everything she could to give the crowd a show worth the cost of their cover charge.

Kary did all this, and still Jimmie sank lower every week. He didn't have the energy to run either the gym or the bar any more, much less both. He stopped coming out to the main floor to talk with them, instead staying in his office at the gym all day and watching the friends through the wall window, saying nothing unless they came to his door and asked directly.

Kary, Garth and Diette put their heads together and discussed going to the bank for a loan. Buying him out and keeping the businesses in the family but they couldn't decide. They weren't sure a bank would take a chance on three twenty-somethings buying two businesses. Especially when only one of the three was working on a degree and none of them owned anything worth putting up as collateral.

So instead they fretted about Jimmie over beers and boxes of pizza on each other's couches and waited. They all knew that nothing, not even this, could last forever.

✦

It didn't.

Adam called her to his office at the midtown Adamson Industry's skyscraper halfway through the spring semester. The secretary, the same one who'd tried to stop her that Sunday afternoon a lifetime ago, gave Kary a dark look when she arrived but ushered the college student through to Adam's office and brought her coffee.

"Kary, welcome."

"Hey Adam, what's all this about? Feels formal." Her coffee was cold.

"Well it is formal. I was wondering if you'd thought about your future."

Her future? That felt very random coming from him. "I'm just trying to make it through to graduation and get out." It wasn't a total lie.

"You graduate next year, correct? Have you any idea what you would like to do afterwards? Jobwise?"

"One that pays the bills would be nice." Job-wise? She hadn't a clue what people with English/Spanish literature degrees did after college besides teach high school or continue their education. She didn't want to do either.

"What about after the spring graduation? Johnnie will be leaving Commonland to pursue his...career and I know that he was the main reason you came to us. Would you be willing to continue with us, even without him here?"

It was almost funny to think about Johnnie being her only tether to the supers now, after everything. At some point in the midst of the unhappy haze before Christmas she'd never wanted to see them again. Now they were the only ones who knew everything.

Johnnie, who stitched her side together and held her while she sobbed so hard she was afraid she'd tear in two like a seam ripped down the center. Adamant, who handcuffed her brother and led him all the way to his new home, a cell in the Barton County prison. Bearkat, who led the Register inquiry into Mynx's decision to switch off her com and refrain from helping Kary and Audra when the college student went in to drag her young friend from that godforsaken warehouse.

Mynx was no longer Bearkat's sidekick and had been struck from the Register. Her actions were proven to have been motivated by jealousy and she was declared unstable as an officially sanctioned super with a permanent Register assignment. Last Kary heard she'd been sent back to the Recluse for extensive training in self-discipline and respect.

Audra.

She couldn't leave Audra. Both of them still woke with nightmares. They meditated for hours together and separately and with the adult supers. They trained until they collapsed. They did therapy with the Register approved psychiatrist who appeared in the House twice a week and still there were days when either or both of them would flashback and they were in that warehouse all over again dragging themselves across dirty floors with blood falling out of their skins like water.

It'd only happened once while Kary was around her real people friends, one flashback at the bar when all eyes were turned on the girl and the man double her size she'd been locked in the ring with. It took Garth and Diette and Jimmie combined to drag Kary off her opponent after she pinned him down, ripped off her gloves, and started beating his skull in with her bare knuckles. They never asked why she snapped that particular night; she never offered an explanation.

Just a dog in a pit.

Johnnie had been waiting outside when her friends hustled Kary out the back exit before the ambulance arrived. He took her down to the river that night and they ran the trails together until she could barely stagger and exhaustion made her mind clean again. Only then did he drive her home and bandage her battered hands.

Adam had paid for the man's hospital stay through an anonymous fund and buried the official incident reports without telling Kary until after, and only then that the incident had been "handled".

"You're my friends." She said it like that was the answer to everything. Maybe it was.

"Are you sure?" She looked at him, puzzled. Adam never asked twice. "I know about you and Johnnie's... extracurricular activities. I know that you have ongoing frustrations with our organization."

Kary looked down at her hands, knuckles still bruised from her latest bout. Her knuckles were always bruised these days. *Frustrations* was a nice way of puting it.

"And I'm sorry, for everything." She looked back up at him. She'd never heard Adamant apologize before.

She phrased her sentence carefully; she knew Adam liked to be careful of what was said in his office. "I thought... someone told me to never apologize for the way we do the job."

From the hint of a smile in the corner of his mouth, she knew he knew she was talking about Bearkat.

333

"Sometimes, even that rule must be broken. So I do, I am, apologizing. And I'll ask you again, are you *sure?*"

Was she?

Kary nodded. Yes, she was.

Adam smiled. "I'm glad to hear that because the second part of my question is a job offer."

Job offer? "You've lost me." Just when she was in danger of going all sentimental on him.

"As you might've guessed, there aren't many people who know us, *me*...as well as you do. I need someone in my corporation who knows my *singular* circumstances. Someone I can trust to make decisions in my absence."

"But I'm just—"

"This would not be immediate of course. You would start with an internship next week, or tomorrow even, and be trained until your graduation next year with an eye toward beginning full time as my personal assistant in preparation for an executive position."

"I don't know anything about... whatever it is you actually do here."

"Little secret? Neither did I when my grandfather hired me." It was nepotism at its finest. Adam was grinning like a naughty child. His grandfather, the fifth Adamant. The man who'd started Adamson Industries in part to fund his super escapades and to provide jobs for other Registered supers where they would not be penalized for the erratic schedules they were forced to keep. Kary had found his journal in the House library and read pieces of it in her odd moments since January.

"Do you really think I'd be good for this?"

"You, Karissa Dogg, are *uniquely* qualified."

Just because yours came from one side and mine came from the other doesn't mean—

334

"May I have time to think about it? The job, I mean."
She needed to consider a few things before she made
covering the secrets of her super friends her permanent
occupation.

"Take all the time you need."

"Guys, if I could buy the gym and the bar would you
manage them for me?"

"What?" Garth and Diette were confused. "How
would you get that kind of scratch?"

"Adamson wants to hire me and I think I can talk him
into lending us the cash."

"Kary, you can't go and *sell* yourself to that sleaze
and—"

"I know what I'm doing." They were worried. They
had no idea that she and Adam were friends. She'd
never told them about the Thanksgiving ruse she and
the supers cooked up. Kary felt a pang at the lie by
omission but not enough to break face. "I just need to
know if you would be willing to *try*. If it falls through
it'll be my fault for—"

"Kary, we'll do it but are you *really sure* you want to be
indebted to—"

"*Yes*." She really was.

Kary quit her job at the tutor center and started
spending those hours at Adamson tower. She bought
the gym and bar outright with a loan from Adam, that
he called a gift, and went into business with her friends.

Jimmie's gym was renamed to *JC's* and with the *under new ownership* sign people began to trickle back through the doors. The bar became *Rocks'* and, like the gym, people began returning to the taproom as their memories faded and the events of December became distant.

The fact that Jimmie never vacated his office in the gym or that he now sat on a stool to the side of the bar rather than leaning behind it didn't seem to bother customers.

Garth managed the hotshot gym rats that came to box on his canvas with an iron hand. He hired new trainers from the circuit retirees he knew, new people from outside Commonland. Fresh blood for a fresh start.

Diette manned the bar and brooked no nonsense from the rough characters that continued to frequent the little watering hole with the fighting ring on one end. After a few months training with Kary and Garth she was able to handle many of those characters without help from her bouncers but Kary kept bouncers hired just in case. As the owner, Kary visited both of her friends as often as her schedule with the supers allowed. By the time end of semester exams rolled around her friends had quit asking if she was *sure* she wanted to work with a sleazy ex like Adam.

The day of Johnnie's graduation was beautiful. Warm and too bright for the pictures she and Audra and Adam snapped of the graduate to turn out properly. If Kary's eyes were watery, it was only because the sun was in them.

She hugged the younger super tight as he left the basketball arena where their university graduated its students. He and the Adamsons were going straight to the House and taking the jet to secret location where Johnnie would go through another ceremony and be inscribed as an official Register super. He would be given his assignment there and expected to go wherever he was sent immediately after signing the Register. Depending on how far away he was sent and how busy his city was, Kary might not see him again for a long time.

"Look for me in a few years, when you've grownup." She muttered in his ear when she squeezed him. Originally, she'd meant it as a joke but when the moment came she found she couldn't make her voice anything but serious.

The others had already gone to the car, slapping Johnnie's back as they passed. They were alone in the center of a crowd of families. She needed to let her friend go so he could get on his way, toward the Register and his future. "And this is for you." She handed him a creased envelope. "It was supposed to be your birthday present but..." things happened.

He opened it curiously. He wasn't going to remember. There was no *way* he was going to remember the joke and she was about to feel so stupid. So ridiculously— *"Better cereal?"* He grinned, reading the expired coupons for sugary brands that Kary never ate. "As long as they mean you'll have some waiting on me, they're *perfect.*" It was his turn to hug her tight and press his lips to her cheek before she could stop him. "Wish me luck."

He bounded off toward the waiting car before she could react; either slap him... *or* drag him down and show him a proper kiss. She wasn't sure which would've happened.

And it was too late to figure out. He was gone, lanky and young and one of the best friends she'd ever had. Gone to a future she wouldn't be a part of. At least not any time soon.

Buena suerte.

Epilogue

Five years later Adamson Industries Vice President, Karissa Dogg, answered her phone at one in the morning. "You know I keep real person hours now, right?" She groaned as she eased up into a seat against the headboard. It wasn't exactly untrue. Being an executive of a multinational company wasn't very conducive to a regular sleep schedule but it was better than her time as a student training like a super. Kary didn't reach over to turn on a lamp.

"So? You're in *Winterdale*. Why didn't you *call* me?"

"I'm on business Audra, shouldn't you be on patrol?" Kary scrubbed her face with her free hand, trying to rub some awake into her skin.

"Nope, uncle says I'm benched 'til she's born."

She? "It's a *girl?*" Kary could hear the satisfaction in her friend's voice when she hummed agreement. "Is she—can you tell yet?"

"She'll be an Adamant too, she'd have kicked me apart if I was a norm."

Kary wiggled in the dark, happy and restless. "That's *great*. How'd Adam take it?"

"He's happy that I'm happy."

"And her father?"

"C'mon Kary, you *know* I haven't talked to him in months."

Kary sighed, she did know. She'd just hoped— "I was just hoping you at least told him the sex of the—"

"He ran out when he heard I was pregnant and ran back when he realized how rich my uncle is."

"Oh." Empty air stretched between them. "I didn't know that second bit. I'm sorry, Audra."

"No big. Not important... So have you *seriously* not heard from him?"

"I've only been here a couple days. He's probably busy." Defending a city solo was no joke, even for a Register power-house who was funded entirely by a multi-billionaire like Adam Adamson and therefore didn't need a real person job.

"*Kary.*" The young super dragged her name out long, whining.

"*Audra.*" Kary mocked her. "I'm going to sleep now, good night." She hung up and turned on the light, swinging her legs out from under the covers of the king-sized hotel bed.

She lived in hotel suites these days, had for a couple of years now. Becoming VP meant she spent her time flying across the country and around the world overseeing the things Adam couldn't as long as he was tethered by the Register to the Commonland city limits. Kary had long since moved out of her apartment and now kept a permanent room in his home, where she lived when she wasn't on business trips. She'd learned early in her career to ignore the people who muttered that she'd slept her way to the top. Being indignant was too much effort.

There was wine on the dresser, a thirty-year vintage given to her by the management of the Winterdale branch of Adamson Ind. Kary considered opening the bottle and finding a glass but opted against it. Instead she pulled a robe over the oversized tournament T-shirt she still slept in and padded barefoot from her room, taking the stairs to the quiet bar on the roof of her hotel.

"Miss Dogg, what can I get you this fine evening?" There was just enough bite in the night air to make the bartender's greeting sound mechanical.

"Decaf please, with Baileys." She leaned back against the bar and watched the stars above her. Winterdale prided itself on regulating light pollution and smog: meaning that even here, on the roof of a historic downtown hotel, the stars were near and bright. She was glad. She liked the idea of him being attached to a city that was conscious of the environment.

"One Irish coffee." The white china mug clicked on the bar at her elbow.

"Thanks Max, charge it to my room." She wrapped her fingers around the warm porcelain and drifted away from the counter before he could make whatever banal response he was trained to give.

She was still sitting at the decorative iron table at the far corner of the roof when Max came over to her at two. "Miss Dogg, we're closing the bar." Her hands were still twisted around the long-empty mug.

"That's fine Max, thank you for the coffee." He was trying to send her away, off the roof, so he didn't have to worry over whatever liabilities were involved with unattended guests staying alone fifteen stories up.

"Miss..."

"I said *thank you*." He left her alone rather than trying to argue with the imperious Miss Dogg; the young woman who, in five years, had become the face of a multinational corporation. She was known by reputation for her intolerance of incompetence, her ferocious loyalty to Adam Adamson, her defense of his many eccentricities, and her ruthlessness in business. There were rumors that she had once bought a hotel she found unsatisfactory for the sole purpose of reforming it.

The rumors were true. She'd sold the Hotel Lombardie in downtown Andersonville just last year at double the price she bought it for and used the profits to start a scholarship program for young fighters back in Commonland.

She'd only told Audra but funding the scholarship had finally silenced Seth's voice in her head.

Kary stayed where she was, alone with the stars.

She wasn't sure what she'd expected from this trip north, besides the usual roster of meetings and company dinners and the endless cycle of schmoozers that came with the job. She hadn't *planned* to see him. They hadn't spoken since his graduation. He still called Adam at the House sometimes but not her. Never her. Kary put the coffee cup to her lips out of habit and took it away when the cold ceramic reminded her that the contents were gone.

Tonta. Communication was her business; she *knew* it was a two-way street. She should have at least tried to call instead of waiting for him to show up like some damsel. Her first trip to Winterdale since the Register assigned him here. She'd been stupid for thinking he'd look up some girl, who'd spent most of their friendship patronizing him, without at least a little prompting.

Her fingers tightened on the cup. She should go back to her room. Go somewhere warm. Quit worrying. *Sleep*. There were meetings in the morning that she needed to be sharp for. Take a hot shower and clear her head. Call Audra back and gush over the baby super that was about to enter all their lives. Do something, *anything*, besides sit here with the cold settling around her like an arm across her shoulders.

Kary stood, pivoting on the ball of her bare foot like a dancer, pacing across the smooth tile of the roof. The heat from the day had leeched from the stone leaving it as cool to her feet as the air on her face. Just before she reached the door she spun again and threw the mug, watching it fall past the boundary wall of the roof down, down out of sight.

The coffee cup was on her bedside table when she unlocked the door of her suite. "It's a girl." She announced to the shadows, not taking her eyes off the mug where it sat under the lamp she'd left lit when she went to the bar.

"Adam must be proud."

She didn't look at him. She wouldn't look at him. "I'll have to call in the morning and congratulate him." As long as she didn't see him, she didn't have to see how much he'd changed. Or how little he'd changed. She wasn't sure which she wanted.

"Then I'll call in the afternoon."

"I like your city." Her voice was stilted. Why had he waited three days before visiting her? Had Adam told him she was here? In the years since college Kary had gotten even better at lying and acting when she needed to. Smoke screening for a high-profile super like Adamant meant her nonchalant façade was *usually* perfect.

Tonight was unusual.

"You do? You know there's a $500 fine for littering downtown."

She worked at her disinterested act but a smile still edged at her mouth. "What if I don't have $500?"

"Then I might have to keep you here. Take you into custody." Hadn't she once made a joke to him about handcuffs? He came closer to her as they spoke. There was a grin in his voice, a grin she recognized even through the timbre he'd acquired these past years.

"Like you *could*." She punched toward his voice. She wasn't in the same shape she'd maintained before she began living on the road but some things never went away.

He caught her fist before it reached his face with one gloved hand, holding it there without hurting her. There was a new scar under his eye, the tail trailing from under his mask toward his cheek. There was stubble on his chin that he hadn't been able to grow before and he was taller than her now, taller by at least a hand-span. Kary had to tilt her head to look at him properly. His smile was the same. His hair just as tousled as the day he first skulked into the tutor center several lives ago.

Kary jerked her fist from his grip but kept her hand out, stretching up to pull the mask from his face with a soft suction sound. His eyes, when the mask and its lenses uncovered them, hadn't changed. They were still as kind and as blue as she remembered. "Hey Bruiser." It was really him, back. Safe. *Here.* The Vice President of Adamson Industries dropped the black mask worn by Aspect the super and slid her hands across his chest.

She tucked herself against him; his arms came around her and they nested against each other like it was an old instinct. His uniform was cold from the night air, the same as her skin. His breath was hot when his face pressed against hers, his lips ran a burning line along her temple. "Hey Johnnie, it's good to be home."

Author's Note

Arg! What do you mean we don't get to see the big kiss?

If it helps, there is a big kiss and more in Kary and Johnnie's future and someday I might get around to writing it. We'll just have to see—my tomorrows are pretty stacked for a while so "someday" could be a ways off.

Thank you to everyone who made it this far, here's where I start my awards show speech so feel free to hop off at any time:

First and foremost, thank you to my parents and sister. You haven't always understood my choice in subject matter but you've always loved and supported me anyway. This one is for you, for everything you have always done. Thank you forever and love you for always.

To the rest of my family, warmest love and biggest thank you's all around. You encouraged me to read all my life and when you learned about this whole novelist dream, you encouraged me in that too. I know who I am because of all of you.

To Silver, bestest friend and the creator of the beautiful cover that's embracing this story. If people buy this novel, it is because of you. We did it, didn't we? Two decades of tolerance, shall we see what the next two look like? And many more besides, my sister in heart if not blood.

Sawyer, you were the first to read Dogg Girl and Sidekick. That night when you walked into my room just long enough to say that you liked it—you made me an author that night. Thank you, from my core outward, thank you.

And to all my friends: Redwater, San Angelo, Cork—thank you. Without your support, your love, and your generosity I and my book would not be here today.

Is that the get off the stage music? Let's wrap this up—

Thank you to Kristi and the entire team at Dreaming Big Publications for seeing what this novel could be and believing in that. Thank you to Jamie and London, editors of utmost patience. Thank you for putting up with my slow edits and overly nonchalant emails. Thank you to everyone there working behind the scenes, I don't know your names but I do know this wouldn't have come together without you.

And to you, darling reader who has made it this far—muchas gracias for sticking around but it's time to go. The ushers want to sweep the aisles so we've got to scoot. I'll see you next time around, whenever that may be.

Ciao lovelies,
JdB

www.ingramcontent.com/pod-product-compliance
Lightning Source LLC
Chambersburg PA
CBHW021442240626
47153CB00001B/255